# COLLAR OF PEARLS

*A Selection of Recent Titles by Betty McInnes*

THE ALEXANDER INHERITANCE
FAREWELL TO FAIROAKS
THE RIVER CALLS US HOME

ALL THE DAYS OF THEIR LIVES *
MacDOUGAL'S LUCK *

* *available from Severn House*

# COLLAR OF PEARLS

## Betty McInnes

This first world edition published in Great Britain 2003 by
SEVERN HOUSE PUBLISHERS LTD of
9–15 High Street, Sutton, Surrey SM1 1DF.
This first world edition published in the USA 2004 by
SEVERN HOUSE PUBLISHERS INC of
595 Madison Avenue, New York, N.Y. 10022.

British Library Cataloguing in Publication Data

McInnes, Betty, 1928-
    Collar of pearls
    1.   Scots - Soviet Union - Fiction
    2.   Soviet Union - History - Revolution 1917-1921 - Fiction
    3.   Historical fiction
    I.   Title
    823.9'14 [F]

ISBN 0-7278-6030-5

Except where actual historical events and characters are being
described for the storyline of this novel, all situations in this
publication are fictitious and any resemblance to living persons
is purely coincidental.

Typeset by Palimpsest Book Production Ltd.,
Polmont, Stirlingshire, Scotland.
Printed and bound in Great Britain by
MPG Books Ltd., Bodmin, Cornwall.

# One

July 1917 had been the sunniest summer month most Dundee folk could recall, but August had redressed the balance with a vengeance.

Captain Andrew McLaren stared out at the rain pattering against the windowpanes of his house in Peep o' Day Lane. Being a seafaring man, with a keen interest in weather statistics, the captain had noted in his diary there had been twenty-eight wet days already this month. Today, the thirtieth, looked set to add to the total. That was a pity; he'd hoped for a blink of sun for his daughter Anna's twenty-first birthday.

Andrew turned away from the sight of the dripping garden and flags hanging limp at the harbour. At least the breakfast room was cosy and cheerful. His dear wife Irina had seen to that. The interiors were tastefully furnished in keeping with the captain's stone-built villa standing in its own grounds.

Andrew McLaren had prospered over the years, and good luck to him, Dundonians said. He had risen from deckhand to shipowner by hard graft and ability. The masts and funnel of the *Pole Star*, McLaren's ocean-going cargo ship, could be seen from the window. It had recently returned from the Baltic, skippered by Andrew's second-in-command, Duncan Wishart. Andrew himself was laid up in dry dock as he put it. A serious bout of pneumonia had left him weak and shaky.

The McLarens were an industrious family, however, and not completely dependent upon the captain for income. In a purpose-built extension facing the back garden, Irina, the captain's Russian-born wife, ran a discreet sideline making handmade corsets for well-off ladies. She was assisted in this enterprise by their daughter, Anna, the McLarens' only child.

Williamina Murray, a middle-aged ex-weaver from Dens Road Linen Works, was the sole employee. Mina Murray's nimble fingers were a valuable asset, while her candid comments delivered in broad Dundee dialect frequently provided a cold shock of reality for Irina's customers.

The captain had risen early that morning. His dear daughter's coming of age was an important occasion not to be missed. While he studied the clock impatiently, his wife poked her head round the door.

'Isn't she down yet?' she enquired.

'I told her to have a lie-in. It's not every day a lass gets the key to the door, y'know.'

Irina came into the room, a small, neat, pretty woman with the fine Slavic features their daughter had inherited. 'You and your funny customs. And you tease me because I am Russian! Which key to which door is our daughter to have, tell me? We have so many!'

'The key to a good life, I hope, love.'

'Hush, here she comes!' Irina had heard a light step on the stairs.

'Happy birthday, Anna darling!' they chorused as the door opened.

Anna Androvna McLaren halted in the doorway. Her eyes widened as she saw the breakfast feast prepared for her. Beautifully decorated boiled eggs stood in gilded eggcups; pink rosebuds tied with white ribbon lay at her place. In traditional Russian fashion there were dishes of salt and loaves of home-baked bread. On the sideboard a samovar steamed, ready to dispense tea.

Best of all were the crystal dishes piled high with pats of fresh butter. Anna knew her mother must have queued for hours to get it. Butter was scarce and everyone made do with whale-oil margarine. The effort involved in preparing such a special surprise brought tears to Anna's eyes. Only in Russian, her fluent second language, could she express her heartfelt thanks.

'Ah, *Mamushka, Papachka, spasibo*!' Anna hugged them both.

After breakfast they lingered over cups of tea. Irina nudged her husband. 'Andrew, the gift!'

He pretended to search his pockets, then produced a small leather box.

Anna opened it and gasped, 'Oh, how beautiful!'

It contained a gold locket and chain. Set side by side in the locket were a red ruby and green emerald. Above the two precious stones was a star formed from glowing diamonds. The significance was not lost upon Anna McLaren, a seaman's daughter.

'Port and starboard lights with the Pole Star above, Dad!'

'Aye.' Andrew smiled. 'Your mum and I thought you'd appreciate a wee bit of guidance so's you don't lose your way.'

Anna fastened the jewel round her neck. Strangely, the gold chilled her skin and, just for an instant, she had an odd sense of foreboding. Then it passed and she smiled her delight.

'Thank you. Oh, thank you so much!'

'There is a letter from Russia which I kept for your birthday,' Irina said.

'From Aleksandr?' Anna's heart leapt.

'No, it's from your grandmother.'

Her parents exchanged a glance. They had believed their daughter's love affair with Aleksandr Rostovich was over. Now, it appeared, they'd been mistaken.

'Seraphima's letters are always a delight,' Andrew said. 'I was very worried when the Tsar was forced to abdicate last March, and even more concerned when refugees from Russia turned up in a cattle boat in June. But your grandmother writes cheery letters. She says Archangel's peaceful and there's nothing to worry about. That took a weight off my mind.'

'Yes.' Irina nodded. 'She writes that luxuries are scarce and Russians tighten their belts. She is making corsets for slimmer ladies now. That made me laugh!'

Eagerly, Anna slit open the envelope. She loved *Babushka* Seraphima dearly and had made many visits to Archangel to see her before the war with Germany intervened. Now her parents deemed that a visit was too risky, although there were still trade links between Dundee and Archangel, principally in timber and flax.

There were romantic links also. Anna's father and mother had met and married there and Anna had fallen in love with Seraphima's lodger, Aleksandr Rostovich, on her last visit before war had broken out. Anna and the young economics student had written faithfully to one another since she'd come home. For months, though, there had been no word from Aleksandr apart from a terse note in March, saying his army unit had been ordered to Petrograd to guard the Tsar.

So what had happened to Aleksandr when Tsar Nicholas abdicated? Today, though, was not the time to brood on such worrying matters and Anna turned her attention to her grandmother's beautiful Cyrillic script:

*My dear Anna,*

*So now you will be twenty-one years old. A Scottish lady! Every day I pause before the good St Stephen's ikon and say a prayer for you, my only grandchild. I imagine the blessed saint smiles. Do you remember when you were little you thought he resembled your brave papa, with whiskers? No wonder St Stephen smiles!*

*But on this, your twenty-first birthday, I pray that you will have a happy life. Though we may never meet again, dear child, I pray that you will find true love and know the joy of children.*

*You have a faithful heart, but you must forget the*

*love you had for Aleksandr Rostovich and be spared
the sorrows of a broken heart.*

*Be strong, no matter what news you may hear of
me. While I have breath, be sure I will pray for your
happiness, dear Anna.*

*For ever your loving* babushka *Seraphima*


Anna stared at the words blankly. It was not what she
had expected.

'Why aren't you smiling?' her mother demanded.

'Something's wrong. She sounds so sad!'

Irina snatched the letter and read it aloud, translating for
her husband's benefit. She glanced at him uncertainly. 'What
do you think, Andrew? *Mamushka*'s moods can change from
light to dark. Is this perhaps a lonely prayer for a grandchild
far away?'

'Perhaps. But her recent letters have been so cheerful, and
this is very different. Maybe something has happened.'

Anna turned to her father. 'I'm worried, Dad. Can't you
do something?'

'What do you have in mind, my dear?' He frowned.
'It's true that the *Pole Star* will make one last trip to
Archangel before winter, but I'm hardly fit enough to go
to sea. I can ask Duncan Wishart to look in on Seraphima,
but that's all.'

'But Dad—'

'That will be enough, Anna!' Irina interrupted hastily.
Her husband's serious illness had given Irina a bad fright.
His recovery had been slow.

'Anyway, my mother may be small in stature, but her
spirit is strong,' she went on. 'Besides, who would harm
a hard-working widow who has done so much good for
Russian women? My father was a doctor and from him
she learned the harm foolish fashion can do to the body.
So she set out to put it right. She taught me all I know about
corsetry.'

She turned to her daughter. 'Anna, the feast is over and

we must get to work. Mrs Hunter has a fitting at ten, and she is an athletic lady who rides bicycles. She demands strong support for stockings and no whalebone to stick into ribs. This makes problems!'

'Try a few elastic bands here and there,' her husband joked. Irina looked thoughtful.

'You know, darling, that is not a bad idea.'

It was Mina Murray who put unsettling thoughts into Anna's mind a few days later. Mina was weaving elastic thread into suspenders on the athletic lady's corset.

'My Archie's no' awfy keen to go on this trip to Archangel,' she said.

Anna and Irina were interested. Archie Murray, Mina's son, was cook aboard the *Pole Star*. He was a reliable weathervane on the way the wind was blowing in Russia.

'There's trouble in Petrograd down the coast, stirred up by a man called Lenin.'

'Petrograd was St Petersburg when I was a girl,' Irina mused. 'Why should this man Lenin make trouble in my country?'

'He wants peace.'

'Doesn't everyone?'

'Aye, but it's the way he's going about it that's worrying. He plans to kick out rich folk, get the soldiers to desert, and make peace wi' the Kaiser.'

'That's madness! Russia and Britain are allies! It'd be just us and the French against the Germans, then,' Anna cried.

Mina gave the finished suspender a satisfying twang. 'Archie says they've shifted the Tsar and his family from a grand palace to a wee place in Siberia for safety.'

'Siberia?' Anna and her mother exchanged glances. The Siberian steppes had a reputation for harsh weather and hard labour.

That night, Anna tossed and turned restlessly. Maybe the Tsar and his family would be safer in exile on the steppes, surrounded by loyal peasants who revered him. But Anna's thoughts were more concerned with Aleksandr. What had happened to him?

She sat up in bed, staring into darkness. If what Archie had reported was true, no wonder Seraphima was troubled. She'd always been a staunch Imperialist. But why had she mentioned sorrow and a broken heart? Anna refused to believe the man she loved was dead. I would have known! she thought. Somehow, I would have known.

Next day there were corsets to be delivered and Anna was glad to cycle off along Broughty Ferry Road, facing into a fresh east wind to clear her head. Afterwards, returning along Dock Street, on impulse she rode into the harbour area and dismounted at the quayside.

Her father's ship was preparing for the Archangel run and the dock was a hive of activity. She propped the bicycle against the wall and watched. If only her father had been in command there might have been a chance of finding out if Seraphima was safe and Aleksandr alive. But she didn't feel confident much would be done with Duncan Wishart in charge.

She remembered the man well from past voyages. As a young girl she'd admired his looks and suffered from a short spell of hero-worship. She'd followed him around aboard ship and he'd made no effort to hide the fact that he found her a tiresome nuisance. She had retired hurt and kept well out of his way since.

'Why, it's yoursel', Miss McLaren!'

She turned to see Mina's Archie, wheeling a trolley piled high with stores. 'Archie! Your mum was talking about you, yesterday.'

'If it wis about Jessie Bell, it wisna me.'

'No,' Anna laughed. 'It was the situation in Russia. You know my grandmother's Russian. We're very worried about her. What d'you think we should do?'

'If she was my granny, I'd get her out fast.'

'How can we, when my dad's ill?' she cried in anguish. A sudden possibility occurred to her. 'Archie, would

Captain Wishart take me with you? My gran will be reluctant to leave, but I'm sure I could persuade her.'

'Nah!' He shook his head. 'The man'll no' take passengers this trip. He'd no' let you set foot on the gangway.'

'And how could he stop me? It's my father's ship!'

She eyed Archie thoughtfully. An idea was beginning to take shape in her quick brain, but she'd need his help to make it happen.

'What are you thinking, miss?' Archie asked uneasily. Experience had taught Archie to have a suspicious mind when it came to the wily ways of women.

'Oh, nothing,' she replied airily. Before she involved Archie, she'd have a plan worked out right down to the last detail.

Just then, Anna noticed that Duncan Wishart had appeared on deck. The captain was supervising cargo being loaded into the hold when he caught sight of Anna. She waved merrily, mounted the bicycle and rode off, laughing.

Grimly, Duncan Wishart didn't return the salute. It was all very well for that flighty little madam to laugh. He had a dangerous journey ahead and the fearsome responsibility of her father's ship and crew. He watched her swerve around horse-drawn jute carts and a dock shunter hauling coal wagons. That young woman is trouble for someone, Duncan Wishart thought, and dismissed her thankfully from his mind.

Irina's heart was heavy with secret worry. Andrew had hovered at death's door that summer so she didn't want to concern her darling husband with her troubles. She knew northern Russians were a free and independent race, and now Imperial rule had ended, she suspected this would be a most fierce and terrible winter for those poor souls in her homeland. It was a turmoil which her beloved mother must face, alone.

If only Andrew had been well he could have brought Seraphima back, but Irina had no faith in Captain Wishart, an unsmiling man with a hardwood chip on his shoulder. Why should he bother about an old Russian woman? Irina finished stitching pockets for the boning on stays for Mrs Murphy – an ample lady who needed strong support. She tested the strength of lacing and busks. She nodded. Yes, Mrs Murphy would be pleased.

Today, there was more worry. Anna was not her usual sunny self. She had been jumpy and preoccupied. Unfinished work lay untouched on her workbench as she gazed out of the window towards the sea. That was unusual.

Then, in the evening she kissed her father for no reason and wiped away a tear. Irina watched, and her worry increased, though she said nothing at the time. Later, after they'd retired to bed, she knocked on Anna's door and went in to find her daughter fully dressed. Anna hastily closed an open drawer.

'My darling, what are you doing?' Irina asked.

'Nothing!'

'It does not seem like nothing to me.'

'I was just looking out some winter clothes. There's a nip in the air.' Anna began brushing her hair. The reflection in the mirror was tense and tearful.

'I, too, worry about Seraphima,' Irina said. 'I worry silently and do nothing, for there's nothing to be done. You must see that?'

Her daughter didn't reply. Irina hugged her. 'Please, my darling, promise me you'll do nothing rash?'

'I love you, *Mamushka*,' was all Anna said in a small, choked voice.

'I know.' Irina smoothed her daughter's dark hair and kissed her. 'Never forget your grandmother is a strong woman, Anna, and we, too, are strong.'

'I won't forget.' She touched the locket at her neck with a faint smile.

Irina had said goodnight and left the room before she realized her daughter had made no promises.

None at all.

\*     \*     \*

9

The plan Anna had evolved worked like clockwork. It was after all quite simple. If Captain Wishart wouldn't take her willingly, then she'd just stow away. She knew every inch of the *Pole Star* and had already decided where she could hide quite successfully.

The day before, she'd returned to the docks and collared Archie.

'There's quite a big store next to the galley, isn't there?'

'Aye, mops and brushes and suchlike.'

'I could hide there before the ship sails. Wishart would be none the wiser till it's too late to turn back. You could help me to sail to Archangel, Archie.'

'Whit?' he'd paled. 'No' me! It's more'n my job's worth. Wishart's a hard man.'

But Anna had faith in the persuasive power of her brown eyes. She laid a hand lightly on his arm. 'Oh, Archie! Imagine how you'd feel if it was your widowed granny out there, all alone. You'd do anything to help her, wouldn't you?'

'We-ell, I am awfy fond o' my auld granny . . .' He wavered.

'Of course you are! You're a kind, brave lad. I knew you wouldn't let me down. Bless you! Eleven thirty tomorrow night, Archie. Keep an eye open for me and make sure the coast's clear,' she'd ordered briskly, then planted a kiss on his cheek and watched him wander off in a daze.

Anna did not underestimate the dangers that lay ahead with this plan of action, but she knew she must face them bravely and, apart from Archie, all alone. However, when the time came for her to leave, her heart had turned to ice, mindful of the worry her unsuspecting parents must bear after her secret departure.

And so, on a dark and moonless night, while her parents slept soundly, Anna crept furtively from the house. When she arrived at the docks, Archie was nervously puffing the contents of a packet of Gold Flake at the foot of the gangway. He whisked her on board and into the locker without seeing a soul. She shut herself in and lit one of the supply of candles she'd brought. Archie, bless him, had provided for her comfort. There was a heap of clean jute sacks on the floor, two ship's blankets and a pillow. He'd left soap, a basin and ewer, and enough stores to feed a dozen stowaways.

Anna stretched and yawned. She'd had little sleep the night before, too busy packing warm clothing and sitting up half the night writing a long, loving letter to her parents. She'd left the letter where they'd find it in the morning, but, by then, the ship would be at sea and far away.

She still hated the thought of worrying them, but at least they would know she was safe aboard the *Pole Star*. Soon she heard the unmistakable sounds of departure, and the steady rhythm of the engines lulled her to sleep.

Archie attended manfully to her needs for the first few days, sneaking her out of the locker into the deserted corridor to wash and stretch her legs. On the fifth morning at sea, however, she was rudely awakened by a thunderous hammering. Rubbing her eyes, she unlocked the door. The corridor was full of men. Archie, ashen-faced, cowered in the background.

'You!' Captain Wishart exclaimed. 'I heard rumours there was a stowaway aboard, but I never dreamed it was you!'

'This is my father's ship, Captain!'

'You are still a stowaway, Miss McLaren!' His eyes narrowed. 'I'm tempted to leave you in there for the rest of the voyage – or on second thoughts turn around and sling you off at Muckle Flugga.'

'But you won't!' Her tone was defiant.

'No, I'm stuck with you.' He gave the cowering cook a baleful stare. 'Thanks to Archie!'

He turned and glared at the audience, which silently melted away. 'We're not carrying passengers this trip, so you may as well occupy a cabin. Collect your gear and follow me,' he ordered.

11

She obeyed in silence. He led the way down a companion-way and showed her into a cabin not much bigger than the locker. He stood in the doorway, blocking out what daylight there was.

'Stay in your cabin till we reach Archangel, or at any rate, stay out of my sight.'

She would have welcomed a little kindness at that lonely moment and, to her dismay, her eyes filled with tears.

'I only stowed away because we're desperately worried about my grandmother in Archangel and my dad's too sick to go. I knew you wouldn't accept passengers, but surely if your mother or grandmother was in such danger you'd do anything you could to help?'

'No, I wouldn't.' His blue-grey eyes were cold as steel.

'You . . . you're a cruel monster!'

'No. I just don't jump to conclusions, that's all.'

The cabin door closed behind him, leaving Anna shocked and shivering.

The first icy breath of winter had already frosted Archangel's cobbled streets. Winter had come early to northern Russia and Seraphima knew it would be long and hard.

She stood in her small shop in Troitsky Prospekt, a hand pressed against her mouth to check a frightened cry. The men were back. A crowd of them steamed the shop window with their hot breath, leering at the hand-embroidered corsets and lacy underwear displayed there. Seraphima's shop was a target for abuse because the ruffians believed her customers were *barynya*, fine ladies.

Oafs, she thought tearfully. Did they not know their mothers, wives and sisters came to her for warm woollens, which she sold for a few kopeks to combat fierce cold?

But Seraphima knew that her beloved Russia would never be the same again since Tsar Nicholas had been imprisoned.

Earlier that day, she'd watched a rag-tag mob go marching down the street, waving red flags and yelling freedom.

Someone had thrown a stone which had cracked a pane in the shop door. Then, to Seraphima's relief the men ogling her window spotted another victim farther down the street and moved on.

It was early afternoon, but Seraphima drew the blinds and shut up shop. At moments like this she was thankful that her son-in-law, Andrew McLaren, was recovering from illness and would not come to Archangel. The brave man would be incensed and try to rescue her, and that would be dangerous for him. For Seraphima was a marked woman. That was why she'd written cheerful letters to give no hint of her terror as the country descended into chaos after an uprising in February 1917 resulted in the abdication of the Tsar.

Foolishly, when the troubles had started, her fears had got the better of her and she'd written to her daughter and son-in-law telling them how much she hated the Bolsheviks who were steadily gaining an iron grip upon the land.

This letter had been returned to her within a day of posting, slit viciously open. A slash of red obliterated her loved ones' names in a dreadful, silent warning.

That night, Seraphima went down on her knees to thank God that Irina and Andrew McLaren did not know, and would not come hurrying to her aid. Her letters since then had been happy and cheerful, so that they would never know.

Somebody was rattling at the shop door, and she froze. Had those dreadful men returned? But the shadow on the blind was slender and the knocking urgent.

'Go away. The shop is closed!' she called.

The knocking stopped and a voice whispered, '*Babushka, ya Anya Androvna!* It's Anna, please let me in!'

Anna! Could it be? Pray God it was not! Seraphima felt faint and her hands shook so violently that she could hardly move the bolts. Was she dreaming? But when the door was opened, her granddaughter fell into her arms.

Anna was carrying a heavy bag and was chilled to the

13

bone. Seraphima's heart rejoiced, but her mind was filled with dread.

'Oh, Anna, what are you doing here?' she wept. She glanced up and down the street and quickly shot home the bolts.

'*Babushka*, we were worried about you,' Anna replied, tearfully. 'Dad wasn't strong enough to make the voyage so I came instead, to beg you to come home with me.' She was recovering, a smile now hovering on her lips.

'You're here alone? Anna dear, this is madness!'

'Hardly alone.' She laughed. 'I brought the captain and crew of Dad's ship with me.'

There was a thunderous knocking and Seraphima shrank in terror against the wall.

'Well, of all the cheek!' Indignantly, Anna opened the door. 'What do you want, Captain Wishart?'

He stepped inside and slammed it angrily behind him. 'What the blazes do you mean, sneaking ashore like this?'

'I didn't think you'd even notice. You made it perfectly clear you don't care what I do. Besides, I can look after myself.'

'Of course you can't. You're a stowaway, entering Russia illegally. You could be a spy, for all they know, and I'm responsible.'

'Hard luck!'

She turned her back on him and spoke to Seraphima in Russian. 'This is my father's second-in-command. If you come home with me dear *Babushka*, I'm afraid we're stuck with the rude oaf for the whole voyage.'

'Less of the rude oaf!' he scowled.

So he understood Russian! That required a change of tactics. Anna bestowed her most charming smile upon him.

'Just joking, Captain, dear! You'll take my grandmother aboard when we leave Archangel, won't you? You can see for yourself how dangerous the situation is for a lady on her own.'

He eyed Seraphima reluctantly. 'I suppose I'll have to

take her since she's Captain McLaren's mother-in-law. But remember, once our cargo's aboard, we must leave immediately. The ship and crew are my concern, not refugees, and I've no intention of spending a winter icebound in Archangel.'

'Don't worry, I don't expect any consideration from you, Captain Wishart,' Anna said icily.

The captain hesitated, then opened the door. He turned his collar up against the cold, gave the two women a cursory salute and set off down the street.

Anna bolted the door. Seraphima looked at her and said, 'The poor man was cold. Why did you not bring him in to the warm?'

'Because there's no warmth in him, *Babushka*. He wouldn't lift a finger to save his own mother. He told me so.'

Later, the two women sat talking and drinking Russian tea from clear glass cups, in the comfort of Seraphima's flat above the shop. Anna remembered this lovely room with affection. There was a tiled stove burning fragrant pine and birch logs occupying one wall, and carved armchairs with bright embroidered cushions and covers arranged around it, and rugs from Turkestan on the parquet floor. It was here that Aleksandr and she had shared their first stolen kiss.

But Seraphima was upset. 'Anna dear, I long to go with you, but what would become of Moussia?' Fondly, she stroked the large green-eyed cat purring on her lap. 'Already the Bolsheviks say I'm an enemy of the common people because I've worked for aristocrats. They're welcome to my belongings, but how could I leave darling Moussia to starve?'

'Don't worry, we'll take her with us,' Anna promised.

The beloved cat seemed a trifling complication. She broached a subject closer to her heart. '*Babushka*, where is Aleksandr? Last time he wrote he was guarding the Tsar. But I've heard nothing from him for months. Do you know what happened to Aleksandr after the abdication?'

Seraphima's eyes filled with tears. 'I'm afraid you must

15

prepare yourself for some very bad news, Anna. The Aleksandr Rostovich you loved is dead,' she told her granddaughter sadly.

'No!' Anna exclaimed. 'It can't be. I loved him so, *Babushka*. I was sure I'd know if he had died!' She broke down, racked with sobs.

Seraphima put her arms around the girl's thin shoulders and held her close. 'I'm so sorry, Anna. But terrible things are happening in these dark days and life must go on, my dear. Come, wipe your eyes. Let's turn our thoughts to escape.'

Anna was still too shocked to take any part in the conversation as Seraphima chattered on in an attempt to ease her distraught granddaughter's grief.

'First, we have a wedding to attend,' Seraphima announced. 'Madame Orlov ordered corsets for herself and the bride and I've agreed to help them dress on the wedding morning. I won't disappoint my good customers. Besides, there's a big bill to settle!' The shrewd businesswomen smiled.

There were flurries of snow over the next two days and frost tightened its grip upon the land. Anna and Seraphima were almost ready to leave Archangel when the Orlov wedding day dawned.

They rose early and set off on foot for Leon Orlov's large house, close by the river. They were muffled in fur-trimmed coats, hats, gloves and heavy felt boots. Anna carried a large lidded basket containing an indignant Moussia, mewing plaintively. The cat weighed a ton, but Seraphima wouldn't hear of leaving her pet behind in the empty shop when bands of criminals roamed the streets.

As a further precaution the two women had sewn jewellery, silver teaspoons and trinkets into their fur hats, along with Anna's precious locket. St Stephen's gold ikon was wrapped in old jerseys and tucked away out of sight in Moussia's basket.

'They're welcome to the rest.' Seraphima shrugged.

16

When they reached the house they found the interior buzzing with wedding excitement. Madame Orlov greeted them with a flush-cheeked baby in her arms. She looked harassed.

'This is Basil, Seraphima, our little . . . er . . . afterthought. He's teething, poor *pyzhik*.' She turned to the nanny. 'Take him, *mamka*. Try oil of cloves.'

Having disposed of the grizzling 'little reindeer' she ordered a maid to remove Moussia to the security of the kitchen quarters.

'Now, come upstairs and meet the rest of the family.'

A middle-aged gentleman in black trousers and white dress shirt met them at the top of the stairs. Anna assumed correctly that this must be Dr Orlov. He bowed.

'Good morning, ladies. Katerina, I can't tie this confounded bow tie!'

'I'll be with you in a minute, my darling. Is everything under control?'

'Perfectly. I ordered the children down the garden to the bathhouse early on, bride and all. They had a snowball fight on the way, would you believe?'

A young boy, rosy-cheeked and tousle-haired, appeared and eyed the visitors curiously. Madame Orlov grabbed him.

'Did you wash behind your ears, Michael?'

'Mama, nobody looks there!'

'I do! Go and wash.'

He wriggled free and disappeared. The fine lady sighed.

'That's one of our twins. Now, let's meet the bride.'

She continued along a corridor and opened a door leading into a room flooded with winter sunshine. A young girl, clad only in lace-trimmed chemise and knickers, was perched on the bed. There was such a striking similarity in looks to the young scamp they'd just met, Madame Orlov's introduction was hardly needed.

'Marga, the other twin.'

'Why must I wear horrid corsets, Mama?' The youngster sulked.

'To restrain your antics during a solemn service, monkey.'

Madame Orlov turned to the young lady seated at a dressing table, moodily studying her reflection. 'And this is Elena the bride.'

'Mama, I'm so plain. What did Dmitri see in me?' Elena said.

'He's a doctor, a kind and clever man. He knows beauty is only skin deep. But don't worry, Anna will make you beautiful. Seraphima will do what she can with me.'

Katerina Orlov grabbed the reluctant twin by an arm and swept her out of the room.

Anna thought Elena Orlov perfectly lovely once the thick dark hair was brushed and braided and arranged on top of her head. However, when it came to fitting the embroidered corset, she discovered Elena's waistline had thickened considerably since Seraphima made the garment.

'Anna, dear, not so tight. Leave room for . . . er . . . expansion.'

The two women stared at one another. The young bride sighed.

'Dmitri and I are very much in love and so we . . . anticipated our wedding. Anna, are you very shocked?'

'No, of course not!' Anna smiled warmly and eased the lacings.

'It is one reason why the wedding is so quiet, you see. Life is very hazardous for all of us now,' Elena said sadly.

By the time Madame Orlov returned, resplendent in shimmering turquoise, the bride was dressed in the beautiful Orlov wedding gown which had been handed down through generations.

'How beautiful you are, my darling!'

Katerina Orlov embraced her daughter and wiped away a tear. She carried a large leather jewel case, which she laid on a nearby table. 'Now, the collar of pearls!' she announced.

As she raised the lid, Anna gasped. A gold collar, set with clusters of diamonds and pearls in the form of orange blossom, was adorned with rows of pearls set in gold, every pearl separated from its neighbour by a matching diamond. Diamond and pearl earrings completed the set. It was breathtaking.

'Catherine the Great gifted this to one of my husband's ancestors,' Katerina explained. 'It's a tradition in our family that every Orlov bride wears it on her wedding day. It's priceless as a whole, but every piece can be detached and worn separately. Superstition says that if one piece is lost our dynasty will end. So we guard the collar of pearls with great care!' She fastened the collar around the bride's slim neck, where it shimmered and glowed with fire of its own.

Katerina kissed Elena on both cheeks. 'Go with God, my daughter,' she whispered.

Anna had never attended a Russian wedding before. The ceremony took place in the family chapel and was a quiet affair attended by the Orlovs, a few friends, and all the servants and estate workers. The bride and groom carried lighted candles twined with orange blossom and the heavy scent of incense filled the air.

Anna was pleased to see that Dmitri, the bridegroom, obviously adored Elena. His young bride would need her husband's love and care in the difficult months to come.

She turned her attention to the groomsmen holding gold crowns above the couple's heads. The taller one, immaculately turned out in the silver and black uniform of the Tsar's Black Hussars, must surely be Ivan, the bridegroom's brother. She had to admire his courage. Revolutionaries were on the lookout for former officers of the Imperial Guard.

By the time the ceremony ended, Anna had tears in her eyes for what might have been, for herself and Aleksandr.

There was a Russian feast in the salon and dancing in the ballroom. Ivan tracked Anna down.

'I've never danced with an *Anglichanka*. May I?'
'I hope you won't be disappointed!'
'You could never disappoint.'

19

He reminded her poignantly of Aleksandr, young and handsome, with a clear, admiring gaze and honest eyes.

'This dance is the *lisgintka*, fast and furious.' He led her on to the floor.

Seraphima was there already, partnered by Vassily, the Orlovs' gatekeeper. Her grandmother winked at her.

The music began slowly and Anna gave herself up to romance, circling dreamily around in the dashing young officer's arms. Gradually the tempo quickened, stirring her blood, rousing in her a Russian exuberance she hadn't known existed.

The dancers whirled, stamped, yelled and clapped in time to the furious rhythm. Anna's eyes were sparkling, ablaze with excitement. Ivan linked arms, whirling her round.

'You're magnificent, my *Anglichanka!*'

When Vassily had approached Seraphima in the dining room, she had hesitated to dance with him. Not that she had anything against peasants – far from it – but she was not from an agricultural background. Her father had been a cod fisherman, lost at sea when she was a little girl. Her widowed mother fortunately had the skill and foresight to design corsets for fashionable ladies. Later, Seraphima carried her mother's business forward, married a doctor and opened a successful shop.

It was no wonder she eyed the old man who lived a solitary life in the gatehouse doubtfully. His large hands were coarse with manual labour, his skin lined and leathery with working in all weathers. But it was a shy and hopeful face and she didn't want to offend him.

To her surprise, Vassily was light on his feet and supple as a birch wand. Seraphima responded to the magic of the dance and forgot she was elderly. She shouted, stamped and whirled furiously with the rest. Alas! Seraphima's balance was not what it once was. The room spun crazily, she staggered into the path of a leaping Cossack and was sent flying. Music faltered and died, dancers halted in horror and Anna screamed.

Seraphima lay on the floor, white with pain, clutching her ankle to ease its agony. In tears and quite unjustly, she screamed at Vassily, 'This is your fault, peasant, do you hear? Your fault!'

'It's not broken, but it's a very bad sprain. I've given her something to ease the pain and help her sleep,' Dr Orlov told Anna when the elderly lady had been carried to the spare room and Katerina had put Seraphima to bed.

'When will she be able to walk?'

'Not for a fortnight, at least. Even then she will have to rest that ankle as much as possible.'

'But Doctor, my grandmother and I have arranged to leave Archangel aboard my father's ship.' Anna was almost in tears.

'I had no idea!'

'We don't broadcast the fact. Seraphima feels threatened.'

'So do I. I've been outspoken in criticism of the new regime and now I'm told I've no right to own land. I've been warned the estate will be confiscated and the house looted any day now.'

He looked hopefully at Anna. 'Would there be room for my family aboard your father's ship, Anna?'

'Of course there would! Plenty room,' she answered readily.

Captain Wishart would be furious when she turned up with more refugees, but she'd fight that battle later.

Leon Orlov put an arm round his wife. 'Listen, my darling, you and the children must grab this chance to leave Russia in safety.'

'But what about you, Leon?'

'I'll give our servants and estate workers their pick of the furniture and leave the rest to the mob. Dmitri and I will stay at the hospital to make sure the patients are looked after. As soon as we can, we'll slip away to the new British naval base at Murmansk and join you later.'

21

'Oh, my darling, you'll be in such danger!' Katerina sobbed.

'I can take care of myself.' He smiled. 'My heart will be at ease, knowing you and our children are safe.'

True to the doctor's diagnosis, Seraphima could put no weight on the painful ankle next day. She lay in bed with Moussia cuddled beside her and supervised the Orlovs' plans for their hurried departure.

When Katerina visited the invalid that morning, she complained it was impossible to decide what to take.

'The collar of pearls must go with us, Seraphima, but it's such a responsibility!' she said. 'Vassily will drive the sleigh to the ship tomorrow night. But what if we're accosted by thieves?'

'You must think of a secure hiding place, madame.'

'These people are cunning, they know where to look.'

'We could hide the pearls where nobody would look,' Anna said.

'Could we? But where?' Katerina looked at her questioningly.

Anna laughed as she divulged her plan.

Some of the worry cleared from the troubled lady's brow as she considered the idea. 'Yes, that's wonderful, Anna! How clever you are.' She smiled. 'So now, shall we get started . . .?'

It was a parting full of sorrow when darkness fell and the lamps were lit next day. Elena sobbed as she clung to Dmitri, her husband of only a few hours, while Katerina and Leon held one another, the knowledge of danger and long separation uppermost in their thoughts.

It had been decided that Ivan must go with the family, since the treatment of former Imperial officers captured by rebels was particularly harsh. Reluctantly, he'd agreed to leave for Britain to fight another day.

Dressed inconspicuously in old clothes, Ivan carried Seraphima to the covered sleigh and wrapped her in warm furs. Seraphima could not look at Vassily, her shame at the injustice done to the poor man was so crushing. But what could she do to amend it? Saying sorry does not obliterate an insult, she thought. Conscience pained her more than an aching foot.

Baby Basil howled when taken from his weeping nanny's arms, but cheered up when installed in the sleigh with Michael and Marga. The twins waved the baby's wooden rattle and Basil reached for the noisy toy and began contentedly chewing the handle.

Vassily had stood impassively at the horse's head during the sad leave-taking. Falling snow mantled the old man's bowed shoulders and he took care not to look at Seraphima.

Normally, Anna would have enjoyed the sleigh ride through the dark, frozen countryside and snowy backstreets Vassily chose as his route to the anchorage where the ships were berthed. Tonight, however, the air seemed tense with menace. Even Moussia, a solid weight in her basket on Anna's knee, was quiet. She could feel the tension within Ivan as he sat beside her. The young officer had much to fear from dark figures gathered at street corners.

They heard shouting and screams in the distance, and the sky to the north was suddenly lit with a torch of flame. Katerina saw it, but said nothing. She prayed with all her heart that it was not their house. Skilfully, the gatekeeper manoeuvred horse and sleigh around shrouded stacks of timber down by the riverside, then stopped at a word from Anna.

'Wait here while I negotiate our passage,' she said with a confidence she didn't feel.

'Take Moussia,' Seraphima urged. 'The captain will be pleased to have a mouse-catcher aboard. Moussia will be an asset to the ship.'

Anna set off with the basket over her arm, heading for the quay where she knew the *Pole Star* was berthed. After she'd walked some distance she became aware that there were no ships of the *Pole Star*'s tonnage left in the frozen water. There were no lights, no drifts of tobacco smoke or smells of cooking, no voices. The whole place was silent and deserted.

Anna reached an empty stretch of frozen river where the *Pole Star* had been. She stared incredulously across a path of broken ice that marked the ship's departure. It took her a moment or two to accept that the cruel, cold man, Duncan Wishart, had abandoned them, just as he'd threatened he would. It had never entered her head that he wouldn't wait. Somehow, in spite of everything, she'd trusted him. That was what hurt, that was what made her cry so bitterly, as she stood all alone on the waterfront with the frozen river ahead and the insoluble problem of the Orlovs and her injured grandmother waiting patiently in the cold.

Moussia began a low mournful howling and started to kick and scratch the basket lid. Anna groaned. Far from being an asset, Seraphima's beloved cat was assuming the proportions of a nightmare.

# Two

An icy wind stung Anna's face and she began shivering, in spite of all the warm layers she wore to combat a Russian winter. She was on the verge of panic after finding that the ship had gone, but biting cold had a sobering effect. The priority now was to find shelter.

Tugging a scarf over her nose and mouth, she turned her back upon the frozen river. She dreaded breaking bad news to the others, but at least the effort of trudging through the snow soothed the cat. Moussia stopped her pitiful miaowing and lay quiet in the basket.

Retracing her steps past silent warehouses and snow-covered stacks of timber, Anna saw a light shining in the window of a cabin she hadn't noticed before. The scent of burning birchwood reached her nostrils and she could make out a pale plume of woodsmoke curling from the smokestack.

She paused. Whoever was in there might know where the *Pole Star* had gone. Her spirits lifted a little at the thought and she headed towards the cabin. She'd only taken a few steps before remembering the risk involved in these uncertain times. Would these people be friendly or hostile?

She halted uncertainly. Maybe it would be better to give the place a wide berth and return to the comfort of the Orlovs' home. As she turned away she saw flames and sparks shoot up in the distance, lighting the dark sky with an ominous glow. The area of the fire seemed perilously close to the Orlovs' estate. If it was their property going up in smoke, they'd have no choice; they'd have to find shelter tonight and investigate a dangerous situation in daylight.

So there was nothing else for it. I shall have to ask someone for help, she thought, eyeing the cabin doorway apprehensively.

Her knocking seemed to fall on deaf ears at first. Then the door suddenly whipped open and a man confronted her. He was brandishing some sort of weapon.

Anna screamed.

'Whee-eest!' the man hissed, glancing around nervously before peering down into her face.

'Och, it's yoursel', Miss McLaren!' he said with relief, lowering a large frying pan.

'Archie!' She hugged the *Pole Star*'s cook with delighted surprise. 'Oh, Archie, dear, I'm so pleased to see you! What's happened to the ship?'

'Aye, well, the skipper waited till the very last moment, but he had to head for open water when the icebreakers came. If he hadn't the ship would've been stuck in the ice till the spring.'

'What a predicament! But why did he leave you behind?'

'Skipper says sneaking you aboard in Dundee was my fault so I can face the consequences. Och, he's a hard man, thon Wishart!' He sighed. 'Onyway, he ordered me to sling ma hammock in this auld hut that's leased to your pa's shipping company an' keep a weather eye open for you an' your auld granny.'

Anna could have wept. Now she had Archie on her conscience as well as the rest. 'Oh, I'm so sorry to get you into trouble, Archie, but I don't see how you can help us.'

'Nae bother, miss! The skipper left plenty cash for you to take the train, and I'm to escort ye.'

'There's a train? Where to?' she demanded excitedly.

'Murmansk. The water doesnae freeze there 'cause of warm currents and Wishart says the ship'll wait for us. He thinks there's railway most o' the way.'

'Can we trust him to wait?'

'Skipper says to keep our fingers crossed.'

'Don't worry, I will!' she said grimly. 'But the bad news is there are more refugees, now. There's my granny who's sprained her ankle, a Russian officer in danger of his life, two ladies, twin bairns and a girny baby. Not to mention this angry cat.'

She tapped the basket and Moussia snarled. Archie recoiled.

'I cannae stand cats!'

'I'm not keen on them myself, at the moment. Anyway, you'd better come and meet the rest of the party. The poor souls are expecting safe passage on my father's ship.'

He followed dutifully, but was struck dumb at the sight of a sleigh packed with people. His eyes widened with panic.

Ivan had been pacing up and down, making anxious tracks in the snow. He came striding towards them. 'Anna, thank God you're safe! I was worried. I was sure I heard a scream. Is this one of the ship's crew?'

She introduced Archie and gave Ivan the bad news. The young officer groaned. 'Then we are truly sunk!'

'No, there's still hope, Ivan. The ship will wait for us at Murmansk. We can take the train.'

'Don't you realize how dangerous that is?' he warned. 'Red Guards target railways. Rich people travel by train.'

'I hadn't thought of that.' She sighed dispiritedly. 'Maybe we should go back to the Orlovs' house and try to find a better way.'

Vassily pointed to the red glow still illuminating the northern sky. 'Maybe there is no house! There were rumours that Bolshevik sympathizers were forcing the Orlovs to leave. Then the house will be burned, by order of the people's soviet.'

'But why should the council burn such a lovely house? What's the point of that?' Anna cried angrily.

'They believe it shows bourgeois citizens that the common people rule Russia now.'

She turned cold. 'What about Dr Orlov and Dmitri?'

27

'Oh, they won't be harmed, miss. Don't worry. Doctors are desperately needed. They say hospitals in Moscow and Petrograd are packed with wounded deserters from the Romanian front.'

Ivan gave the old man a pitying glance. 'If this is true, Vassily, your home has gone too, I'm afraid.'

'A house is sticks and stones, *barin*.' He shrugged. 'Home is where the heart is.'

Vassily turned away and spoke soft words to the patient sledge-horse.

There was consternation when news of the disaster was broken to the others. Elena, the young bride, was inconsolable for the husband she'd been forced to leave behind and the scared young twins huddled together for comfort.

Baby Basil sensed trouble and howled miserably while Seraphima tried to soothe matters with a sentimental lullaby which made all the Russians weep.

Presently, Katerina Orlov dried her eyes and turned her attention to practical matters. 'The temperature's dropping,' she observed. 'If those evil men have indeed destroyed our home we'd better find shelter for the night.'

'I know where we can go,' Anna said.

She emphasized the cabin's comfort and endowed Archie with rank, authority and thereby courage, which was perhaps bending the truth a bit, but served to revive everyone's flagging spirits. They beamed upon Archie with hope and admiration.

His understanding of Russian was limited to phrases picked up in riverside bars on previous visits, but he recognized admiration when he heard it and swaggered importantly as he led the way.

Madame Orlov was taken aback when she saw the rough timbers of the sturdy wooden building. 'This is no better than a peasant dwelling, Anna dear!'

'But it's warm, ma'am!' Anna pointed out through chattering teeth.

When they'd disembarked and the men had carried

Seraphima inside, Vassily drove the sleigh round the back and stabled the horse in the woodshed.

The main living area was crowded when they were all assembled in there, but at least there was a plentiful supply of logs. Archie packed the stove till it blazed and the weary travellers began to thaw out and relax.

Basil started a fretful wailing in Katerina's arms. His mother knew he needed a nappy change, but this had been the nanny's job and the poor lady had only the sketchiest idea of how to proceed.

She and Elena struggled clumsily with towelling and safety pins, but at last the baby was comfortable and smiling again. He tossed the wooden rattle to the floor and chuckled as his mother rushed to retrieve it. Basil immediately realized that this was an absorbing new game.

Seraphima dozed in the adjoining bunkroom with Moussia purring in attendance. The cat had been released from the hated basket and placated with strips of dried cod which Seraphima kept handy for emergencies.

Archie eyed the animal warily. The cat seemed to sense dislike and took devilish delight in rubbing her head lovingly against Archie's trouserleg.

There weren't enough seats to go round, but the refugees settled down gratefully on the sawdust-covered floor. A weary silence fell as they contemplated their plight.

Archie was a cheery soul who hated to see long faces. Determined to lift everyone's spirits, he turned to a subject close to his heart. Food. Opening the storeroom door with a flourish he revealed a cupboard packed with cans of food, sacks of potatoes and flour, strings of onions, tins of biscuits and chocolate bars.

'Tell the poor souls this food comes wi' the compliments o' the *Pole Star*'s captain, miss. Let them know they'll no' starve.'

Anna translated and that raised a cheer. Soon the aroma of frying onions drifted through from the adjoining galley while Archie concocted a simple meal. He'd decided a nourishing potato dish better known in his home town as 'stovies' would do the trick.

The refugees were impressed by the delicious results of Archie's cooking, under such difficult circumstances. Ivan and Anna sat side by side, demolishing heaped platefuls of the inspired dish.

'You're right, my *Anglichanka*, your Captain Archie is a most capable chap,' Ivan said admiringly.

Anna hid a smile as she watched the young cook relaxing in his hammock, having shown the twins how to collect dirty dishes and do the washing up. The children thought guddling with hot soapy water a fascinating new game and were tackling the task with gusto.

'Marga, a wee bit mair hot water in the tub for rinsing, like I showed ye, hen,' Archie called encouragingly.

'I must admit Captain Archie knows what he's about,' Anna said, laughing.

'Our escape is in very good hands,' Ivan agreed seriously.

He dared to slip an arm around her waist and Anna did not object. She welcomed the comfort of his arm and rested her head gratefully on his shoulder as they sat close together in the firelight.

Danger had sharpened the emotions and she was certainly attracted to Ivan. But was it for his own qualities, or because he reminded her of Aleksandr? Tears welled up in her eyes at the memory of her lost first love.

Ivan traced a teardrop down her cheek. 'Why are you crying, dear one?'

'Just a sad memory.' She sighed.

'But you were born to smile!' he said softly, and kissed her.

Anna relaxed in his arms and gave herself up to the magic of the moment.

Katerina Orlov sat in the shadows watching the young couple, but took no pleasure in the sight. How could she, when her adored husband was not with her and her eyes ached with tears? Stop it! Don't fall in love, she longed to warn them. Love will make you vulnerable.

Katerina sighed. As if these beautiful young people would listen to a sad, middle-aged woman! She looked down at the baby, breathing rythmically on her lap. Elena lay curled up, fast asleep, beside her, exhausted with weeping. If Vassily were to be believed, the Orlovs were homeless, all their beautiful possessions looted, the house burned.

But not all the riches! With a sudden glow she remembered the Orlovs' most precious jewel, the wonderful collar of pearls, was safe from thieves in a place where nobody would think of looking.

Katerina studied Basil's guileless little face. This dear baby of her middle age was the most precious jewel of all, more precious to her than diamonds and pearls. She hugged the baby to her breast, suddenly overcome by a terrible fear for this innocent child. Would he be taken from her? Then the painful pent-up tears ran down her cheeks . . .

Dawn had broken when Captain Duncan Wishart returned to the bridge of the *Pole Star*, though it was not yet time to commence his watch. A restful night's sleep had eluded him, all because he'd abandoned Andrew McLaren's cherished daughter and mother-in-law in war-torn Russia. He tried to comfort himself with the thought that he'd had no choice. Pack ice had been tightening a stranglehold on the *Pole Star*'s hull. With an icebound winter in prospect and no sign of the two women, he hadn't dared to wait another moment once the icebreakers came in. But no doting father would believe that!

Well, at least he'd done his best to retrieve the disaster. He'd sent Archie Murray ashore as escort – and the ship had lost the best cook they'd ever had as a result. The crew were grumbling already. Life had taught Duncan Wishart hard lessons. The most important was whom to trust, and he trusted Archie.

Archie might not be the brightest star in the navigational

almanac, but he'd survived a streetwise education in Dundee's pubs, not to mention the city's darker wynds and closes.

And, having had the opportunity to observe Anna McLaren's composure during a stormy, dangerous passage outwards from Dundee, the captain had grudging respect for that young woman's fortitude. Her courage, he'd decided, bordered on sheer brass neck, which would be useful ashore. He'd judged those two would make a formidable partnership. He only hoped the judgement proved sound.

He turned his attention to the sea. The ship had long since passed islands at the mouth of the frozen Dvina and was in the open waters of the White Sea, but Wishart had lookouts posted and had ordered a cautious rate of knots in case of submerged ice floes or enemy mines.

The reinforced hull had been built in a shipyard famed for Arctic whalers, but Captain Wishart would take no risks with Andrew McLaren's vessel. He owed everything to that fine man. It was a debt he knew he could never repay – except perhaps by bringing Andrew McLaren's reckless runaway daughter home safe and sound.

Wearily, he rubbed his eyes, gritty with staring at a grey sky and unfriendly sea. Visibility was fading, a storm was on the way and worry clouded his mind.

'Launch coming up astern, cap'n,' the lookout called.

Shaken out of his reverie, Wishart glanced round in surprise. It was a sleek white craft, a red flag fluttering at the stern. It sounded a warning klaxon and a signal lamp winked imperiously at him. It was obvious those aboard intended coming alongside.

What on earth was going on? He gave the order 'slow ahead' and the ship's engines subsided to a mere whisper of steam, enough to preserve steerage way and allow them to board.

He went on deck to supervise the unfurling of the Jacob's ladder and watched as four men accomplished the tricky transfer from boat to ship.

These were military types, dressed in Red Guard uniform. The officer in charge saluted and Wishart nodded.

'Comrade, we have reason to believe you have illegal passengers aboard,' the officer said in good English.

'You've been misinformed, my friend. We've no passengers on this trip.'

'You have no objection if we search?'

'Be my guest,' Duncan Wishart said pleasantly.

They were very thorough, even breaking open packing cases in the hold, but of course they found nobody. Wishart followed them curiously as they entered the tiny cabin Anna McLaren had occupied. Although it was empty of her few belongings, a faint essence of her perfume lingered on the air. He'd noticed it often himself, and he watched with interest as the officer raised his head and sniffed delicately.

'Ahh! You carry lady passengers?'

'Sometimes ladies, sometimes gentlemen – whoever will pay the fare. But not this trip,' Duncan answered levelly.

The man gave him a cool glance and rapped out an order. The search was intensified. It was over an hour later before the men assembled on deck.

'Satisfied?' Wishart enquired.

'Very satisfied, comrade.' The officer smiled but his eyes were cold. 'I will tell the commissar the person he seeks is still ashore. That makes it easier for us.'

'Who are you looking for?'

'That is not your concern.'

A cold smile, a mocking salute, then the four soldiers climbed down the ladder to the waiting boat.

Duncan Wishart leaned on the rail and watched the launch speed back the way it had come. He was deeply troubled. Were they after Anna or Seraphima? The women had no papers or exit visas and somebody must have tipped off the authorities.

And what about Archie? He'd be in serious trouble if they caught him ashore without the necessary documents. The revolutionary forces might even use Archie's capture as an excuse to confiscate the *Pole Star*. If they could catch her!

Wishart raced to the bridge and whistled down the voice pipe to the engine room. 'Full steam ahead!' he ordered, recklessly.

Andrew McLaren had never before known such anguish and anger as he had experienced on finding his daughter's farewell note that fateful morning. He'd thrown it down on the table in angry despair. The anger was not directed at Anna, of course. He could never blame the brave lass for trying to save her grandma. He'd have done the same himself, if he'd been able.

'I know who's to blame for this, Irina!' he'd cried bitterly. 'It's that man Wishart!'

Irina had tried to soothe him. 'My darling, if Anna has made up her mind to rescue her beloved *babushka*, I doubt if even Captain Wishart could stop her.'

'That's hardly the point! The man was duty bound to tell me what the lass had in mind. Why the devil didn't he warn me on the quiet?'

'Perhaps he did not know.'

'Of course he knew! He's captain of my ship, isn't he? It's his job to know!'

'Anna does not say in the note that he knew,' Irina had argued, studying the letter intently. 'She only writes that she will travel with him, and tells us not to worry, because Wishart is a fine seaman and knows Archangel well.'

Andrew's rage had known no bounds and his distress would not be comforted. 'Say what you like in his defence, my dear, but the fact remains he's risked our daughter's life taking her there. It's a serious breach of trust and Wishart will never work for me again,' he'd declared furiously.

Strangely enough, though, despite the worry and anguish that occupied his every waking thought, Andrew McLaren's health had improved vastly since that unhappy day.

November was raw and chilly, but today a blink of sun

tempted Andrew to wrap up warm and stroll down to the harbour. There was always the forlorn hope he'd see the *Pole Star* come steaming in.

He was disappointed, but sunshine persuaded him to walk through the harbour area, revelling in the familiar sights and sounds of the busy port. He continued past the red sandstone splendour of the West Station until he reached the riverside promenade which stretched towards the girders of the railway bridge that spanned the Tay. There, he paused and rested for a bit, leaning his elbows on the sea wall and staring pensively across the river to the Fife coast.

The ferryboat, known affectionately locally as 'the Fifie', swung out from the ramp nearby and began plying its way across to Newport, but Andrew's gaze was fixed moodily upon a black and white hulk anchored off Wormit on the opposite side.

This was the *Mars* training ship for boys, a former man-o'-war built in the 1840s, whose reputation for strict discipline sent a shudder down young Dundonians' backs and provided provoked parents with a potent threat: 'Behave yoursel', or I'll send ye tae *Mars*!'

Leaning on the wall, Andrew recalled the skinny little eleven-year-old urchin the first mate had hauled before him by the scruff of a dirty neck, nearly twenty years ago.

'Found 'im hiding in the for'ard locker, cap'n.'

Andrew had scowled at the wee wretch. 'What are ye up to? Thieving?'

'Naw! I wouldnae. I'm goin' tae sea.'

'Oh you are, are you?' Andrew had eyed him more tolerantly. 'How's your maths?'

'What?' his mouth had hung open.

'You can't navigate a ship without maths. What about knots, can you tie a clove hitch?'

'Naw.'

'Och, you're no use to me. Come back when you're six foot and educated. Now run away home to your ma.'

'I never had a ma,' he'd said.

'Everybody had a ma, sonny.'

'I didnae. And I've had a bellyful o' foster folk.'

Andrew had taken him by one too-thin arm and marched him on deck. He'd pointed across the river.

'See that ship?'

The lad had turned pale with fright. 'It's the *Mars*. It's for bad boys.'

'No, it's not. It's for training wee skelfs like you to be of some use aboard ship. If I put your name to the board and you were accepted for training, would you go?'

The boy had hesitated a while. 'Aye, mister, I would,' he'd said eventually.

'Very well, it's a bargain. What's your name?'

'Duncan Wishart, sir.'

Today, Andrew turned away from the river with tears in his eyes. There was a painful lump in his throat as he remembered how proud he'd been of that half-starved wee waif in the end. But all the same his mind was made up. Duncan Wishart would never work for him again.

The refugees wakened next morning to a fresh snowfall and Archie whistling 'Pack up Your Troubles'. The stove was stoked and there was the sizzle of bacon frying. Hot water steamed in the boiler in the kitchen and a large container of snow was melting nearby.

Katerina Orlov could hardly believe her eyes. The rude little hut was almost civilized.

The greasy smell of frying reached poor Elena's nostrils. She clapped a hand to her mouth and rushed outside, disappearing into the snow.

Archie stood at the door and watched with interest. He glanced at Anna and raised his eyebrows. 'The poor lassie. So that's the way o' it, is it?'

'I'm afraid so.'

Young Michael's spirits had revived after a sound sleep. The snow looked soft and tempting. He nudged his twin sister. 'C'mon, Marga. Let's go out and have a snowball fight.'

'No thanks. I don't want to play childish games.'

He stared in astonishment. Marga was a tomboy. There was nothing she loved better than a snowball fight. 'Are you sick?'

''Course not.'

'Elena is.'

'She's having a baby. It makes you ill. Boys don't know anything!' Marga sighed.

'C'mon *sestritsa*. We could build a snowman,' he cajoled.

But she turned her back and carried on brushing her hair.

Michael went outside in a temper and began kicking the snow about. He was lost and lonely. What on earth was wrong with his sister? The truth was that Marga had fallen in love. It had happened suddenly when Captain Archie took her hand and swished her fingers through soapy washing-up water, and it felt wonderful and strange.

'Not too hot for ye, is it, hen?' he'd asked kindly.

She and Michael were taught English at school, but not the English that Captain Archie spoke. His brown eyes had been warm and his voice deep and soft but the words had sounded strange. She liked this 'hen' though. She didn't understand what it meant but she'd noticed it was an endearment used only for herself. It was a special word between them, maybe because he loved her too.

Play? She had finished with playing. She had grown up. She was in love!

After breakfast Archie cornered Anna in the privacy of the kitchen. 'The sleigh's gone an' so's the horse. Looks like the old man's pinched them,' he said quietly.

'What?' She realized she hadn't seen Vassily that morning. He must have crept out when everyone was asleep. This was a serious blow. They couldn't travel far on foot.

'Oh, Archie, what are we going to do?'

'Search me.' He shrugged.

Seraphima wept when the news was broken to the shocked

refugees. 'It's my fault! I insulted the poor man and this is his revenge.'

'Nobody is to blame, my dear,' Katerina comforted her. 'Not even Vassily himself. Our world is turned upside down and the poor old man has nothing to show for faithful service to the Orlovs. Maybe he's entitled to the horse and sleigh. After all, he looked after them for years.'

But Ivan could not take such a lenient view. 'He's a thieving, callous wretch!' he stormed angrily. 'I've a good mind to go after him and drag him back.'

Anna stood up hastily. She couldn't let Ivan barge into town in this frame of mind. He'd draw attention to himself, and although the clothes he wore were shabby old cast-offs, he still had a soldierly bearing. Somebody might put two and two together.

'No, Ivan, I'll go myself and see if I can find out where he's gone. I might be able to persuade him to come back and at least drive us to the station,' she said. 'You're a stranger in town and would attract attention. The locals have seen me in the marketplace with Seraphima. Nobody will think it odd.'

The others were not happy with this suggestion, but nobody could think of a better plan. They clustered round the doorway to watch Anna leave and wish her luck.

Anna found it quite a relief to be on her own again after the hectic events of the past few days. It was easy enough to follow Vassily's tracks, until she reached the cobbled streets and they disappeared into hard-packed snow.

Her spirits sank. She could see she'd set herself an impossible task, but she went on nevertheless. There might be news of him in the market. Food was scarce, but people still gathered out of habit to gossip and hear the latest news. Anna saw a woman stallholder she recognized and bought a weary cabbage as an excuse to enquire about Vassily and the ominous fire they'd seen. The woman was eager to talk.

'Such a shame! The pretty house is a blackened shell this morning and I heard Dr Orlov and his son-in-law are to be sent to Petrograd. There's been fighting round the Winter Palace, and there's a shortage of doctors to tend the injured.'

'Oh no!' Anna cried.

'Aye, miss, I'm afraid the country's in a bad state. There are rumours the British will send troops to Archangel if Lenin makes peace with the Germans. But it's more than your life's worth to speak out. The *Cheka* has moved into town on the quiet.'

'The *Cheka?*'

The woman put her mouth to Anna's ear. 'Secret police, my dear.'

But there was no word of Vassily.

Anna plodded dejectedly past the ancient cathedral where she'd worshipped with Seraphima and Aleksandr in happier times. She paused beside the public bathhouse with its lines of numbered doors and cautiously studied the exterior of her grandmother's shop. To her amazement the blinds were up, corsets and delicate underwear displayed in the window as usual, the wooden storm doors open. Everything looked as it should do on a normal working day. But how could it be?

Anna had helped her grandmother secure the shop and the flat above before they'd set off for the wedding. They'd locked all doors and drawn the blinds. So who is in there? she asked herself. This was an intriguing mystery. Cautiously, she skirted fresh heaps of snow shopkeepers had cleared from the boardwalks and was making her way towards the shop when a neighbouring shopkeeper clearing ice from his doorstep glanced up and saw her.

'Miss, don't go in! The *Cheka* are in there!' he warned softly and quickly bent to the task once more.

She halted abruptly and stared at the shop's innocent facade. Only it didn't seem quite so innocent now. She realized, with a chilly sensation of dread, that it was a trap cunningly set for Seraphima or herself. There was only one consolation. They obviously did not know where to find her, yet.

Unless Vassily told them, of course.

# Three

A nna was terrified. Her first instinct was to turn and run, but she knew someone would be watching from inside the shop. She paused, and in leisurely fashion, studied cheese, salted herring, pickled cucumber and rounds of dark rye bread in nearby shop windows. She was glad she'd bought a cabbage in the marketplace. To the casual observer she would simply look like a woman out shopping. Muffled in layers of clothing designed to ward off frostbite, she was confident she would not be recognized.

She bought some provisions, then crossed the wide street at an unhurried pace, dreading all the while a tap on the shoulder or a grip on the arm. But nothing happened.

She'd given up hope of finding Vassily. Now her priority was to warn Seraphima and the others that their hiding place was no longer safe. Anna quickened her pace as she made her way along avenues lined with bare trees mantled with snow. Glancing over her shoulder to make sure nobody was following her, she broke into a run.

Sun shone on dazzling whiteness all around her and the golden domes of churches sparkled with layers of silver frost. Tramcars were snowbound that day so the town lay in the unique stillness of a northern winter. There was silence broken only by a tinkle of distant sleigh bells, the snorting efforts of sledge-horses and the sigh of runners slicing through hard-packed snow. Her fear seemed out of place amidst such peaceful tranquillity.

By the time she arrived back at the cabin she was gasping for breath, and she tumbled through the door, startling them all. Archie pounced on the food, but the others gathered round her and listened with growing horror and distress as she relayed what had happened.

'But who can be in my shop? How did they get in? I have all the keys!' Seraphima wailed.

'Someone must have broken in and ransacked the place after you left for the wedding,' Ivan said grimly.

'It didn't have the appearance of a burglary,' Anna frowned. 'The shop was open for business as usual and the window display was beautifully arranged. It looked more like a trap, and in that case the authorities must realize we haven't left Archangel'

'Perhaps.' Ivan nodded. 'And although they obviously don't know where to find us yet, I bet Vassily will tell them. We must get out of here.'

Katerina Orlov had been devastated by the news that her husband and Dmitri were destined for Petrograd. 'I will leave Archangel without a backward glance now they've destroyed our beautiful house,' she declared passionately. 'But I won't leave Russia unless my darling Leon goes with me.'

'Wheest!' Archie held up a hand. 'There's someone outside.'

Anna heard furtive sounds, a faint jingle of harness and the beat of hooves muffled by snow. Her heart lurched. Had she inadvertently led their enemies to this hiding place?

Before she could make a dive to lock the door, it swung open to admit a man clad in thick furs. He pulled off gloves and began unwinding a scarf covering his nose and mouth.

Ivan sprang forward and pinned him to the wall. 'How many have you brought with you, you wretch?'

The scarf fell away from the man's face as they struggled, and Seraphima cried out, 'Vassily! We thought you'd deserted us.'

The old man pushed Ivan aside. 'There is nobody else, *barin*, only me.' Sadly, he studied the frightened, suspicious faces. 'I've worked as a free man for this family for many

41

years and could have left any time. Did you really think I would desert you now?'

'What were we to think?' Katerina cried angrily. 'Where have you been?'

'To sell the sleigh.'

'What? How dare you do this without my permission!'

'Would you have given it, *barynya*?' he asked patiently, 'It was a beautiful sleigh made for rich people and it attracted envious glances when it passed with its bells jingling. It was not a vehicle to choose if you wish to escape unobserved.'

Katerina was silenced. She saw the force of the argument, but it didn't make the loss any easier to bear. 'Oh, Vassily, the lovely sleigh!' she whispered.

She couldn't stop the tears. The sleigh held precious memories of happy times. She saw herself as a young bride in her husband's arms as the horses raced across the frozen river to take them on a blissful honeymoon. She remembered joyful visits of parents, now long gone. She heard an echo of children's happy laughter as the horses sped along the ice . . .

It was a sad sacrifice, but a wise one. Katerina wiped away a tear and met Vassily's sympathetic eyes. The old man understood the loss. It was breaking his heart too.

Strange, she thought, how this humble old servant had become a valued friend, whose sorrows matched her own.

Anna listened to this unexpected development with dismay. Speed was important. The sleigh had been well balanced and fast, even when drawn by a single horse. She glared at the old man. 'Now we've no transport, thanks to you! How are we now going to cross the river to the railway station when the ice is thick enough?' she demanded.

'Oh, we won't wait for that, *barynya*, we'll leave right away. I've made other arrangements.'

He opened the door and pointed to a strange vehicle standing outside. The old horse-drawn cab was totally enclosed, with a door and a grubby sealed window on either side. The whole contraption stood on low runners and the driver's seat was more or less open to the elements.

'It's a *vozok*!' Elena laughed. 'It's the most battered old *vozok* I've ever seen!'

It was the first laughter they'd heard from the sad young bride. Everyone joined in, even Vassily.

'Nobody will give it a second glance!' he chuckled. He turned to Katerina Orlov apologetically. 'I took the liberty of buying furs with the roubles left from the bargain. The cab is lined with thick felt and you'll be quite warm. It will be cold as we drive south.'

South? They stared at him. That meant following a well-used main road which led to the rail junction at Vologda and eventually to Petrograd.

Katerina was astonished. 'Is that wise? What if we're stopped?'

He studied their crumpled clothing and dishevelled hair and his eyes gleamed with amusement. 'If anyone asks, we are a peasant family travelling to a wedding. We'll drive south to a spot I know where the river will be safe to cross. There's a small railway station used by peasants and hard-up farmers not far away. If you don't mind travelling the hard way, nobody will bother you.'

Ivan looked at the old man with respect. 'It's a sound plan. Rich people never travel like that.'

'Yes, it will work, *barin*.' Vassily grinned.

I wish he hadn't said that, Anna thought nervously. It seemed like tempting fate. She recalled Duncan Wishart's advice and hastily crossed her fingers.

A commissar stood looking out of the window in Seraphima's warm flat above the shop, concealed from view by lace screens. He had been watching the comings and goings in the street all day from this vantage point.

Olga, an efficient female Red Guard recruit, was downstairs in the shop, dealing with would-be customers, but the people he hoped would come had not appeared. Early darkness was already closing in and the lamps were lit.

There were footsteps on the stairs and a tall man entered, cheeks pinched with cold. The commissar turned to him eagerly. 'Any sign of them, Boris?'

'None. They've vanished into the snow drifts, Commissar.'

Boris removed his fur hat and overcoat and flung them down on Seraphima's chair. He wore a shabby suit, but Duncan Wishart would have recognized him instantly as the army officer who had made a thorough search of his ship.

He warmed himself by the stove, rubbing cold hands together. 'The sleigh has been found, though.'

'Where?'

'Here in Archangel,' Boris replied. 'A carpenter bought it from an old peasant. It had been stolen, most likely. The house and stables were burned to the ground, as you know.' He glanced at the commissar. 'Looks like the prey has escaped the talons,' he said lightly, trying to hide his curiosity.

'Please don't align me with Imperialist eagles, if you don't mind!' the commissar said, laughing. He turned back to the window. The sun had sunk blood-red into blackness, but the heavy snowfall made darkness bright. 'You say the ship's bound for Murmansk?'

'So the deckhand said,' Boris confirmed.

'We have guards posted in Murmansk. The ship will be kept under close observation. In the meantime, you can escort the two doctors to Petrograd and make sure everyone knows where they're going. That way, we have all possibilities covered.'

'Very clever. What do we do about this place?'

'We ask Olga to shut up shop and then we commandeer this comfortable bolthole for our cause. They won't come now, Boris. Something tells me they're miles away.'

The commissar drew Seraphima's red velvet curtains across the window, shutting out the night . . .

*     *     *

44

Dundee had not been troubled by snow as yet, only frost and rime that trapped smoke from a forest of factory chimneys and brought yellow acrid fog down upon the city. It wasn't good for a man with the scars of pneumonia on his lungs. Irina had forbidden Andrew McLaren to set foot outdoors, and he chafed against the restriction.

It was little wonder that the moment a soft west wind cleared the air and restored a sparkle of sun to the river, the captain grasped the opportunity.

'I'm away out for the day, love!' he announced one morning.

'Where are you going?' Irina asked anxiously.

'A trip on the train and a visit to Wormit.'

'That is an expedition. You will wait while I make sandwiches.'

Andrew set off swinging his walking stick. He had a plan in mind which he had not divulged to his dear wife. He had long been a patron of the *Mars* training ship for boys, and had no difficulty securing an invitation to go aboard. He intended to satisfy his curiosity concerning Duncan Wishart.

As Andrew's anger at the man's behaviour had smouldered into brooding resentment, he realized he knew very little about his protégé's early life. When, at last, a tense telegram arrived from Wishart reassuring him that Anna was safe, and in the process of retrieving her grandmother, Andrew was greatly relieved. However, inactivity had never suited Andrew McLaren. He had become increasingly curious to learn more about the man he held responsible for his daughter's safety.

After the short train journey across the Tay bridge, Andrew found the cutter from the *Mars* waiting for him at Woodhaven pier. It was manned by small boys with identical close-cut haircuts, dressed uniformly in navy trousers and jerseys and supervised by an officer. He was rowed smartly across the three hundred yards separating

45

ship from shore and was warmly greeted on deck by the captain.

After a short tour of the solid old man-o'-war, the captain seated Andrew in his stateroom. 'So what can we do for you, Captain McLaren?' he asked.

Andrew explained his mission and the captain frowned thoughtfully.

'Twenty years ago? That's a bit before my time. However, there should be a full report on the lad somewhere in the records, if you'll just bear with me for a moment.' He pulled a large ledger from a shelf and pored over it.

'Ah, yes! I thought I recognized the name. Duncan Wishart was one of our success stories. Conduct exemplary apart from a tendency to argue, which earned him the tawse now and again. Top marks in English and Mathematics, distinction in Seamanship and Navigation. He could have been accepted for training by the Royal Navy, but preferred to go into merchant service. He did very well there, gaining his mate's ticket and reaching the rank of captain at an early age.'

He looked up with a smile. 'A very bright lad!'

'But what was his background?'

The captain referred to the book again. 'Foundling. Parents of infant were unknown.'

'A foundling?' Andrew was startled. 'I knew he was an orphan and had a series of foster homes, but I didn't know he'd been an abandoned baby. Where was he found exactly?'

'That I don't know. The police might have it on record, though. You could try there.'

Andrew stood up. 'Thanks, Captain, I'll do that.'

As he boarded the waiting cutter he had a lot on his mind. He was quite determined to discover more about Duncan Wishart's unusual start in life.

Vassily's plan was working well, but traffic was heavy, making progress slower than expected. The full extent of the upheaval taking place within Russia was becoming clear.

Bands of army deserters were making their way north, hoping to grab a share of land once owned by the rich. An equal number of servants and estate workers were fleeing south to the cities in hope of finding work. The highway was jammed with horses, carts and sledges piled high with people, household goods and looted artefacts. Nobody took any notice of the old horse-drawn cab.

Archie had packed as much food as possible into the interior before they left, but Katerina had objected to several ripe cheeses whose rich aroma played havoc with Elena's nausea. Obligingly, he'd wrapped the cheese in tarpaulin and stowed the package outside on the luggage grid.

During one of many stoppages, Archie decided everyone would benefit from a nourishing snack. Rye bread and cheese would be just the ticket. He climbed out into freezing cold air, welcoming the freshness. But just as he was unwrapping the cheese, a hand fell on his shoulder. He found himself surrounded by a group of army deserters with gaunt cheeks and hungry eyes.

'We'll have that!' one said. Archie was familiar with the phrase from Russian hostelries. He'd heard it in answer to the question: What'll you have?

'Oh, no, you'll no'!' he stated.

'You want a fight?' The man doubled his fists.

Archie studied the poor undernourished specimen.

'Och, awa' hame to your ma, you wee nyaff, an' tak' yon bunch o' tattie-bogles wi' ye,' he replied, not unkindly.

The desperate men reminded him of scarecrows guarding cornfields in his native Angus.

The deserters stared, open-mouthed. Vassily came to the rescue. The Russian group turned to him. 'We only asked a bite of cheese, comrade, but this man talks strangely. I know a little English, but this is not it.'

'He is Dundonian. They are fierce fighters,' Vassily warned.

47

The men backed away and scurried off.

'Haud on, loons. You could do wi' a feed!' Archie yelled. Grinning, he hurled the cheese after them. The twins could understand Archie's Scottish dialect reasonably well by now, based upon English lessons at their former school, and little Marga applauded the generosity. Her vulnerable heart swelled with renewed love for her hero. She could only utter a shy word of thanks later on, when he handed round slices of cheese and pickled cucumber neatly arranged on rye bread. Archie had a special word for little Basil as he handed him a baby's bottle filled with sweet rowanberry cordial.

'There, my wee man. That'll put hair on yer chest!'

Michael nudged Marga. 'Hair on a baby's chest? What a fool!'

Marga slapped her twin brother's cheek. He yelled, more surprised than hurt, but the precious bread and cheese fell to the floor and was lost amongst the furs.

Moussia, released from the basket, pounced greedily.

'Mama, did you see what Marga did?' Michael struggled with tears. Marga had been his playmate and companion since birth. He'd shared his hopes and dreams with her, admitted his weaknesses and fears. She understood his terror of darkness, and always made sure the lamp was lit beneath the saint's holy ikon in the bedroom at home. Home! A heart-rending tide of homesickness washed over him. There was no home now, no *Papachka*, no comforting lamp to lighten the darkness any more.

His sister was staring at him as if she hated him. He didn't know why, except it had something to do with the loathsome sailor. Since they'd met him, Marga had behaved like a stranger.

There was a window separating cab from driver. It slid back and Vassily's face appeared in the opening. 'We've made such slow progress we must find shelter for the night. But don't worry, my old friend Petya lives nearby. He won't turn us away.'

Elderly Petya and his wife were astounded to find Vassily with a group of strangers standing in the doorway of their cottage. The couple recovered swiftly, however, and the visitors were ushered inside.

Their home was small and humbly furnished but spotlessly clean, and Mrs Petya was charmed to have a baby in the house. She removed Basil from his mother's arms and attended to him, cooing and singing.

Archie brought in stores from the cab, which Vassily had concealed behind the cottage. The horse he stabled in the byre adjoining the living quarters.

After a satisfying meal, their hostess produced a jug of *kvass*, a drink made from fermented brown bread and raisins, and the men settled down round the scrubbed pine table to chat and drink beer.

This was dangerous! Anna thought. Tongues were loosened and guards dropped. Petya and his wife seemed a pleasant pair, but how could you tell where loyalties lay these days?

'So it's a wedding you're off to. Anyone I know?' Petya asked Vassily.

'You remember Lidya Androvna, my cousin's youngest girl?'

'No, I don't. I thought you'd lost touch with all your relatives years ago. You seem to have collected a few, all of a sudden.' Petya laughed, waving a hand at his guests.

'These are my late wife's relations. It makes sense for us to travel together,' Vassily said easily.

Michael resented this remark. The young lad refused to be classed with the sailor who'd bewitched his twin. He pointed at Archie accusingly. 'Except that man doesn't belong with us. He's from an English ship and shouldn't be ashore at all.'

There was an awkward silence, during which Marga glared at her brother. Vassily blew scented smoke towards the ceiling.

'He has permission to attend the wedding, of course.'

49

'Oh, of course!' Petya laughed jovially, handing round the stoneware jug of beer.

Anna did not sleep well that night, although the stove kept the cottage warm as she lay on the wooden floor with the others, wrapped in furs. She had noticed their host eyeing the well-tended hands of his women visitors, in stark contrast to Mrs Petya's hard-worked hands and broken fingernails.

Ivan shook her awake while it was still dark and the lamps newly lit. 'We should be ready to move at sunrise, Anna. Vassily says the river crossing isn't far.'

He pulled her to her feet and held her in his arms for a few comforting moments. They had slept in their clothes and the young officer was already sporting a growth of beard.

'It suits you,' Anna smiled, stroking his cheek.

'It's a good disguise. I look just like a bandit.' He laughed, kissing her.

She rested her cheek against his shoulder to hide her disquiet. A beard could not disguise what he was – a handsome young officer with an aristocratic bearing that singled him out in a crowd.

Meanwhile, around them the others were gradually preparing for the day ahead. Seraphima's ankle was much better. She was up and moving around freely with the aid of a stick, keeping an anxious eye on Moussia, who'd been released from the basket. Archie had given Mrs Petya a bag of oatmeal to make a pot of porridge – a rare treat – which she was stirring on the stove.

Katerina Orlov had slept lightly. In the early morning, a chilly draught had roused her and she had realized someone had quietly opened and closed the door to the byre. She'd tucked the furs more securely around the baby and slipped back into a fitful dose, but now she remembered the incident. Looking around, she saw no sign of Petya.

'Your husband was up early,' she remarked to the peasant woman.

'He had work to do.'

Katerina met Anna's eyes and saw the same worried

thoughts mirrored there. She smiled at Mrs Petya. 'We'll have a plate of porridge and be on our way.'

'Petya said to tell you there's no hurry.'

'I think there is.'

The woman gave her a quick glance. 'Very well. Give me the baby and sit down and eat,' she ordered. She patted Katerina's arm and spoke softly. 'I'll make sure the little one is changed and fed for the journey. Don't worry, no harm will come to him.'

They ate bowls of porridge washed down with milk, while Vassily quietly harnessed the horse and prepared the cab. Moussia was put into the basket, protesting loudly, and the travellers took their places in the *vozok*.

Anna whispered to Vassily before the door closed, 'Can we trust Petya?'

'Can we trust anyone? All I know is that someone is looking for us and I don't know who or why. That's enough for me.' He took his place on the driving seat and shouted to the horse, '*Gei, gei, gei*, Osopa!'

They went trotting briskly on their way as the red rim of the rising sun gleamed for a moment through thick forests of dark pine.

When they reached the crossing place, the route across the frozen river was being well used by carts, sledges and footsore pedestrians. Archie made a small clear space in the frosted window and looked out.

'Look, Anna, it's packed like Woolworth's on a wet Saturday out here. I thought the auld man promised us a nice quiet train trip?'

'He didn't. He said we'd travel the hard way. It's safer.'

'Surely a wee bit comfort in First Class wouldn't go amiss? It's no' as if we're carrying the Crown Jewels, is it?' he grumbled.

Anna smiled to herself. If he only knew! The Orlovs' family heirloom, the priceless collar of pearls, was hidden where nobody would think to look.

'And what about this poor lassie in her condition?' he

went on, turning to Elena, who sat between them, pale and tired. Archie smiled at the young bride. 'Lay your head on my shoulder and have a sleep if you want to, missis. That was an early start.'

Elena looked into the young sailor's warm brown eyes with gratitude. 'Thank you, Archee. You are ver' kind man,' she told him in halting English. She rested her head wearily against him and closed her eyes with a contented little sigh.

Tenderly, he put an arm around her and arranged the furs warmly across her shoulders.

Marga couldn't believe it. She'd been sitting nursing a grievance against her brother, and now Elena, a married woman, was flirting shamelessly with Archie! Oh, how she longed to leap out of her seat and drag her sister away from him. How dare Elena do this? Marga's eyes flooded with hot, jealous tears.

Katerina watched, and her heart sank. What was happening to her united family? Marga was glaring at Elena, and Michael sulked next to Seraphima. He had refused to sit anywhere near his twin. To Katerina's distress, it seemed the cab's interior was buzzing with disruptive emotions.

As Vassily edged the horse cannily down the river bank and the runners began rumbling hollowly across the icy Dvina, only the baby slept peacefully, blissfully unaware that his loving family was slowly falling apart.

When they arrived at the small wooden railway station just before midday, they found it overwhelmed with frightened people. Rumours were rife and it was whispered that it was only a matter of time before Bolsheviks came north to deal severely with any opposition.

Ivan decided it was essential to shepherd their small group to the front of the platform to board the trucks the moment the train arrived. He'd travelled the hard way before and suspected the trucks would be little better than cattle trucks, fitted with rough timber bunks and benches strewn with straw.

Now the time had come to say goodbye, Katerina hated to part with Vassily, the last link to their former life. She held the old man's hand, at a loss to convey all that was in her heart. 'You could come with us, Vassily. Please come.'

He shook his head and smiled gently. 'And who would care for my horse? How could I rest in a foreign land if I thought Osopa was ill-treated?'

She had no answer to that. Unhappily she searched the lining of her muff and gave him a set of small spoons set with precious gems. 'These will buy you more than roubles will.' She smiled.

With tears in his eyes, he knelt and scrabbled on the slushy path at her feet. When he stood up he held two handfuls of mud which he spread tenderly over her soft white hands and manicured nails. 'There, dearest *barynya*. That is safer for you.' Meanwhile, by pushing, shoving and ignoring resentful protests Archie and Ivan had secured tickets and managed to usher the women and children closer to the platform edge. After that, there was nothing for it but to sit on the wooden boards and wait, huddled in the few furs they'd managed to bring from the *vozok*, along with a rucksack of rations, suitable for a long journey, that Archie had got together for them all.

Seraphima was proud of herself. She'd managed well despite the ankle. Moussia was yowling in the basket, so she loosened the lid a fraction to give her air and soothed her with her voice.

Peace descended, apart from the lilting sound of many peasant voices and the fretful crying of babies.

And so the long day wore on.

The train, when it came, did so quietly, with only the tremor of the rails to alert everyone. Then pandemonium broke out as it steamed into the station.

Ivan grabbed Anna, Katerina and the baby, Archie snatched Elena with one hand and the twins with the other and swung them aboard.

'*Babushka!*' Anna yelled, struggling to reach Seraphima.

'I can look after myself, Anna. Go on now, dear, you get aboard!' Seraphima pushed forward, using the cat basket as a battering ram. She had almost reached the truck when the leather thongs holding the lid burst under the strain and the terrified cat leapt out.

Seraphima screamed. She caught a glimpse of her beloved pet darting frantically through the crowds. Seraphima turned back, all thought of boarding the train now gone. Fighting her way through, cheeks wet with tears, she shouted despairingly as she hobbled on.

'Moussia, Moussia, my darling, come back!'

There was no sign of the cat anywhere; Moussia had disappeared.

# Four

Anna had scrambled aboard the crowded wagon, but when she turned round to offer her grandmother a helping hand she couldn't see Seraphima anywhere.

'*Babushka*, where are you?'

There was no reply. Thoroughly alarmed, Anna tried to climb down.

'Please let me through . . . I must find my grandmother!' She cried frantically.

None of those swarming aboard would let her pass, and she was shoved roughly aside. Ivan quickly hauled her to safety on a straw-covered bunk and held her there despite her protests.

The Orlovs and Archie had taken refuge nearby, surrounded by the assorted bundles they'd brought with them. Katerina Orlov clutched a large kettle, guarding it like the crown jewels. They were all safely aboard, only Seraphima was missing.

'Ivan, please, let me go!' Anna struggled desperately as the engine let out a warning blast.

'Anna, listen to me!' He held her fast. 'If you go now you'll miss the train for sure.'

Doors were slamming shut all along the line and, seconds later, their heavily laden wagon gave a convulsive jerk and began to roll along the track, gathering speed.

Anna buried her face in Ivan's shabby coat and sobbed.

'Don't cry, my love, please don't!' he begged. 'Your grandmother probably boarded the train farther down.'

'What if she didn't?'

'She'll follow us to Murmansk on the next train and turn up safe and sound. Seraphima is a determined lady!' He smiled encouragingly.

Anna dried her tears and lay quiet in Ivan's arms, but she couldn't share his optimism. Where was Seraphima? What had happened to her during those few vital minutes Anna had lost sight of her grandmother? Oh, if only she'd stayed by her side. If only!

Wearily, she drifted into a troubled sleep, lulled by the dull rhythm of the wheels and the soft murmur of many Russian voices . . .

Seraphima hobbled to the outskirts of the crowd and found herself on a deserted road rutted with deep snow. She looked up and down hopefully but there was no sign of the cat. The sprained ankle was agony, but the aching sense of loss was much worse.

'Moussia! Moussia!'

Her cries were thin and weak in the icy air. She knew they would hardly reach the few scattered cottages which made up the small farming village, but Seraphima guessed the terrified cat would make for signs of habitation. Moussia was a cherished household pet. She would not know how to survive outside.

Seraphima headed for the nearest cottage. The snow was much deeper here and she floundered into a drift, tripping over the cat basket she was carrying. She fell face down, stupified by pain and numbing cold and with little strength left to struggle on.

At that despairing moment she felt herself lifted up and helped to her feet. In a daze, she heard a man's deep chuckle as he brushed caked snow off her coat and hat.

'A snow-woman, by St Nicholas!'

Then she heard the shrill warning blast of the engine's whistle. The sound brought Seraphima to her senses. 'The train's leaving!' She gasped.

'Quickly! There's still time – I'll carry you!' The man grabbed her but she fought him off.

'No! No! My cat's lost. I can't leave without my cat!'

'Mistress Seraphima, be sensible!'

And then she realized who her rescuer was. 'Vassily!'

'Yes, but hurry!'

Even as he spoke they heard the train steam out of the station. Silently, they watched the long line of coaches disappear into the forest. Pale woodsmoke drifted through the pines.

'Well, ma'am, that's that!' Vassily said. He glanced down at her. 'The cat's safe. you know.'

'What?' At once Seraphima brightened up. 'Where is she?'

'In there.' He pointed.

The horse and ungainly old cab were parked behind bushes at the back of the station buildings. She stared at the old man questioningly.

'I waited out of sight till the train came,' he admitted. 'I wanted to be sure all was well with you.'

'And Moussia recognized the cab!' Seraphima closed her eyes and gave joyful thanks.

'Yes. The little cat came scratching at the door.' Vassily nodded. 'She's safe inside, hiding under the furs.'

Seraphima almost hugged him but remembered just in time how badly she'd treated Vassily. The awful memory ruined a happy moment.

'Why didn't you bring her to me right away?' she cried tearfully. 'I might have caught the train!'

'You might!' He shrugged.

He retrieved the cat basket then picked Seraphima up as if she were as light as a feather and carried her to the cab. Moussia crept sheepishly from beneath the furs and settled thankfully on her mistress's knee, purring loud relief.

Vassily sat opposite, watching.

'Now I've found Moussia, I'll catch the next train,' Seraphima decided.

'I've been thinking about that.' He frowned. 'Maybe you shouldn't.'

'Why not?'

'I think you have enemies.' He hesitated. 'I heard someone say the secret police are on the lookout for two ladies from Archangel.'

'Could that be the Orlovs?' She looked at him with dread.

'No.' He shook his head. 'There was no mention of that family.'

'So you believe it must be myself and my granddaughter,' she said flatly.

'That's what I think.' He nodded.

This information chilled Seraphima, though it was not unexpected. She knew she was a marked woman. Vassily was quite right; darling Anna would be safer travelling alone. The corset-maker from Archangel was a well-known face, but Anna could escape notice in a crowd.

'Very well, so be it!' Seraphima squared her shoulders. 'But how am I to reach Murmansk now?'

'By road. I'll drive you there.'

'You?' She stared at him. 'But it's a long, slow journey by road in these conditions. The ship won't wait!'

'Your granddaughter will make it wait,' he said. 'It's her father's ship and she will have the authority. She came to Russia to take you home. She won't leave without you.'

Seraphima eyed Vassily doubtfully. He was quite right, but there was still one problem. 'We would have to travel together – alone!'

'Not alone. There is the cat.' He grinned, then caught her stern expression and hurried on hastily. 'I'll be driving by day, of course, and we'll stop for the night at resthouses I know along the route.'

'I have my good reputation to consider . . .' She studied the elderly peasant, undecided. What was she to do? Her ankle was badly swollen after this escapade and she could not walk another step. Although, how could she ask Vassily to attempt this long, hazardous journey on her behalf when they were on such bad terms? It didn't seem right to ask the man to do it.

'Mistress Seraphima, it may not be an easy choice.' Vassily sighed. He could see the dilemma. 'But it's a choice an enemy might not expect you to make.'

Seraphima was silent.

'Very well!' Vassily stood abruptly. 'I'll leave you to consider the risks of travelling with a peasant while I see to my horse.'

He spoke coldly and left Seraphima feeling miserable.

Her gaze fell upon the cat basket and she suddenly remembered the precious ikon of St Stephen, hidden inside. Reverently, she unwrapped the ancient ikon that had graced the walls of her home ever since she could remember. The saint would be watching over all those she loved, as he always did.

The sequence of events now held fresh significance for Seraphima. Moussia's escape, her pursuit of the cat and Vassily's presence with the cab seemed ordained. Even missing the train might be part of the scheme of things, although Seraphima could not see the grand design just yet.

She smiled, said a prayer, shed a few tears and felt at peace again. When Vassily returned he found the lady sitting serenely, the cat fast asleep on her lap.

'Well?'

'I'll travel with you.'

'Good.' He nodded. 'We should leave at once.'

She stopped him with a hand on his arm. 'Thank you, Vassily – for everything.'

He shuffled his feet and muttered, looking hugely embarrassed. On closer scrutiny, though, Seraphima noted that the hurt had gone from his eyes and she was heartened . . .

The train journey seemed to take forever, mainly because Anna was impatient to reach the first stop to search for her grandmother. She slept fitfully, but was on her feet the moment the train ground to a halt.

There was a frantic rush and much pushing and shoving as passengers struggled to disembark in the pitch blackness of a winter's night. Anna and Ivan joined the crowd, hand in hand. He refused to let her out of his sight.

Katerina Orlov handed them the precious kettle. 'There will be boiling water somewhere,' she told them. 'There always is.'

When Ivan lifted Anna down into the trampled snow they found themselves in a forest clearing, surrounded by a few wooden buildings occupied by railway staff. There was great activity taking place by lantern light to replenish the tender with wood for the onward journey.

Meanwhile, the engine, a mighty black ninety-ton monster, gulped vast quantities of water from an insulated storage tank.

They searched, but there was no sign of Seraphima in the other carriages or amongst queues of passengers snaking into the railway cabins, seeking hot water for washing and tea-making.

Anna clung to Ivan, in tears. 'She isn't here!'

'She'll be on the next train. Try not to worry.'

He put an arm round her as they joined the end of the queue. 'Better make sure Katerina has nothing precious hidden in here,' Ivan said, lifting the kettle lid and glancing inside.

'She wouldn't be so obvious!' Anna smiled. She knew the precious collar of pearls was hidden where nobody would look.

'You're right.' Ivan replaced the lid. 'And I was convinced it contained the crown jewels, the way she was guarding it!'

'She knows hot water's more valuable than jewels.' Anna laughed.

He drew her close to him, protecting her from the bitter night air. Anna relaxed in the warm circle of his arm. How safe she felt beside him! Yet she knew safety was only an illusion. It couldn't be guaranteed for anyone embarking on this long journey.

Captain Duncan Wishart had made good time on the voyage to Murmansk. The voyage had proved uneventful, rather to his surprise. His imagination had conjured up all sorts of possible threats after the ship had been searched in the White Sea, but they'd encountered no mines, storms or enemy warships en route.

He stood on the bridge and narrowed his gaze towards the small huddle of buildings which comprised Murmansk, resting between two low hills by the mouth of the River Kola. He noted the comforting sight of a grey British frigate or two in the ice-free harbour.

'Slow ahead. Steady as she goes!'

The river pilot was aboard, but it was an easy enough approach. The *Pole Star* idled gently into her allotted berth. There was a smell of oil and fish and icy cold air and the reassuring sound of unfrozen water lapping the quay. So far, so good.

However, once arrival formalities had been dealt with by the British naval authorities and Duncan was free to explore the port, he found no sign of Anna McLaren, her grandmother, or Archie, his ship's cook. He stood on the bank of the dark river, wondering what to do for the best. Admittedly the *Pole Star* had made good speed, but he had confidently expected Archie to be waiting on the quay with the two women in tow.

Duncan was surprised to discover how concerned he was about the welfare of Anna McLaren. Troublesome though she was, she was not easily forgotten and he had been quite looking forward to seeing her safe.

He shivered suddenly as he turned away from the cold water reflecting the dark sky. The Red Army's search of his ship must have unnerved him more than he'd suspected, for he had a heavy sense of foreboding in the pit of his stomach now that the two women and Archie hadn't turned up.

These thoughts were occupying his mind when he rounded a corner and bumped into a pedestrian muffled to the nose in typical Russian fashion.

'Sorry, old chap!' Duncan steadied the man.

He didn't reply, but their eyes met before the man nodded, ducked his head and went quickly on his way.

Duncan Wishart stared after him in astonishment. The captain of the *Pole Star* could never forget the cold, keen eyes of the man who had searched every inch of his ship. So what was a Red Guard officer doing in civilian clothing in a far-off bastion of Allied naval power?

Duncan had felt uneasy before, but now he was seriously worried. The Red Guard was obviously hunting Anna and her grandmother for some reason he found hard to understand. Russia was on the brink of civil war. Why bother about two innocent women when army deserters, released convicts and homeless refugees were everywhere on the move? It made no sense!

Duncan Wishart returned slowly to the *Pole Star* to wait – and worry . . .


Irina McLaren couldn't settle to work, so anxious was she about Anna and Seraphima. The papers carried reports from Russia and the news grew grimmer with every passing day. Lenin was making peace with Germany and had thrown the Allies into panic. Britain was considering sending forces to northern Russia to organize resistance against the Bolsheviks.

'And my mother and our daughter are in the middle of this trouble, Andrew!' Irina wept.

'Maybe they'll be safe aboard ship by now, love,' her husband said.

'You mean you've heard good news?' She brightened up.

'N–not exactly.' He hesitated. 'There was a message

from Wishart at the telegraph office. The *Pole Star* arrived safely in Murmansk, your mother and our daughter are fine but there had been a delay and he was awaiting developments.'

'That's all? My mother and daughter are "fine"? What does he mean – "developments"?' She stared at Andrew angrily.

'Problems with cargo or exit visas, I expect.' He shrugged. 'It's wise of Wishart to head for Murmansk, it's an ice-free port. He's on the spot, my dear, we have to trust his judgement.'

'Trust him?' she shouted. 'You know nothing about this man, not even who his parents were. You tell me he was a foundling with no good background, and you took pity on him. This man risked our dear daughter's life and you swear he will never work for you again. And you ask me to trust him?'

'Irina, darling, listen—'

'No! I have listened for weeks! I am sick of listening to you! I want my daughter back and my mother safe, that is all I want. Do you understand me?'

Andrew had never seen his wife so angry. She was Russian and volatile, always exciting, but always loving. Her flashing temper was soon done with, quickly turning to tears or laughter in his arms. They'd weathered many squalls and loved one another all the more for them, but this was a tempest, a hurricane, and he was afraid.

'Irina . . . please . . .' He tried to take her in his arms, to calm her with a kiss.

'Don't you touch me!' She shoved him away.

He reeled back against the wall. He'd tried so hard to help her through the heartbreak of their daughter's disappearance, and this was the thanks he got! Well, now he'd had enough.

'Don't worry, I won't!' He stared bitterly at his wife, tears on his cheeks. 'You're not the only one that's hurting, Irina, the only one that's broken-hearted and in need of comfort.

I've struggled to keep hopeful and cheery for your sake when I felt more like breakin' down and crying. Well, I needn't have bothered. I can see you're too selfish to heed anyone's suffering but your own!'

He turned on his heel and walked out on her. It was the first time in all the years of their marriage they'd failed to kiss and make up. He shrugged on a coat from the coatstand and grabbed any old hat, then headed outside into Peep o' Day Lane.

It was a cold day, and icy sleet driven by a cutting wind stung his cheeks. Blinded by tears, Andrew didn't notice the discomfort. Doggedly he walked along Dock Street, heading instinctively for the everlasting comfort of the sea.

By day and night the long trainload of weary travellers had passed through vast forests and featureless open spaces. Now and again, the landscape was dotted with villages and peasant cottages and little churches with clusters of wooden domes. All were embedded in the first snow of winter.

Under different circumstances, Anna would have found the scenes from the tiny square window quite beautiful. However, her appreciation of beauty was dulled by so many stops for wood and water, and frequent shunting to sidings to let faster trains speed through, some with red flags fluttering from the windows. All she longed for now was to arrive.

Katerina had given up all attempts to control baby Basil. He roared and struggled and would not be contented upon her knee. In desperation she put him down on the straw-covered floor and he was immediately delighted. He crawled off swiftly to charm the neighbours. Katerina, trusting to the Russian love of babies, had neither the strength nor inclination to fetch him back. Besides, she was becoming increasingly concerned about Elena. Her daughter was finding the jolting discomfort of the wagon a sore trial.

'Oh, Mama, what if it harms the baby?' she whispered.

'It won't.' Katerina smiled. 'Women are not so weak,

64

my dear. It's an illusion we foster to flatter the men-folk.'

Elena managed a smile, but it was difficult. If she had to endure the rattling, itchy discomfort of this awful truck much longer she thought she would scream.

Archie was teaching the twins his version of English while Marga was attempting to show Archie how to play cat's cradle.

'This is what you call an awfy mixter-maxter,' he said rue-fully, holding up fingers trapped in a confusion of string.

Marga was doubled up with laughter at the tangle, and even Michael – not Archie's greatest fan – giggled help-lessly.

Elena envied them. Maybe when Dmitri joined her in England and their baby had arrived safely, she could laugh and be happy again. Maybe!

Suddenly the train stopped with a grinding screech of brakes. The passengers were thrown about and there was much screaming and shouting.

'Basil!' Katerina dived for the floor, scrabbling frantically through the straw.

'He's here, *barynya*. I have him.' A peasant woman held Basil on her lap, none the worse. She handed him over.

'Oh, thank you!' Katerina hugged the baby. She knew her hair was untidy, hands as dirty as her shabby clothes, and yet she'd still been recognized as a 'lady'.

'How did you know?' she asked the kind woman softly.

'Ma'am,' the woman patted her arm, 'it takes more than dirt to hide good breeding.'

It was intended as a compliment of course, but how it frightened her! It meant that no matter how she tried, she could not hide. Katerina crouched on the bench, wondering why they'd stopped. The junction at Belomorsk was their destination, but this barren area could not be it. She pacified the baby with the wooden rattle which was never far from her hand.

They could hear shouting, and doors were opening and slamming shut.

'It's thieves! Brigands!' a voice whispered fearfully.

'They won't bother us.' Another laughed. 'We've nothing worth stealing.'

But the door was soon flung open. The thief had the look of a dark-eyed renegade Cossack, a curling lovelock on his brow. He grinned. 'Morning, comrades! Any rich aristocrats hiding here?'

Nobody moved. His black eyes narrowed and he looked thoughtfully around the interior. They came to rest on Katerina. She straightened her back, raised her chin and stared back at him.

'Ahah!' he said, and bounded in, laughing. 'I'm collecting contributions for the cause, fine lady.'

'Here you are then.' She reached into her pocket and held out a wad of paper money.

'Oh, come now, ma'am!' He frowned. 'We both know that's not worth anything.' His eyes lighted on the kettle at Katerina's side and he lifted the lid and glanced inside. 'Now that's a nice kettle. Just the thing for me and my mates.'

'You can't have it.' Katerina was adamant.

'Did you say – *can't*?' The man scowled.

'Yes. You may have my diamond rings and gold bracelets, but you can't have my kettle. I need it for the child.'

The thief stared, his mouth hanging open. Basil waved the rattle in his astonished face and chuckled. The robber had been made to look foolish and a titter of laughter ran through the wagon.

'Fair enough!' he agreed, trying to maintain a semblance of dignity. Katerina ripped open the lining of a fur hat and handed him the contents. He scooped the jewels into a pocket and left hurriedly, slamming the door.

'That was brave!' Anna told her admiringly.

'This kettle is more precious than jewels,' Katerina shrugged, then smiled impishly. 'And he didn't get the collar of pearls.'

66

When the train reached Belomorsk they said goodbye to their travelling companions, most of whom were heading farther south. Anna and the rest of her party would continue the train journey north-east across the Kola peninsula towards Murmansk.

If only Seraphima had been with them, how happy she would have been! Ivan made enquiries at the ticket office and discovered their train wasn't due for several hours. It was a nuisance, but there was a warm stove in the waiting room and copious hot water available for washing and making tea. They settled down in reasonable contentment on the wooden benches to wait, eat and sleep.

There was much coming and going on the platform outside, however, and the baby was restless. Basil refused to sleep and wouldn't even lie quietly and play with the rattle, preferring to fling it pettishly to the floor. He brought the roof down when his mother scolded and restrained him. Having become accustomed to crawling around the railway wagon to be petted and admired by friendly strangers, he screamed and struggled energetically till Katerina was at her wits' end.

She knew Elena was worn out and needed to sleep and the others were not much better, but how could they have any peace with Basil screaming? In desperation Katerina picked the baby up and carried him outside. Anna followed her, to lend a hand.

It was better outside. Cold air cooled Basil's flushed cheeks and there were plenty of interesting sights to attract his attention. Anna could see Katerina was exhausted and she held out her arms to relieve her of the burden of the baby. Katerina gratefully handed him over and the two women walked slowly along to the far end of the station, where, to Basil's delight, an engine was being replenished with water and fresh supplies of wood.

The women saw at a glance this was a special train. It sat on the line bound for Petrograd but contained only three gleaming coaches. Brasswork shone and it was evident that ordinary passengers and refugees were not expected aboard.

As if to prove the point, soldiers with red tabs on their uniform prevented the two women from coming too close. Katerina and Anna turned away obligingly. They had no wish to draw attention to themselves and Anna hurried ahead with the baby. However, as Katerina began to follow her, a hand fell on her shoulder.

'One moment, please. I believe you are Katerina Orlov?' Dressed in shabby civilian clothing, this man would not have been noticed in a crowd, but the soldiers were standing to attention.

'Yes, I am.' Katerina hesitated, desperately trying to remain calm. 'Why do you ask?'

'That will be explained later, madame.' He smiled, but his eyes were cold. 'Let's just say, for the moment, that if you want to see your husband, you and your daughter will kindly step aboard the train.'

'Of course I want to see him!' she cried. 'But this young lady is not my daughter, she is *Anglichanka*, a guest in our country returning home because of the troubles.'

The man looked as if he'd wearied of hearing that tall story. 'If that is true she'll have a visa and the relevant documents to show me.'

'No, I'm sorry, I-I don't have them with me . . .' Anna faltered.

'I thought so.' He sighed. 'How can an *Anglichanka* speak such perfect Russian, tell me?'

He motioned to the soldiers. They closed in and urged the two women towards the waiting train. Katerina resisted desperately. 'But you don't understand! I can't leave my children . . .'

'You have your daughter and the baby,' he said coldly. 'The rest are old enough to look after themselves.'

One of the soldiers leaned forward unexpectedly and grabbed Basil out of her arms. Laughing, he carried the howling little boy into the carriage. Katerina gave a wild shriek and followed them. The others bundled Anna hastily aboard after her and slammed the door.

Ivan had been dozing, but some sixth sense awakened him like a chill in his heart. Something was wrong, he was sure of it.

He looked around. The others were sound asleep, but there was no sign of Anna. Madame Orlov and the baby had gone too.

Dimly, he recalled the baby crying and the two women quietly removing him. But surely they should have returned by now? It was bitterly cold outside.

He rose and went out, stepping over several huddled figures waiting patiently. Ivan noticed the train just leaving on the Petrograd line, but it was obviously not intended to carry civilians. He'd seen others similar to this one during his army career. They were military trains, lightly armoured and carrying high-ranking officers and staff in comparative luxury. It seemed totally out of place here.

Frowning, he stopped to watch the train pass through the station. At that moment, to his horror, he saw that Anna was aboard. She was standing at the window of a lighted coach, and as their eyes met, she pressed her hands against the glass and her lips formed his name in silent entreaty. With her head leaning against the pane, she watched him despairingly as the train sped on.

Then the line of carriages vanished into the darkness and Ivan was left with only an impression of her frightened face to haunt his worst nightmares . . .

Anna stood at the window of the compartment and watched all hope of rescue fade into the distance. Katerina sat with Basil on her knee, devastated by events, but still clinging to a thread of hope. They'd promised she'd see her husband again.

'Anna, I'm sorry!' she sobbed. 'You shouldn't be involved,

69

but they won't believe a word I say. It's Elena they want, because of Dmitri.'

'Then I'm glad they didn't get her.' Anna sat down beside her and held her hand. 'Archie and Ivan will make sure that Elena and the twins reach Murmansk safely. When these people discover their mistake, I'm sure we'll be released, and the doctors too.'

'I'm so glad you're with me, my dear,' Katerina said tearfully. 'You're such a comfort!'

There were voices in the corridor. A soldier of the Red Guard slid the door aside and looked in. 'You Orlovs will stand respectfully,' he ordered. 'The commissar will see you now.'

The two women rose and stood close together, swaying to the motion of the train, the baby silent, for once, in his mother's arms.

A man entered, waved the soldier away and closed the door before turning to confront them. 'Ladies . . .' He began pleasantly, then stopped and stared.

Anna's head swam and she felt faint. 'Aleksandr!' she whispered.

He was older, harsher looking, but there could be no doubt. It was Aleksandr, the man she had loved.

# Five

'I don't understand!' Anna stared at Aleksandr, hardly able to believe her eyes. 'My grandmother told me you were dead.'

'That does not surprise me!' He laughed, but the sound was harsh to her ears.

'Please sit, ladies.' He turned his glittering smile on Katerina Orlov, who met his scrutiny stony faced. 'We have much to talk about. Finding my dear Anna is a miracle!'

'It's hardly a miracle, Commissar,' Katerina retorted grimly. 'Your men decided we were mother and daughter. They forced Anna on to this train against her will.'

'Ah, that was Cupid taking a hand, madame!' He took a seat in the luxurious compartment, his eyes never leaving Anna's face.

'I heard you were in Archangel with Seraphima, and I went there hoping to find you. I searched everywhere with no luck!'

'Was it you in Seraphima's shop, then?'

'Yes. I kept a key. I was her lodger, remember?'

'Of course.' A rush of memories brought colour to her cheeks. 'I should have guessed.'

Katerina stirred impatiently. She set baby Basil down on the floor and confronted Aleksandr.

'I want to see my husband and son-in-law. Where are they?'

'I wish I knew.' He shrugged.

'What do you mean?' she demanded.

71

'They began work at Petrograd hospital, but now they can't be found.'

'So they've escaped your clutches!'

'I wouldn't put it quite like that, ma'am,' he said mildly. 'We're confident they haven't left the city. I'm sure you'll help us find them.'

'No, I won't!'

'You'll help, without even lifting a finger.' He sighed. 'When word gets around that you and this charming little chap are our guests, the doctors will return of their own accord. You should be obliged. Soon you'll be reunited with your husband.'

Anna was horrified. 'This is outrageous, Aleksandr! You can't use Katerina and the baby as hostages!'

'I think you'll find I can do whatever I want, my dear!' His cold tone and steely gaze chilled Anna to the bone. Then he smiled, and when he spoke again his attitude was conciliatory. 'There's no question of hostages, Anna. You are my honoured guests, travelling with me to visit Russia's most beautiful city. Fate has engineered your presence here, not I!'

He leaned across and gripped Anna's hand. 'Trust me, *Annoushka*! Trust me, and nobody will be harmed.'

Anna hesitated. How could she trust him? Seraphima had warned her against him. She'd even gone as far as fabricating the story that he had died.

Aleksandr's eyes were blue, his expression piercing. Anna had almost forgotten the power he'd exerted over her as a vulnerable young girl. She was startled, and more than a little scared, to discover she was just as vulnerable to that power today.

Ivan stood transfixed for several moments after the train carrying Anna disappeared into the distance. Then he turned and ran back to the station waiting room. Floor and benches were littered with weary travellers and he paused in the doorway to make a careful check. There was no mistake.

Anna had gone. And where were Katerina Orlov and the baby? They were nowhere to be seen. Had they been taken too? He shook Archie awake and explained in halting English what he had seen.

'Anna's awa' on a train to Petrograd?' Archie frowned. 'She's a sensible lassie. Why would she do a daft thing like that?'

'It was a military train. The Red Army has taken her. She entered Russia without a visa, as you know. Maybe they believe she's a spy. That is very serious.'

'What?' Archie was wide awake now. He stared at Ivan. Wishart would have him in irons if he found out Archie had lost Anna McLaren as well as her granny.

'There is more bad news,' Ivan admitted. 'Katerina and the baby are missing. I'm sure they have been taken, too.'

'Och, no!' Archie groaned.

Their agitated whispering had wakened Elena. 'What has happened?' She sat up.

Ivan explained the situation to his sister-in-law as gently as he could.

Elena paled, but took the news calmly. 'How can we get them back?'

'I'll catch the next train to Petrograd,' Ivan planned. 'I have good friends in the city who'll help me find them and bring them to Murmansk.'

Elena glanced worriedly at the twins, still fast asleep. With their mother and Ivan gone, the youngsters would be Elena's responsibility. Captain Archie was brave and resourceful, it was true, but he didn't speak Russian.

'Tell me what I can do to help,' she offered bravely.

'It will take time to rescue everyone – your father and Dmitri as well. I'll telegraph Murmansk when I've succeeded. You must go on as planned and make sure the ship waits for us.'

'Of course!' She squared her shoulders as she'd seen her mother do.

'Good girl!' Ivan was loath to leave his sister-in-law, but

73

what else could he do? He kissed her fondly on both cheeks – maybe for the last time. Who could tell?

'Now we will sit down together till your train comes.' Elena smiled through her tears.

The old Russian custom of quiet contemplation before a journey had never seemed so poignant. Silently, Elena prayed the twins would be safe in her care, for there was a dangerous secret which Ivan did not know. She knew where the collar of pearls was hidden – and the fate of the precious heirloom weighed very heavily on Elena.

She managed to persuade her brother-in-law to take her diamond and ruby engagement ring, along with some small items of jewellery her mother had sewn into the twins' hats. Ivan was reluctant, but she insisted. He might need bargaining power to help free her loved ones.

'But your engagement ring, Elena!' he protested.

'I know it's valuable.' She smiled. 'But the plain gold band my husband placed upon my finger on our wedding day means more!'

At that moment the train bound for Petrograd came steaming into the station and there was no time for argument. They hugged one another tearfully before Ivan hastily joined the crowd jostling for a place.

'So it's just the four of us now!' Archie observed gloomily after they had watched Ivan's train leave. 'Heaven knows what Wishart will say!'

'Captain Archie, are you afraid of this Wishart?' Marga asked her hero curiously.

'No' me, hen!' he replied smoothly. 'It's just I'm afraid the man's coarse language is no' fit for young ladies' ears.'

'Don't worry, Captain.' Elena smiled. 'We will not understand. Our school did not teach Scottish.'

Archie found Ivan's sudden departure had made him jittery. It had been reassuring to have the big fellow around. Now, he sat in the waiting room and studied his sole responsibilities with some trepidation – a bonny pregnant woman, a flighty young lass and a sullen boy! An anxious load had suddenly descended on Archie's unwilling shoulders.

Well, there's comfort in food! he said to himself as he examined the packages they'd brought with them and produced bread, cheese and pickled cucumber, to be washed down with cups of tea.

By the time a train arrived to take them on the last lap of their long journey, Archie was refreshed and resolute.

The wind had risen and fresh snow was falling fast when the train pulled out of Belomorsk, but at least they travelled in more comfort this trip. Passengers were packed in like herring in a barrel, of course, but there was safety in numbers. Mindful of Ivan's warning about spies without visas, Archie had no desire to stand out in a crowd.

As the slow journey progressed it became apparent that the twins were more badly affected by the loss of their mother and baby brother than Elena and Archie had suspected. Squeezed listlessly into the far corner of the compartment, both youngsters looked very pale and out of sorts. They persistently refused nourishment, which was unusual and worrying.

Tedious hours later the train passed through a featureless white landscape, the wind whipping fine snow into dense mist that clouded the windows.

A man seated opposite turned his attention from the blizzard to the silent twins. His grave scrutiny made Archie nervous.

'What's he gawping at?' he whispered to Elena.

'Shh! Be pleasant. Smile!'

This had the desired effect and the man leaned across. 'Forgive me, but these youngsters seem quite ill.' He spoke in hushed tones.

'I don't want to start a panic in the coach, ma'am, but we'll be stopping at Tanilov in the next few minutes and if I were you I'd get them to a doctor. It could be influenza – there's a serious epidemic at the moment. If so, they should be in hospital.'

Thoroughly alarmed, Elena thanked him and hurriedly explained her fears to Archie. 'The train is stopping. We must get off at once!' she cried.

'What?' He looked at her as if she'd taken leave of her senses. 'Don't be daft, Elena, they'll catch their death o' cold out there! No, we'll sit tight till we reach the ship. Captain Wishart will know what to do.'

'But you are Captain!' She stared in astonishment.

'We-ell . . .' Archie struggled with the truth. 'Captain of the galley. I'm . . . er . . . the ship's cook . . .'

'Ship's cook? And you let us believe you are in command?' Her eyes flashed angrily. 'You are only a servant!'

'Servant, is it?' Archie cried, stung. 'You're a fine one to talk, my lady! You never did a decent day's work in your life!'

'How dare you!' Elena retorted furiously.

The train was jolting to a halt. The man who'd advised Elena had disappeared and others were preparing to leave the compartment. Elena roused her ailing brother and sister and gathered their belongings.

'We are leaving now, my darlings!' She turned to glare at Archie. 'You can tell your captain we will come when we are ready!'

'Elena, wait!' This had gone far enough. He grabbed her desperately. 'Please don't go! I . . . I may never find you again.'

She stood motionless as the young man's arms tightened around her.

'We should stay together,' he whispered. 'You know that we should, don't you, lass?'

'Yes, I know it.' She looked up into his face. 'Please, Archie, come with me?'

Vassily and Seraphima had made good progress on the long journey to Murmansk. Osopa, the sledge horse, trotted steadily along a well-used route of hard-packed snow, over which the cab's low runners glided smoothly.

76

Vassily knew his way across country, and used every possible shortcut. Meanwhile, the two travellers had settled into quite a comfortable routine.

For days the sky had been pale blue and cloudless, the wind a tiny breath, temperatures falling to the lowest Vassily could remember. Only a glint of eyes behind snow-goggles could be seen as he drove, but by nightfall, in the resthouses, Seraphima could see the elderly man's eyes were red-rimmed and sore.

He made light of the discomfort, but it distressed her. So, as they journeyed on she fell into the habit of banging on the communicating window and ordering the driver to take shelter in the cab at regular intervals.

As the days passed, they began to look forward to these small breaks in the monotony. It was pleasant to relax in the cab's felt-lined interior warmed by the portable stove, while the cat chewed on softened ship's biscuit and the horse rested outside in the sun's pallid rays, chomping contentedly in a nosebag.

'Tell me about your childhood,' Seraphima urged Vassily one day.

'There's not much to tell, ma'am.' He laughed, but looked pleased all the same. 'My parents slaved to send me to school. They thought I had brains and would have a prosperous future ahead of me, bless them. But, as you can see . . .' He spread his work-hardened hands and shrugged.

She didn't know what to say, but he went on reminiscently.

'My mother was a gifted woman – like yourself, ma'am. She knitted warm garments in beautiful colourful patterns which she invented herself, to sell to the better-off. When I was little, I used to commit the patterns to memory and count out the stitches for her.'

'But that was very clever of you!' Seraphima said in surprise.

'Oh, I always had a good memory, ma'am, I never forget.' He lowered his gaze and fell silent.

77

Seraphima nibbled a ship's biscuit to cover an awkward moment. She couldn't find words to express her gratitude to the man she'd insulted so cruelly, but mention of his mother's accomplishments had given her an idea. She would knit a warm scarf for him, in a bright and colourful pattern of her own invention.

The plan cheered her, although it would be difficult to assemble the materials she'd need and knit the scarf without Vassily knowing. She wanted to surprise him with the gift at the end of the journey. He could wear it when she'd gone – and perhaps remember her more favourably.

Vassily finished the hot drink she'd prepared and stood up to resume the journey. He paused a moment, sorry to leave this kind lady alone in the cab with only the cat for company. It must be wearisome for her, mile after mile with nothing to do. If only she had something to occupy her mind, time would pass quickly!

Then the perfect solution came to him. She should have a book to read, of course! Vassily frowned. But where would he find such a thing?

Captain Duncan Wishart was not a man who took kindly to waiting. He found the long dark days spent in Murmansk unbearably tedious. Members of his crew were growing restive and he couldn't blame them. Most were married men who had expected to be home with wives and families by Christmas.

As days dragged by and this looked less likely, Duncan was met with hostile glares and sullen faces when he did the rounds. Much more of this and he'd have a mutiny on his hands.

Recalling his own apprenticeship on the *Mars*, he kept the men busy. The *Pole Star* had never looked so trim. But for relaxation as Christmas approached, Duncan trawled the district for talent and organized a concert to be held in the largest warehouse in Murmansk. To his delight he discovered a soulful choir of Russian fishermen and an aged but agile troupe of Cossack dancers.

On the night of the entertainment the warehouse was packed to the rafters. The Russian performers went down well with a local audience, but the first mate's version of a Scottish sword dance, followed by his crew's energetic interpretation of the eightsome reel, almost brought the house down.

Then Duncan stood up to sing 'A man's a man for a' that'. He had a fine tenor voice and there was rapturous applause for Robbie Burns's, sentiments and shouts for an encore.

To his amazement his mood changed, and he launched tenderly into: 'Oh, my love is like a red rose—'. He couldn't understand it. He'd had several girlfriends and had even imagined himself in love once or twice, but he usually steered well clear of love songs. The glass of vodka the Cossacks had pressed upon him must have been stronger than he'd thought.

> That I will love you, love you still,
> 'Til all the seas run dry.

Why was his sight blurred and what was causing an unaccustomed ache in the region of his chest? As the last sentimental notes faded into the hushed silence of an enraptured audience, Duncan Wishart vowed that he'd avoid vodka like the plague in future.

He escaped from the stage to tumultuous applause and the strains of 'Auld Lang Syne'; a fitting end to a successful concert.

There was a man standing in the shadows as Duncan passed by. 'A sad song, my friend!'

He recognized the voice instantly. He would never forget it. It belonged to the Red Army officer who had made such a thorough search of the *Pole Star*. Tonight the man was dressed as a fisherman and merged easily into the crowd of locals.

'It was you I met the other night.' Duncan frowned accusingly. 'You've been spying on my ship!'

'Yes.' He shrugged. 'It was most boring. I'm glad the surveillance is over.'

'What do you mean, over?'

'Mission accomplished. We have found Anna, your love.'

'Not my love!'

'You're right!' The officer laughed, amused. 'Not yours. Your red, red rose belongs to another now. I have just received the good news by telegraph.'

'What?' Wishart had gone cold. 'Where is she?'

'Relax, my friend.' The Russian patted his arm. 'You need not wait in this dark hole any longer. Nobody will come. Go home, Englishman!'

'Scot!'

'Whatever you are!' He laughed carelessly.

The audience was leaving the warehouse in droves. A noisy group pushed past and when Duncan looked again, the Russian had disappeared in the crowd.

He was left with an agonizing dilemma. Had they really captured Anna, or was this merely a ruse to make him abandon her? It would be easy enough for the Reds to pick her up with Seraphima when she arrived to find the ship gone.

So what should he do? Leave Murmansk for the sake of his crew, or keep faith with Anna McLaren?

Irina and Andrew McLaren had patched up the first serious quarrel to threaten their marriage – but only after a fashion. The loving relationship had been sadly damaged that day hurtful words were spoken and Andrew had walked out in a rage.

Since then, husband and wife had become withdrawn from each other. It was an unhappy situation, made worse by Mina Murray, Irina's assistant, Archie's mother.

Mina held Andrew personally responsible for her son's late arrival. 'Where's my bonnie laddie, Captain?' she wailed. 'Why's that ship o' yours long overdue this time?'

He had to confess he'd no idea.

'A'body in Dundee kens Wishart was sent tae the bad boys' ship,' Mina grumbled on. 'Bad blood will out. So why trust my son and your ain precious daughter to a bad penny like him?'

It was useless to protest that many perfectly decent young lads received an excellent training and sound discipline aboard the *Mars* training ship. The women had made up their minds. Duncan Wishart was condemned – and that judgement offended Andrew McLaren's sense of fair play.

He gave the matter much thought and decided it might help the situation if he could establish who Duncan Wishart's parents had been. It was a long shot after thirty years, but worth a try, and the Dundee Orphan Institution in Ferry Road seemed an obvious starting point.

He was ushered into the matron's office and found Mrs Davidson a pleasant lady, eager to help when Andrew outlined Duncan Wishart's case.

'You say the young man's now aged around 30?' she said thoughtfully. 'So he would be born in 1887 or thereabouts. Mr and Mrs Peddie would have been master and matron at that time, if memory serves me right.'

She crossed to a filing cabinet and returned with a large folder, which she pored over for a few minutes.

'Ah, yes!' She glanced up. 'A baby judged to be only hours old. That must be it. Your young man was found abandoned beneath Wishart Arch in Dundee on 18th November 1887. Do you know the place?'

'Aye.' He nodded, suppressing a shudder.

The ruined archway had once formed part of the eastern boundary of the town. Legend had it the fiery preacher George Wishart had delivered a sermon from the old gateway to townsfolk gathered within, and poor plague victims cast outside the walls to recover or die. It was a cold cheerless place to lay a tiny unwanted bairn.

'When the mother can't be traced we try to name the baby after the place it was found,' Mrs Davidson explained. 'We feel it gives the child some sort of link with the past.' She referred again to the folder. 'The baby was found in the early hours by a Sergeant Duncan, who wisely brought him straight to us.'

'But the boy told me he was fostered!' Andrew frowned.

'He was. Being newly born, a foster mother was found for him. Matron Peddie notes he was placed with a family in Peddie Street – which seems to have amused her!

'After that, we somehow lost track of little Duncan Wishart. The record's incomplete. That's all I can tell you. I'm sorry.' Regretfully, she closed the file.

'It's not much to go on.' He sighed, disappointed.

'Wait a moment, though.' The matron rose and opened a cupboard. She rummaged around and came out holding a small package. 'Just as I'd hoped! There *is* something.'

She held up a baby's tiny, knitted bonnet. 'His name label's still pinned to it, see? *Duncan Wishart*. He would be wearing it when he was brought in. We often keep a small item of clothing when there's no other means of identification. After all, you never know!' She handed it to Andrew with a smile. 'The young man might like to have it now, Captain. It's so beautifully knitted one can tell it was knitted by someone with a loving heart. That could be a comfort to him.

'Poor woman! She must have been in desperate straits to abandon her baby. It brings tears to your eyes, doesn't it?'

'Aye,' agreed the matron.

He took the little bonnet gently in his hands and slipped it into a pocket before bidding the kind lady goodbye.

'I'm sorry I wasn't much help, Captain,' she said, accompanying him to the door.

'Don't you worry about that, ma'am.' He smiled. 'I've learned someone cared enough to knit a wee bonnet for his birth, and he was found by a soldier named Duncan beside the Wishart arch. At least I can tell the man where he got his name!'

He had raised his hat and gone off down the street

before the matron realized there was something she hadn't made quite clear. She nearly called him back then decided against it. It was a trivial matter after all, hardly worth mentioning . . .

The official train carrying Anna, Katerina and the baby had thundered on throughout the night, heading south.

The carriage was a relic from Tsarist rule and luxuriously appointed. Aleksandr had seen to it they were treated royally, though Katerina viewed all attempts to win their favour with deep suspicion.

However, they couldn't resist the lure of a hot bath. Basil was removed by a stewardess to be bathed and fed, while the women washed their hair and luxuriated in scented bathwater.

'You know why they did this, don't you?' Katerina whispered when they returned to the sleeping compartment. 'I bet the seams and hems of our outer garments have been thoroughly examined.'

Anna made a dive for her clothing and made a hasty check. 'Nothing's missing!'

'Of course not, my dear. But now they think they know what we have with us – the fools!' Katerina smiled.

White bedlinen and soft blankets were another luxury and Anna fell soundly asleep. When she wakened, however, it was still dark, yet Katerina was up and dressed. Basil lay fast asleep in a nearby crib.

Katerina put a finger to her lips. 'The next stop will be Vologda, if I remember rightly. The train is certain to stop there to refuel. Even when Leon and I journeyed to St Petersburg before the war the station was very important and busy. If we mean to escape, Vologda is the best place.'

'Would it be possible?'

'It's worth trying.' Her eyes were alight with determination. 'I won't be used as bait to trap Leon, if I can help it.'

Anna dressed quickly. Quietly easing up the blind, she

83

could make out lines of telegraph poles outlined against the snow and a dark huddle of domestic and industrial buildings on the skyline.

Katerina was right, they were heading into a well-populated area and the train was definitely slowing down. If they could slip away, it should be possible to get lost in the crowd.

The two women were ready and waiting in the dark compartment when the train glided smoothly into the station at Vologda. Basil was wrapped up warmly, still asleep in his mother's arms as Anna slid open the door and glanced out into the corridor. It was empty and there wasn't a sound anywhere as the two women tiptoed out.

Holding their breath, they reached the carriage door and eased it gently open. Anna went first, helping Katerina and the baby down. There were plenty people milling around, even at that early hour. They stared at one another. They'd done it, they were free!

A firm hand clamped Anna's elbow, another rested on Katerina's arm. The women whirled round. Aleksandr smiled, an impassive Red Army guard just behind him. 'So!' He laughed. 'It seems we all need a breath of fresh air, ladies. There's a pleasant little cafe I know, where the spiced buns are the best I ever tasted – except for dear Seraphima's, of course! Will you join me for breakfast?'

'No.' Katerina declined stiffly, struggling to hide bitter disappointment. 'I will return to our compartment.'

'Of course. I understand perfectly, madame.' Aleksandr said sympathetically. 'The weather is too cold for the little one.' He motioned to the soldier, who stepped forward and took the sleeping baby from Katerina's arms.

'Still, I'm sure Anna will keep me company.' He smiled, his hand insistent upon her elbow. She went quietly.

They hardly spoke until they were seated in the small cafe. Anna folded her arms on the table and looked at him levelly.

'We were trying to escape, you know.'

84

'I know.' He laughed. 'I was expecting Madame Orlov to try.'

'But not me?'

'Oh, you are loyal and kind.' He covered her hand with his. 'I knew you would go – but reluctantly. You would not want to leave me.'

'You have a very high opinion of yourself, Aleksandr.' Her voice was steady, but the touch of his hand had set her heart racing.

'I've never seen the point in false modesty. I know what I want – and I have the courage to take it. It has got me where I am today.'

'I can see you're very powerful,' she allowed, withdrawing her hand. 'But why abduct poor Katerina Orlov and her baby?'

'She's hardly poor, my dear.' There was a glint in his eye. 'I have orders to apprehend that family. They are rich people planning to leave Russia with a historic jewel that is not theirs to keep.'

'The collar of pearls!'

'Exactly. It was a gift from the Empress Catherine. It belongs to the state.'

'If you can find it!'

'We will.' He studied her thoughtfully.

She looked away, sipping the hot tea the waitress had brought. 'So how long do you intend keeping me prisoner?' she asked lightly.

'Prisoner?' His eyes widened and he laughed in disbelief. 'But you're not a prisoner, Anna dear, you're free to come and go exactly as you please.'

He reached for her hand again, as if he knew only too well the power of his touch, and her foolish heart lurched.

'My darling, don't you understand?' he said softly, looking deep into her eyes. 'I'm still in love with you!'

# Six

Aleksandr's declaration of love was the last thing Anna had been expecting – especially here, in a crowded cafe.

The initial shock of finding him alive had subsided, leaving her with a confusing mixture of emotions. But, above all, she realized the situation required caution. She had loved Aleksandr the student. Aleksandr the commissar was still an unknown quantity.

'Thank you, I'm flattered.' She smiled. 'But isn't this rather sudden?' She was determined to lighten the atmosphere.

'Not so sudden! I never stopped loving you,' he replied.

For a moment he studied her thoughtfully. 'But maybe you have changed,' he went on. 'Do I have a rival? The captain who commands your father's ship, perhaps?'

'Wishart?' Anna was astonished. 'Whatever gave you that idea?'

'He brought you to Archangel.'

'Not willingly.' She laughed. 'I stowed away. He was furious.'

'Still, he waited for you.'

'Not long enough!'

'The river froze. He had no choice.' Aleksandr shrugged. 'In any case, it was Seraphima's fault you missed the boat. She insisted you attend the Orlov wedding.'

'How do you know all this?' she asked, shaken.

'My darling, I make it my business to know!' he declared. 'I also know that Wishart, your lover, waits for you at Murmansk.'

'He's not my lover!'

'Isn't he?' The smile was teasing but his eyes were like ice. 'Then why does he sing of love? Who is the bonnie lass he vows to love till the seas go dry?' He leaned forward and gripped her wrist. 'Tell me, Anna, who is she?'

'I don't know. Let go – you're hurting me!'

He released her.

Rubbing her painful wrist, she tried to imagine Duncan Wishart singing love songs. She wished she'd been there to witness the miracle.

'Anna, I'm sorry.' Aleksandr apologized. 'I admit I'm jealous. My adjutant took pains to telegraph the details from Murmansk just to tease me. Besides, it seems your brave captain has grown weary of waiting and has decided to leave port after all.'

'No, he wouldn't!' She paused. Secretly, she'd feared this might happen.

'There's a limit to every man's patience, my dear,' he said wryly.

'This man's love is worthless when put to the test!'

Anna pushed the half-eaten breakfast roll away. Her appetite vanished as she considered the serious predicament she was in. Somehow, she had to prise Katerina and the baby from the Red Army's grasp and find Seraphima and the scattered Orlov family. Once they were all together in Murmansk, she must persuade some other ship to take them home to Scotland. What a daunting prospect!

'A *kopek* for your thoughts?' Aleksandr sipped a tumbler of tea, watching her over the rim. His expression was faintly amused.

'I was thinking these rolls are not so good as Seraphima's,' she replied, not giving anything away.

'Ah, yes. Seraphima.' He nodded. 'Tell me, did you come to Russia to rescue your outspoken grandma, or were you hoping to find me?'

'Both reasons, Aleksandr. I hadn't heard from you for many months and I was frantic with worry.' She met his gaze honestly. 'I was devastated when Seraphima told me you were dead. Now, though, I think I understand what she meant. The student I fell in love with doesn't exist any more, does he?'

'No.' He sighed. 'That innocent young idealist died long ago!' He glanced at his watch and stood up. 'It's been a most interesting conversation, my darling, but we should be going.'

He moved round to help her on with her coat. His hands lingered on her shoulders and his smile was tender. Memories of the love they'd once shared threatened to overcome her and she made her way swiftly to the doorway.

Outside, there was another shock in store for her. Two armed Red Guards were on duty.

'And you say I'm not your prisoner!' She whirled round furiously to face Aleksandr.

'Did you think I'd run away and abandon Katerina and the baby?'

'Anna.' He looked down at her, grimly amused. 'You will find that I'm a man who does not take chances.'

He offered her his arm. After a moment's hesitation she took it and walked back to the waiting train, with two guards marching formally a few paces behind her.

Vassily and Seraphima had continued to make good progress, thanks to calm weather. There was a hard skin of frozen snow upon the roads and the cumbersome *vozok* ran lightly as a sleigh. Osopa, with her padded hooves, had an easier time of it.

That day, they reached the first large town Vassily had dared to enter. He only approached the town centre because he could see from a crush of farm vehicles jamming the roads that it was market day. One more cab wouldn't attract attention.

'I need to buy stores and fodder for the horse, ma'am,' he explained to his lady passenger, carefully avoiding her eyes. He also intended to buy a fine book in this still prosperous town as a present for her and he wanted the gift to be a surprise.

'I'll go for a walk round the market-place, then, Vassily,' Seraphima announced.

This was her chance to buy wool for the scarf she planned to knit for him.

'We-ell, I'll come with you,' he offered. It was disappointing; he couldn't carry out his plan if Seraphima was there.

'No, no! You buy the stores,' she said. 'I won't go far, but the exercise will be good for my ankle.'

'All right.' He agreed reluctantly. 'Be careful not to fall. Take your stick.' He handed her the stave he'd whittled for her in his spare time, and off she went.

Vassily made sure the cat was safely confined and the horse securely tethered, then set off on his quest. He was lucky. In a quiet side street he came across an untidy little shop packed with all sorts of old rubbish. There, in the window, lay the most beautiful book Vassily had ever seen. The red leather cover was dusty and the gold lettering on the spine dull with age, but the book looked interesting and was a handy size for a lady to hold. Vassily pushed open the shop door and went inside.

A few streets away, a buxom farmer's wife was pulling hanks of smoothly spun wool out of her pack for Seraphima's critical inspection. There was plenty of it in a creamy shade, along with a selection of wool dyed in beautiful soft natural colours. Seraphima also bargained for two pairs of bone knitting needles, and, after spirited haggling, parted with two gold bracelets in exchange for all her purchases.

She left the peasant woman admiring the gold glittering on her hardworking wrists and hobbled gleefully back to the *vozok* hugging the precious bundle.

Seraphima was sitting innocently feeding Moussia titbits when Vassily returned. The hanks of wool were safely hidden beneath the seat. Vassily was in a happy mood.

The book tucked away in his coat pocket had cost him the last of his savings, but it was worth it.

Whistling merrily, he prepared to drive out of town, much to Seraphima's surprise.

'I thought we would stay here tonight?'

'The town will be much too rowdy after market day, ma'am.' Vassily shook his head. 'There's a small village farther on which will be more peaceful.'

On the outskirts of town Vassily glanced up at the sky. He didn't like the look of it. Blue sky had turned the colour of lead and the wind was rising. He sniffed the air. He could smell snow. '*Gei, gei*, Osopa my beauty!' He urged the mare into a fast trot and she obeyed willingly, ears laid back, sensing the coming storm.

After a mile or two Vassily cursed his own foolishness as swirling snowflakes obliterated the road ahead. Earlier that morning, he'd noticed telltale signs of a change in the weather, but he'd been so set on buying Seraphima's book, he'd ignored the warning. Now the wind had risen to gale force and the horse was labouring through gathering snowdrifts.

Searching for shelter, Vassily turned off the road beside a thick clump of snow-covered trees and bushes. Frantically, he seized the shovel and began to dig into a deep snow-drift, fashioning high walls of hard-packed snow to protect himself and Osopa from the cutting wind. Sheltered there and huddled against the warmth of the horse, a man could survive the night.

'What are you doing, Vassily?' Seraphima poked a worried face round the door of the *vozok*.

He explained they couldn't hope to reach the village resthouse now, but she wasn't to worry. She'd be quite comfortable in the cab for the night, and he'd prepared shelter for himself and the horse outside.

He paused to stare at the lady in astonishment, for she was laughing so heartily there were tears on her cheeks.

'Vassily, are you crazy? Osopa is a sledge horse used to

all weathers. She'll be fine in the snowy stable you've dug for her, but there's no question of you sleeping with the horse. You will spend the night inside the cab with me.'

'I could not! It . . . it's not proper, ma'am!' He was shocked.

'Nonsense! Who bothers about that sort of thing in a blizzard?'

'But . . . Seraphima, ma'am!'

'Will you please step inside before Moussia and I freeze to death, you awkward man?' she ordered. 'The stove is lit and I've made tea. It's cosy in the cab and I refuse to listen to any argument.'

Sheepishly, Vassily shook snow off his coat and knocked ice off his boots, then removed his hat politely and clambered inside.

Irina McLaren examined the baby's bonnet her husband had brought home from his visit to the orphanage. Andrew had gone out that evening to a meeting of the Seamen's Fraternity and left the grubby bonnet lying on the hallstand. Irina had picked it up with a shudder of distaste as she read the name tape.

She wished her husband hadn't brought it here. It was an unpleasant reminder of the dubious origins of the man she blamed for her beloved daughter's disappearance.

Taking the bonnet into the brightly lit lounge, she was surprised to discover it had been knitted on fine needles by an expert knitter who had taken meticulous care. Something odd happened to Irina's heart at that moment and her eyes filled with tears. She was picturing the unknown woman who had knitted this exquisite bonnet with love in her heart for the unborn baby. A mother . . . a grandmother, perhaps . . .

'And she was forced to abandon him in the end!' Irina whispered softly. 'What heartbreaking sorrow!'

And the baby, the boy, the man who grew up never knowing that loving care. Ah, what a tragedy that was!

Presently she dried her eyes and went to the scullery,

where she carefully washed away years of grime from the bonnet, restoring it to pristine whiteness. How beautiful the intricate pattern looked now! She smoothed the baby's tiny bonnet with a gentle hand. The poignancy of the small item had afforded Irina much greater understanding. It might even go some way to softening her harsh opinion of Duncan Wishart, the man.

How strange that was!

The blizzard had swept westward from the Siberian steppes and severe weather covered most of north-west Russia. It had reached the small town of Tanilov on the Kola peninsula where Archie, Elena and two sick youngsters sheltered from its ferocity in a small noisy cafe. They'd been tantalizingly close to journey's end when they'd left the train. Now they were located opposite a doctor's surgery, waiting for it to open.

'I was daft to leave that train!' Archie sighed.

'But you say we must stay together!' Elena heated cold hands on a tumbler of tea.

'Aye, so I did,' he agreed gloomily.

This was not what he'd had in mind, though. He'd meant stay together – on the train. He studied the twins anxiously. They did look ill. Their poor wee wan faces were paper-white, their eyes bright with fever.

'How're you feeling, hen?' He leaned across to Marga.

'My throat hurts bad, Archie!'

The young girl groaned.

'So does mine,' her twin said.

Elena was distraught as she studied her sick brother and sister. 'It could be this bad influenza, Archie!'

'Wheest! Keep your voice down.' Archie looked round anxiously. 'If they think we're infectious they'll throw us out!'

'I wish they would. I hate this place.' Michael sighed.

The cafe smelled of hot, greasy fat. It made him feel sick. He'd noticed two men at a corner table, watching them.

It made him uneasy. He thought one of them had been sitting opposite him in the railway coach, but he couldn't be certain.

'There's a light on in the surgery at last.' Archie had been keeping watch. He stood up and began gathering their belongings. 'Come on. If we hurry, we'll be first in the queue.'

Out in the street, the full blast of the storm hit them. Elena staggered with the force of the wind and stinging snow, and Archie put an arm round her. He took Marga's hand and shouted to Michael. 'Stay close behind us, son!'

Michael obeyed, puzzled and angry. This Scottish tongue was strange. He would not want to be Archie's son. He couldn't stand the man. Trailing along sulkily, he soon dropped some distance behind.

'C'mon, you wee tyke, get a move on!' Archie yelled impatiently from the doorway.

Michael stuck his tongue out and slowed to a dawdle. Archie disappeared into the surgery, his arms around the two women. Michael joined the group of patients knocking snow off their boots in the lobby. Two men stopped beside him, scraping their boots as they muttered together.

'Are you quite sure it's the bride, Elena Orlov?' one asked.

'It's her all right. I followed her all the way from Belomorsk.'

Michael gave them a startled glance and shivered when he recognized the two from the cafe.

'What about the foreign sailor and the young ones?' The other man asked.

'They're of no importance.' He shrugged. 'Luckily, the kids fell sick and I persuaded Elena to get off the train before she reached Murmansk.'

Michael was trembling with fear as he crept away, desperately hoping he'd escaped their notice. He wormed his way through the damp, coughing crowd in the hallway and found Archie and his sisters seated on one of the long wooden benches lined up in a room lit dimly by a single electric bulb.

'Elena, listen—' He began urgently.

'Where've you been, you daft wee gowk?' Archie scowled and grabbed him. 'I've warned you no' to wander off.'

'You must do as Archie says, Michael,' Elena added reprovingly. She'd been worried when he'd lagged behind, and now they were all on edge.

'Why must you be so stupid?' Even Marga, sick as she was, took up the scolding chant.

Michael swallowed tears. His throat ached, his head ached and the scolding hurt him. This foreign sailor was unkind! How could his sisters not see it?

'What were you going to tell me, dear?' Elena spoke in gentler tones, concerned by Michael's odd behaviour. He was trembling and sweating. 'Michael, tell me, what is it?'

'Nothing, Elena, nothing . . .' He gave her a strange, desperate look that alarmed her.

Michael's head was spinning. Why should he warn her? There was no sign of the men and Archie would say he'd made up the story to excuse his dawdling. Well, let Archie protect the womenfolk if he was so clever! Michael was much too ill.

The doctor had begun to call patients into the consulting room. The system was to shuffle along the bench to fill up the empty spaces. They shuffled along towards the end.

As they moved along, Michael's heart gave a massive thud. He'd just seen the two men enter the room. They must have joined the end of the queue so that they could keep an eye on Elena and grab her later. Now that danger was so close, a strange thing happened to him. Love for his sisters flooded through Michael's muddled head and cleared his thoughts. This was no time for sulking!

He couldn't stand Archie, but he had no doubt that he would know what to do. Michael blurted out the whole story to him in a breathless whisper. Archie's eyes widened as he listened.

When the boy saw that Archie believed his story without question, a relaxing warmth spread through his body. He watched the Scottish sailor observe the two men. It was beautifully done with a casual glance that wouldn't arouse suspicion.

Archie knew he had to tell Elena what was up. He didn't know why these men should want to capture the poor lass, but Russian ways were beyond his comprehension. He hoped she wouldn't give the show away by yelling the place down.

She did not, bless her. 'What shall I do, Archie?'

Another shuffle along the bench brought them to the passageway. Archie surveyed the surroundings thoughtfully. 'This is the plan,' he said. 'When I tell you, run for the door and get outside fast as you can.'

'But they'll see me!'

'No, they'll no'!' He grinned. 'Trust me! As soon as you're out in the street, head for the station. I checked before we left, and there's a local train leaving on the hour. You still have your ticket. When you reach Murmansk seek out the *Pole Star* and tell the skipper I'll be along to cook his breakfast tomorrow.' With a large slice o' luck! he added silently.

'But Archie . . .' She turned to him. 'We should stay together. I–I do not want to leave you.'

'I know.' He did not want her to go. He leaned forward and kissed her forehead. 'When I tell you to go, dear Elena, run for your life!'

'But the twins . . .?'

'I'll look after them, never fear.'

He gripped her hand. Her fingers twined with his. It felt good, but it was just for reassurance, nothing more. Gently, he unclasped her hand.

'Ready?' he whispered. He leaned back casually and flicked off the light switch, plunging the room into darkness.

'Run!'

Elena darted away. The baby stirred within her, as if the little one was startled by the sudden movement and the ensuing commotion in the pitch-black room. The thought of the baby gave Elena strength. She ran out into the street, gasping as icy air hit her lungs.

Running through deepening snow slowed her progress and she glanced wildly over her shoulder. The was no sign of pursuit, but she knew the men would soon discover she'd gone and come after her – unless Archie could devise a way to stop them.

She wondered why they were so determined to capture her, and then a frightening thought occurred. They knew she was the Orlov bride. Perhaps they also knew she'd worn the priceless collar of pearls. If they caught her, they might force her to tell them where it was hidden.

Once she'd rounded the corner of the street Elena couldn't be seen from the surgery and the men couldn't be certain which way she'd gone. Maybe they wouldn't guess she was heading for the station. They'd never expect her to leave Archie and the twins behind and go to Murmansk alone.

She quickened her pace but found she was facing into the teeth of the howling blizzard. The going was treacherous underfoot and the station seemed miles away but she plodded on, for the baby's sake . . .

After two days and nights, the train with Aleksandr and the two women aboard had arrived in Petrograd. In spite of the circumstances, Anna felt a thrill of excitement as the engine glided into Finland Station shortly before midnight.

Anna, Katerina and the baby were dressed and ready. Baby Basil, swaddled in layers of fur, clasped his favourite wooden rattle. Katerina hugged him. He was so precious!

They were marched through the deserted station with a military guard on either side.

96

'This is how you treat guests?' Katerina curled her lip.

But she was silenced when they arrived outside and found a gleaming black limousine waiting.

'A Rolls Royce!' Anna gasped.

It seemed strange to find a British car in the chaos of revolutionary Russia, and stranger still when Aleksandr opened the car door and helped them inside.

'You've gone up in the world, Aleksandr Rostovich!' Anna remarked when they were comfortably seated.

She remembered one glorious summer's day, when she and Aleksandr had walked hand in hand for miles. There had been no limousine handy then! They'd walked till the patched soles of Aleksandr's ancient boots gave out. Then he'd laughed and plugged the holes with pages from an economics text. They were young and carefree and so very much in love. She wondered if he remembered. Maybe he did; he had reached for her hand and held it tight.

'I know where we are!' Katerina cried suddenly. 'This is Rastrelli Square. We're approaching the Smolny Institute, my old boarding school!'

'Ah! So you were one of the Noble Maids!' There was a hard edge to his voice. 'Only the idle rich could afford to send their daughters to the Smolny Institute.'

'My father wasn't so rich,' Katerina said heatedly. 'And he was never idle. He worked very hard to do it.'

'Madame, this area produced bitumen many years ago, not privileged daughters of the wealthy,' he countered mockingly. 'I assure you that workers who slaved to supply the imperial shipyards with tar worked much harder than your industrious papa!'

The car swept through the snow-covered square and into a driveway fringed with tall trees and dark bushes. Anna had a fleeting impression of a complex of buildings built in the grand manner before the Rolls halted in front of one resembling a duke's palace.

'My old school!' Katerina breathed emotionally.

'Not any more, madame!' Aleksandr laughed. 'Welcome to the headquarters of the Military-Revolutionary committee.'

He led them through a maze of hallways and corridors, and showed them into a small suite of rooms overlooking the back.

'I have work to do, so I'll leave you to settle in.' He smiled. 'If you need anything ring the bell. Someone will come.'

After he'd gone Anna darted to the door. To her relief it wasn't locked. The key was on their side.

'This was the housekeeper's flat when I was at school,' Katerina remembered. 'It was out of bounds to Noble Maids.'

'Fair enough! Now it's out of bounds to members of the Military-Revolutionary committee.' Anna grinned and turned the key in the lock.

The blizzard reached the city next morning and raged for three days. The two women were content to stay indoors to rest after the long journey. Katerina spent most of the time encouraging Basil to walk and talk.

'When we escape from these people it will be a help if my dear little one can toddle,' she said.

Eventually, the sun came out on a scene of pristine white. From early in the morning, gangs of men appeared on driveways and paths of the Smolny complex, clearing snowdrifts. Anna was standing at the window admiring the view when Aleksandr knocked.

Katerina unlocked the door. 'Oh, it's you!'

They hadn't seen much of Aleksandr recently. A female orderly brought food and anything else they requested.

'Dada!' Basil beamed.

'You will see him soon.' He laughed and ruffled the toddler's hair.

'Do you have news for me, Commissar?' Katerina asked anxiously.

'Not yet. But there will be, when word gets around you're here.'

Anna turned away from the window. His arrogant tone angered her. 'The driveway's clear. I'm going for a walk.'

'I had planned to take you sightseeing by sleigh.' Aleksandr put a hand on her arm.

'Another time, perhaps. This morning I feel like a walk in the fresh air.'

She lifted her chin and met his eyes coolly. It was a deliberate challenge to his authority – and he knew it.

'Rather too fresh, my dear,' he said softly.

For a moment the grip on her arm tightened, then he laughed and stepped back.

'Go on, then, you hardy Scot. Watch out for frostbite!'

He waited patiently while she wrapped up warmly, then escorted her downstairs to the front entrance. He didn't seem the slightest bit perturbed as she set off on her own.

The morning was bitterly cold but the air was wonderfully crisp and clean. She could almost imagine that she was happy and carefree as she made her way along the driveway.

The labourers were working nearby, widening an adjoining path. Borne on the breeze a faint sound reached her ears, barely more than a whisper.

'Anna!'

'Ivan!'

She recognized the voice instantly and was filled with joy – and a great deal of trepidation. Alert to the danger, she didn't look round or indicate that anything out of the usual had happened. She paused and scooped up snow with her gloves, tossing a snowball lightheartedly at a bronze statue modestly draped with snow.

She could hear Ivan shovelling, not far away. The whisper came again.

'Are Madame Orlov and the baby with you, Anna?'

'Yes.' She threw another snowball. 'They're treating us well. I know the commissar, Ivan, and that helps. We were sweethearts before the war.'

'So that's why they grabbed you!' She heard the shovel strike stone angrily.

99

'No, it wasn't . . .' Anna sighed. If she stopped to explain she'd arouse suspicion.

'Listen, Ivan!' She went on urgently. 'I'll make sure the commissar takes all three of us for a sleigh ride soon. If you can arrange a diversion during the trip we could slip away quietly.'

'It could be done. Be ready for anything!' He laughed softly. 'Tell Katerina I know where the doctors are and will make contact with them soon.'

'Ivan dear, please take care!' she whispered worriedly, dusting snow off her gloves.

'You know I'd risk anything for you. I love you!'

'I . . . I know.'

Love complicated everything. Anna wished he hadn't followed her here. Ivan was in very great danger and she felt responsible. She'd never forgive herself if anything happened to him.

'Look, I must go now,' she whispered.

'Tell me you love me, please!'

'Ivan, I can't. This is not the time, or the place,' she murmured unhappily. She walked away from him, plodding through the snow.

Ivan forgot the danger of prying eyes and leaned on the shovel staring after her. He felt unsettled and perplexed and he knew that was a dangerous state of affairs. It might make him act recklessly.

Aleksandr was waiting in the hallway when Anna returned.

'Pleasant walk, Anna dear?'

'Yes, thanks. Everything looks beautiful.'

'I was glad to see you so happy.'

'Happy?'

She gave him an alarmed glance. So he had been watching her. What had he seen?

'Yes, my darling.' He laughed. 'Throwing snowballs like a little girl. How delightful!'

'It . . . it was fun.' She forced a laugh. 'You should have walked with me, Aleksandr.'

'I wish I had, my dear.'

He smiled, but she couldn't trust that handsome, smiling face. Had those sharp eyes noticed Ivan? And if so, what would he do about him? Anna shivered involuntarily. She had remembered this was a man who never took chances. He'd noticed the shiver, of course.

'Darling, you're frozen!' He put an arm round her and pulled her close, looking down into her eyes. 'I warned you, Anna. It's dangerous to go outside . . . alone.'

# Seven

The weather in Petrograd remained calm and the sky was clear blue the day after Anna's meeting with Ivan. She studied the Smolny gardens anxiously. There was no sign of Ivan today and no labourers clearing the pathways. She frowned uneasily. It seemed to her anxious eye that there was still much snow-clearing to be done.

Aleksandr arrived mid-morning, tapping discreetly on the door and asking permission to enter. Anna let him in.

'Do you fancy a sleigh-ride this morning?' He was bright and cheerful. 'The good weather may not last. We should seize our chances, Anna. I want to show you my beautiful city.'

'I'd like that, Aleksandr.' She nodded. 'But only if Madame Orlov can come.'

'Of course she can, my dear!' He laughed. 'And the little one too.'

Katerina had been listening, Basil seated on her lap. 'I'm surprised you spare the time to drive prisoners around, Commissar,' she remarked. 'Are you hoping my husband and son-in-law will fall into the trap?'

'Madame!' He sighed and shook his head. 'What a suspicious mind! There's no ulterior motive intended and you're certainly not prisoners. You are my guests.'

Anna watched him. Once it would never have crossed her mind to doubt him, but she was older and wiser now. The labourers had gone and that bothered her.

Would Ivan be keeping watch? Would he have time to act, setting up a diversion on this sightseeing run? Whatever

102

happened this trip, she decided they must grab any chance of escape.

The two women were warmly dressed and nervously alert as Aleksandr helped them board the sleigh. He carried Basil, swaddled in layers of clothing. The toddler clutched the favourite wooden rattle in his mittened hand.

Anna wondered what precious memories the beloved toy held for the little boy and why he clung to it so tenaciously. Did it symbolize his lost home, and all that had seemed safe and secure?

'See Dada!' The toddler declared happily. He beamed at Aleksandr and hit him a sharp tap on the nose.

Katerina froze. She and Anna had discussed the possibility of rejoining her husband. Had Basil listened and understood, young though he was? Would the commissar's suspicions be aroused?

'He calls every man he sees "Dada",' Katerina intervened quickly. 'The poor little boy is confused.'

'Indeed he is, madame!' Aleksandr remarked dryly.

He handed over the child and sat opposite, ordering the driver to start. His sleigh was an old-fashioned *troika* built on luxurious lines. The horses were superbly matched and gleamed like black satin. Anna was impressed.

The driver cracked the whip above the leader's head and the three-horse team raced away, snow flying beneath their hooves.

'*Gei! Gei!*' Whooping, the driver gave the horses their head. Woe betide anyone loitering in their path!

Anna clung on to a red and gold hanging strap. Her spirits plummeted. What hope did Ivan have of stopping a carriage like this? Besides, she could see that Aleksandr was watching every move.

'This is the best way to view old St Petersburg in all its glory, my dear!'

He smiled as he leaned towards her, his eyes warm with simple pleasure. For a moment, he was the young man she'd known and loved, and she returned the smile warmly.

Then he turned and scowled at the driver, shouting, 'Rein in those brutes, you fool! How can we see the sights at this crazy speed?'

Her illusions were shattered. This was not the Aleksandr she'd loved. This man demanded instant obedience, and would make sure he got it . . .

They were surrounded by so many wonderful buildings! Anna felt quite dazed by the splendour of it all. Had circumstances been different, she would have been enchanted. As it was, she remained on edge.

Aleksandr noticed, of course. 'Anna, I've just shown you the Winter Palace where the revolution began.' He sighed, sounding thoroughly exasperated. 'I don't believe you heard a word I said! Obviously, historic events and beautiful buildings don't interest you in the slightest.'

'Oh, they do!' she insisted. 'It's just that there's so much to take in, Aleksandr.'

'Maybe art treasures are more to your taste.' He shrugged. 'An art gallery will be warmer. Little Basil's nose is cherry-red.'

Aleksandr ordered the driver to stop outside an unpretentious little gallery in the city's main avenue, the famous Nevsky Prospekt. The commissar helped his passengers out and ushered them inside the building with obvious pride.

'This is my own pet project,' he explained. 'I was given orders to assemble works of art hoarded in mansions and palaces owned by the rich. The treasures displayed here belong to the council of the soviets and the Russian people, now.'

'So that's why you hope to get your hands on our collar of pearls!' Katerina declared.

'It isn't yours to keep, madame.' He spoke grimly, then smiled. 'But don't let's argue. Let me show you what's been gathered so far. It may help to change your mind.'

He guided them through rooms and corridors hung with priceless works of art and lined with display cases containing jewellery, silver and fine china. It was an awe-inspiring collection.

Katerina hugged her little son tightly, wondering what fate had befallen the previous owners of these wonderful treasures.

They'd almost reached the end of the tour when a disturbance broke out on the floor below.

'What on earth . . .?' Aleksandr frowned. He glanced at the two women. 'I must see what's going on. Wait here for me, please.' With that, he headed downstairs.

'Is it Ivan, do you think?' Katerina whispered.

'It must be!' Anna replied.

They glanced around quickly. Katerina pointed to a doorway. 'That looks as if it should lead to the back premises. Let's try it.'

They found themselves in a dusty corridor at the head of a flight of stairs and began to make their way down cautiously. Basil began to whimper in his mother's arms, but she kissed him and he subsided, reassured.

At last they reached the ground floor – only to find the passageway blocked by an iron-studded door. They stared at the barrier in dismay.

'Look! There's a key in the lock!' Anna cried delightedly.

It turned with a loud grating sound, but the heavy door swung open, letting in a rush of freezing air. They were outside! They found themselves in a snow-covered yard leading into a warren of narrow lanes. The two women smiled at one another gleefully. Ivan had seized his chance to provide them with the perfect escape route. Anna had no doubt he'd be nearby, waiting for them.

'Ivan, where are you?' she called softly.

A snowball caught her on the shoulder. Icy crystals stung her cheek and she flung up an arm to protect her face. Another followed.

'Ivan, stop playing games!'

She was grabbed and hugged, a chuckle of laughter caressed her ear. She lowered her arm. For a moment icy crystals frosted her eyelashes. Then her vision cleared.

'Aleksandr!'

'Don't you remember how I love playing practical jokes, my darling?' His eyes were alight with laughter.

She'd forgotten that mischievous side of his character, but had his tricks always been so cruel? He'd obviously planned every detail of their 'escape' just to tease them. Dismayed, she realized she'd mentioned Ivan's name, and that was something Aleksandr would never forget . . .

In the calm after the blizzard, Vassily crept from the cab at first light. He left Seraphima sound asleep. Osopa the mare, warm beneath a horse rug in her snowy stable, turned her neck and seemed to give him a knowing stare.

'Don't look at me like that!' He scolded. 'My lady was cold in the night so I held her and gave her warmth, that was all. Don't you know that I would rather die than lay a whiplash on your back, my beauty, or harm my lady Seraphima?'

Osopa knew it. The mare had complete faith in the man.

At that moment, Seraphima was stirring. She stretched out a hand and touched living warmth – but it was only Moussia. Only? She sat up hurriedly. What was she thinking?

She hugged the furs around her as memory flooded back. It had been very cold last night, so cold she'd feared frostbite.

'Vassily, I'm freezing!' she'd whispered through chattering teeth.

There had been silence from the opposite bench, then a rustle as he crossed over.

'Is that better, ma'am?' he'd whispered eventually.

'Yes. Oh, yes!'

She had snuggled close to the blessed warmth. She remembered drifting off to sleep, clasped in Vassily's arms.

She groaned. What must he think of her? How could she face him after this? But when she'd risen and lit the stove, he came in cheerfully as if nothing out of the way had happened.

'Good news, my lady!' he announced. 'The snowfall isn't as bad as I feared and the worst of the weather is centred farther south towards Petrograd. The villagers are out in force clearing the roads. See what I bought from the farmers!'

Proudly, he produced eggs and rashers of smoked bacon, a rare treat. Breakfast was a feast. It was such a happy occasion Vassily judged the time right to present Seraphima with his gift.

'I know the long journey is wearisome for you, ma'am,' he began awkwardly. 'I thought a book would amuse you and help to pass the time, so I bought this for you.' He placed it diffidently in her hands.

'Oh, Vassily!'

Seraphima gazed at the beautifully bound volume through a haze of tears, deeply touched by such thoughtfulness.

'You don't like it?' Dismayed, he saw the tears.

'I love it!' Seraphima blinked them hastily away. She leaned across and kissed his cheek. 'Thank you for this lovely gift, my dearest friend.'

He nodded, embarrassed and delighted. He couldn't face her in case she noticed the blaze of emotion that had heated his blood. He went outside to prepare Osopa for the onward journey.

Vassily sang softly as he worked. He was surprised to discover he crooned a love song he'd learned as a youngster at school. He'd forgotten he knew the words – till today.

Inside the *vozok*, Seraphima was examining the book with a tender smile. It was an impressive volume, covered in beautiful tooled red leather traced with gold. But the title: *Tsar Ivan the Terrible's Reign of Terror*. Seraphima's eyes widened. It did seem a very strange choice to amuse a lady.

Andrew McLaren had noticed a softening in his wife's

107

attitude towards Captain Duncan Wishart which rather matched his own. She'd been dead set against the man at one time. Now, though, Irina was noticeably silent when Andrew's frustration got the better of him.

The month of December dragged on towards Christmas with no word of their daughter and her grandmother, and no mention of the *Pole Star* or her crew. Andrew found Wishart's reticence irresponsible. At last, in his wife's presence, he'd lost patience and cursed the day that Duncan Wishart had been born. Irina had given him an odd look, and walked out.

She headed into town on that freezing afternoon and halted beside the Wishart arch, where she'd stood for some time, contemplating the spot where the abandoned infant Wishart had been laid. Then, she'd spent hours knitting baby clothes, warm socks and pullovers for orphaned children.

Andrew had noticed resentfully that the baby's bonnet he'd brought home, after fruitless efforts to trace Wishart's parents, had been given pride of place in the display cabinet. What a load of sentimental nonsense!

Still, thanks to his wife's industry Andrew had an impressive bundle of knitted garments to take to a meeting of the Seamen's Fraternity. The meeting had been convened in aid of the orphans' Christmas treat and the master and matron of the orphange were invited as guests of honour. Andrew was pleased to meet Mrs Davidson again.

'My goodness, Captain, your dear wife's been busy!' She laughed when he handed over Irina's parcel of exquisite little garments.

'I've put in wee dollies and model boats and a jar or two of lollipops as well, ma'am.' Andrew smiled. 'Bairns never consider warm woollies suitable as Christmas presents.'

'Indeed they don't!' She smiled, then frowned thoughtfully. 'You know, Captain, I was thinking just the other day about that baby you mentioned – Duncan Wishart. There was something I meant to tell you at the time, and for the life of me I can't remember what it was!'

108

'Don't concern yourself, Mrs Davidson,' Andrew smiled. 'I know all I need to know. The bairn was found at the Wishart arch by a soldier called Sergeant Duncan. At least the laddie got a fine handle to his name from it!'

'Now that's what I was trying to remember, Captain McLaren!' she exclaimed. 'Sergeant Duncan wasn't a soldier.'

'Wasn't he?'

'No.' She shook her head. 'He was a policeman. He found the baby while on his beat.'

'A policeman! Well, well!'

Andrew felt a tingle of fresh excitement. This item of news opened up a new area of investigation. Maybe police records would have something to add to the little that was known about the foundling.

Archie had waited till the pandemonium in the doctor's darkened waiting room had reached panic proportions. When the young sailor judged that Elena had had plenty of time to make her escape, he reached across and switched the light back on.

The doctor had come rushing out of the consulting room to see what all the noise was about. When the light came on again he began to shout loudly in an attempt to restore some sort of order.

Meanwhile, Archie had propelled the two sick youngsters in his charge to the head of the queue. 'Tell the doctor we're next,' he whispered to Michael.

Sure enough, they were ushered into the consulting room. First, Archie took a quick glance over his shoulder and was relieved to see Elena's pursuers had not left the waiting room. Obviously, they assumed Elena was still inside with her young brother and sister. His spirits lifted still further when the two men took up seats near the front and settled down to wait. Every minute would buy Elena extra time to catch the Murmansk train.

The doctor opened the consultation with a flood of brisk Russian.

'You're interpreter, Michael,' Archie told the lad. 'For Elena's sake, take your time.'

The doctor gave the twins a thorough examination then selected a bottle of red liquid from the medicine cabinet and handed it to Michael.

'What's the verdict?' Archie asked.

'Marga is more ill, but it is not Spanish flu. It is bad tonsillitis and we must take medicine three times a day.' The young lad eyed the bottle doubtfully.

'Doctor say to tell you we must not go out for a week, or we will become complicated.'

'You can say that again!' Archie gazed at the two sick bairns who were his sole responsibility now. 'Ask him where he thinks I'll find a billet at this time o' night.'

The doctor and Michael conferred. 'There is hope!' The young lad turned to him. 'Above this room there is an empty furnished apartment which we can have.'

'This man's uncommon kind to complete strangers.' Archie frowned suspiciously. 'Ask him why.'

'I told him my father was Dr Leon Orlov,' Michael explained. 'When he heard what happened to us he was angry and sad and wanted to help. He has children, too, and fears this could happen to him, one day.'

Archie offered to pay in advance but the doctor waved the money aside. He opened a door to the rear of the consulting room and showed the way upstairs.

Archie gave a satisfied grin when he saw the accommodation. The apartment was small and basic but would be a cosy bolt hole till the children were well enough to travel.

He crossed to the window and parted the curtains cautiously. Elena's would-be abductors were arguing on the far side of the street. She and her companions had apparently vanished into thin air. After a heated discussion the two men set off in the direction of the station.

Archie hastily consulted his watch. The train should have

left Tanilov ten minutes ago. With luck, Elena would be safely aboard, heading for Murmansk . . .

After their eventful sightseeing trip, Anna and Katerina's daily life had settled into a wearisome pattern of eating and sleeping. Aleksandr hadn't been seen for several days.

Then, one morning, he turned up out of the blue. 'Care to come for a walk?' He smiled at Anna. 'The sun's shining today.'

'I hope you're not planning any more practical jokes!' she said scathingly.

'Certainly not!' He laughed. 'I promise to be on my best behaviour.'

So she took him up on his offer. The Smolny Institute had begun to feel like prison. Besides, there were questions she intended to have answered. And, oh, what a joy it was to walk in the fresh, cold air again. Bright sunshine always lifted her spirits.

Aleksandr took her arm as they walked along the snow-covered paths. In spite of everything, she felt unaccountably happy. She savoured the moment.

Then he went and spoiled everything. 'This man, Ivan Ivanovich – are you in love with him?'

'I could be. Why?' She stopped and faced him.

'Because he loves you. Why else would he travel hundreds of miles to find you, putting his life at risk?'

'How do you know this?' She found it impossible to suppress a shiver.

'Anna dear! There's nothing wrong with my eyesight!' He smiled. 'I watched you play-acting in the garden and was intrigued to recognize Ivan Ivanovich, one of ex-Tsar Nicholas's Black Hussars.'

'So what?' She shrugged defiantly. 'In that last scribbled note you sent, you told me you were one of the Tsar's guards yourself.'

'Oh, my dear!' He burst out laughing. 'I'm afraid you picked up the wrong end of the stick! I was the officer in

111

charge of Red Guard soldiers guarding the Imperial family when they were under house arrest in Alexander Palace.'

She stepped back and stared at him. Disillusionment was complete.

'Anna, don't glare at me as if I had committed a dreadful crime!' His tone was aggrieved. 'They are potential trouble-makers, but no harm will come to them.'

'Why not let them leave Russia, then?'

'Who would want them?' He shrugged.

She walked on, deeply disturbed by this revelation. After a moment, he caught up with her, matching his stride with hers, their footsteps muffled in the snow.

'What's happened to Ivan?' she asked.

'He's detained in the Bastion in reasonable comfort.' He gave her a quick glance. 'I still respect bravery in an enemy, Anna, even though I think the man's crazy.'

'You believe it's crazy to risk your life for someone you love?' she asked bitterly.

'No, my darling, I do not.'

They had reached a ruined summerhouse built in the form of a tiny Greek temple, the white marble chipped and streaked green with mould. He took her hand and led her inside. Deep in the shadows, secure from prying eyes, he took her in his arms and kissed her.

Some of the old magic still lingered, but Anna resisted. 'Aleksandr, please don't!'

'I have an important question to ask, and a kiss was appropriate.' He looked down at her. 'Will you marry me, Anna?'

'What?' She gasped. 'But, Aleksandr – why?'

'I love you. I need you.'

'Why me?' She was bewildered. A proposal of marriage was the last thing she'd expected.

'You are kind and loving,' he said softly. 'You will never change, my darling, whatever happens in this crazy world.' He hesitated, his expression softened and then he held her closer.

'Oh, Anna, sometimes I'm scared of what I might become, without you. Sometimes I dare not contemplate the future,' he admitted brokenly. He clung to her and she felt his tears wet upon her cheek.

'Listen,' she said 'There is a different path for you to take. Come to Murmansk with me. Begin a new life in Scotland.'

'Will you marry me if I do?'

'Perhaps.'

'Perhaps is not a promise!' he cried angrily, his mood changing in an instant. He let her go. 'Perhaps means nothing!'

'All right, Aleksandr! There's another way.' She lifted her head and looked at him. 'Set Ivan free and let Seraphima and the Orlov family leave Russia in peace. If you would do that for my sake, I'll marry you.'

'So many strings attached to happiness, my darling!' He frowned.

'So what do you say?'

'Perhaps.' He smiled.

'Oh, Aleksandr!' She despaired. He was playing games again, throwing words back in her face like snowballs.

'Very well!' She faced him angrily. 'You tell me I'm free to leave. Let's put that to the test, shall we? Goodbye to you, Aleksandr Rostovich!'

He made no attempt to stop her going, but selected a cheroot from a jewelled cigar case and stood, deep in thought. Scented smoke curled lazily upwards and was lost in freezing shadows as he watched her walk away along the frozen pathways, with head held high. He wondered what she would find if she carried out her threat and arrived in Murmansk. If she ever reached the port, that was, which he doubted . . .

If Duncan Wishart admitted to any one fault, it was a tendency to be too stubborn for his own good. It had got him into trouble before, and he was deep in trouble now.

113

The *Pole Star* was still berthed in Murmansk, with a full-scale mutiny brewing and an irate shipowner fuming in Dundee over the safe return of both his ship and wayward daughter.

The entire crew – except for Archie, of course – was gathered facing their captain in the saloon. The mood was angry.

'If it will satisfy you,' Duncan offered, 'I will telegraph Captain McLaren and leave the decision to sail up to him. I will abide by it, of course.' He sighed.

'Och, that's just a ruse, Cap'n Wishart!' the bosun observed. 'We all know the man'll no' abandon his own daughter.'

'The lassie deserves to be taught a lesson after a' the trouble she's caused!' another voice cried.

'That's so.' The bosun nodded. 'Miss McLaren disobeyed her father and stowed away. Stowaways deserve what's coming to 'em.'

'May I remind you,' Duncan Wishart remarked icily, 'that the young lady stowed away because she was concerned for her grandmother's safety. In my book, that was rather brave and resourceful.'

'Och awa'! It's no' her grannie she was after!' Someone yelled rudely. 'The whole o' Dundee kens the lassie has a Russian boyfriend. I vote we up anchor and leave on the tide.'

This met with roars of approval. Duncan Wishart waited grimly till the noise subsided. 'Very well. It seems you're all agreed we should pull out.' He glanced slowly around the assembled men. 'I must say I'm surprised and disappointed. You swore solidarity. You told me the entire crew was united. You claimed comradeship with one another – and I believed you meant it!'

'So we do, Cap'n!' the bosun protested indignantly.

'But what about Archie, your shipmate?' Duncan leaned forward, fixing the now silent crew with an accusing stare. 'Could you sleep easy in your bunks if we sail for Scotland

and leave Archie behind? Remember, the lad went ashore to bring Anna McLaren and her grandmother back safely to the *Pole Star*. And I believe that's what Archie will do – if you'll only give him time. It wasn't his fault the Dvina froze early this year, was it?'

Nobody spoke. Archie was a popular member of the crew, the best ship's cook they'd ever had. He'd been sadly missed . . . as had his steak pies, his Scotch broth, his creamy rice puddings . . .

They couldn't meet their captain's eye now that he'd reminded them of Archie's plight. They might have reservations about rescuing the feisty McLaren lassie and her granny, but it was out of the question to abandon Archie, a popular shipmate.

'Well, lads,' the bosun sighed, 'I suppose it wouldna do any harm to wait a wee while. What d'you say?'

There was a subdued, shame-faced murmur and Duncan Wishart heaved a sigh of relief. The threatened mutiny had been averted.

Waiting was still a wearisome, worrying business, though. Duncan Wishart couldn't be certain that the Red Army had Anna in its clutches. He'd already decided that could be a cunning move on someone's part to persuade him to up anchor and leave.

Standing in the dim confines of the *Pole Star*'s silent bridge, the captain pondered the rumour that Anna had a Russian boyfriend. Now, he found that most disquieting!

He and Anna had enjoyed many heated arguments and lively discussions during the voyage to Archangel. In the dark silence of this winter's night, Duncan admitted he'd enjoyed pitting his wits against that bright young woman's quick intelligence.

She was headstrong and passionate and if she loved this man, Duncan Wishart frowned as he told himself moodily, nothing, not even the threat of danger and imprisonment, would stop Anna McLaren from going to him.

He stared ahead, watching blown snow catch on the

glass. Another snowfall was threatening to mantle the ship, although his crew kept the decks and rigging clear, ready to move at a moment's notice. He felt depressed all of a sudden, ready to give up hope. Where on earth were Anna, Seraphima and feckless young Archie?

His attention was caught by a movement down on the quay. He leaned forward to see better, clearing a patch of frost. He could just make out a shrouded figure battling through snow, staggering against the force of the rising wind. It was a young woman, all alone.

'Anna?'

He ran out into the storm, clattering down the companion-way, feet skidding as he reached the deck.

'Anna!'

The full force of the wind caught him as he ran towards the stumbling figure. He could see she was totally exhausted, hardly able to plough a crooked path through the snow. Heaven alone knew how she'd managed to make her way from the station.

'Anna, hold on!' he shouted again, redoubling his efforts. The emotion driving Duncan Wishart was new and surprisingly intense. He lunged forward and caught her in his arms just as she stumbled and fell.

'Anna, thank God!' He closed his eyes and held her close. Safe at last!

'No!' She began struggling weakly. 'Please! Please don't!'

He might have known! He let her go. There's gratitude for you! He stepped back, smiling – and found himself facing a complete stranger.

'I am sorry,' the young woman sobbed. 'But I am not your Anna, I am Elena Orlov, and Archie has sent me to you.'

With that terse explanation Elena fainted, sinking down into the snow at his feet . . .

# Eight

After leaving Aleksandr, Anna stormed into the apartment to find Katerina Orlov on her knees, playing with Basil.

'Look, Anna!' Katerina laughed. 'He dances when I sing. Have you ever seen such a clever little lad?'

The besotted mother did not notice warning signs of Anna's emotional encounter. Katerina was discovering the joys of motherhood. She could hardly believe she'd blithely handed all her precious babies over to a nanny. Of course, it was the custom for wellborn Russian ladies to distance themselves from the more intimate care of the very young, but Katerina had already decided it was a bad custom.

'Watch this, my dear!' She sang a Russian version of Jingle Bells while the toddler jigged around, before landing with a thump upon his bottom. His doting mother scooped him up and enveloped him in proud hugs and kisses.

'Yes, very clever.' Anna frowned abstractedly. 'But we should leave this place and head north. Tomorrow morning!'

'What? Leave the institute?' Katerina was dismayed. 'How can we? The commissar would never let us go.'

'Why not? Why shouldn't we call his bluff?'

'Because, dear Anna, we tried to escape once before and look what happened!'

'Circumstances have changed.' She sighed. 'Ivan's been caught. He's in prison.'

'Oh, no!' Katerina wailed. 'That's terrible news!'

'Yes.' Anna nodded. 'Now we must take the initiative.'

'We can't abandon Ivan!' Katerina cried tearfully. 'And what about my darling Leon and Dmitri?'

'I was coming to that . . .' Anna crossed the room and knelt on the floor beside her, aware that some walls have ears. 'The longer we stay the more danger the doctors face,' she whispered. 'Your presence is the bait, but if we walk out tomorrow that solves the problem. As for Ivan, I intend to do some hard bargaining with Aleksandr, first.'

'We-ell,' Katerina shook her head doubtfully. 'You make it sound easy, but I'm sure the commissar will find a way to stop us.'

The two women rose early next day. They had little baggage, so packing was easy. Basil had sensed excitement in the air and was charging around the apartment. The little boy's development had progressed by leaps and bounds under his mother's constant attention. Till recently a nurse had been the most important person in Basil's existence. Then fate had thrown mother and son together and a delightful journey of discovery had begun for both. They were charmed with one another.

Basil knew something important had happened. He looked up hopefully into his mother's face. 'See Dada?'

'Hush, my darling!' Katerina put a finger to her lips, in terror.

Repulsed, he toddled sulkily across the room, whacking the carpet with his beloved one and only toy. The wooden rattle made an angry sound which suited the mood.

When Aleksandr knocked a little later, the little boy was at the doorway in a flash just behind Anna, surveying the visitor warily.

The commissar ignored him. 'So, you really are leaving!' He eyed coats, hats and boots strewn around the room.

'Did you think I was joking?' She lifted her chin. 'Madame Orlov and the little one are coming with me.'

'See Dada!' Basil declared loudly.

'Oh?' Aleksandr lifted an eyebrow. 'I doubt that very much!'

'What . . . what do you mean?' Katerina gasped.

'I mean, madame, that the child will not see his father for many months. I came to tell you the two doctors have been taken into custody.'

'No!' She put a hand to her heart. 'Please – I must see them!'

'Out of the question!' He shook his head. 'Our leader takes a dim view of those who are unwilling to serve the common people. Your husband and son-in-law will be detained till they have a change of heart.'

Defeated, Katerina hugged the child. 'This changes everything. I cannot leave the city now.'

'A wise decision, madame.' Aleksandr nodded. 'Of course, as a British citizen Anna is free to leave at any time – if she wants to.' He glanced at Anna, mockingly.

Duncan Wishart had carried Elena aboard the *Pole Star* and yelled for Jock MacIntosh. Jock was the father of ten healthy bairns and the nearest the ship had to a fully fledged medical man. The sensational news that the captain had brought a woman aboard flashed like a bolt of lightning around the crew.

No, it wasn't the McLaren lassie! It was a Russian stranger the skipper had found swooning on the quayside, and rumour had it Archie had sent her. Archie was known to have an eye for the lassies, so what had the rascal been up to ashore?

Elena was carried to an unoccupied passenger cabin where Jock could examine the fainting lass in peace. Jock was well qualified to do so, having delivered two of his own bairns and weathered family epidemics of measles, whooping cough and chickenpox – not to mention the growing-up antics of five lively daughters. Jock disappeared into the cabin with the first-aid kit and shut the captain outside. Duncan paced the corridor.

He was badly shaken by the incident and his heart still pumped with new and disturbing emotions. On the quayside he'd been so sure it was Anna he'd experienced wonderful moments of delirious joy. Then had come this heart-crushing disappointment. What was happening to him?

'Hsst, Cap'n!' Jock's whiskery face appeared in the doorway. He stepped into the corridor and shut the door. 'The lassie speaks no' bad English though I cannae make head nor tail o' her story. She's scared oot o' her wits, poor soul. Says she's being followed by bad men and Archie sent her to us for safety.'

'Why would he do that?' Duncan frowned.

Jock glanced up and down the corridor and lowered his voice. 'Lassie's pregnant, Cap'n.'

'Wha-at? Was it Archie?'

'Naw.' He shook his head. 'She's five or six months gone. It couldna be Archie.'

'Thank heaven!'

'You can say that again. His ma would murder 'im.'

'How is the lass, Jock?'

'Cold and exhausted, but she'll be right as rain tomorrow after a good night's sleep. I brought a clean nightshirt for her but she refused help and made me leave the cabin. You'd think I'd never seen corsets afore, and me wi' a wife and five fashionable daughters!' Jock grinned.

The captain visited Elena next day.

'Jock says you're much better today. That's good. ' He sat down beside the bunk.

'I feel well. Mr Jock is good doctor.'

'He's had practise.' Duncan smiled.

Elena thought the captain had a nice smile. She guessed there were warm depths to this man. Yesterday when he had imagined she was Anna he had been transformed, like a man in love.

'I'm sorry I am not your Anna,' she said.

'She's not mine!' The smile disappeared. 'Anna went off with her Russian boyfriend and left the crew of her father's ship to be icebound in Archangel.'

'That's not true!' Elena protested. 'I am to blame! Anna's *babushka* had promised to attend my wedding, and Seraphima would never break a promise. Not even to save herself.'

'Stubbornness runs in the family!' He nodded with a sigh. 'So they missed the boat!'

'Yes, but you left Archie ashore, and Archie saved me from very bad men.'

'You were very brave to come here all alone.'

'No, I was not brave for myself!' she protested earnestly. 'I will soon be a mother and my only concern was for the precious baby. You understand?'

'Yes. Of course . . .'

But how could a foundling understand a mother's love? His thoughts turned to the mother he had never known. Had *her* concern been for the precious baby when she crept out into a cold November night carrying her shameful bundle? How could she leave a tiny baby lying in a wet and filthy street, defenceless and unloved? Why did she do it? he wondered for the countless time with sudden painful anguish – why?

In Dundee, Andrew McLaren had spent days pondering the course of action to take next. It was a police sergeant and not a soldier who had found the baby, and that changed everything. He hadn't told a soul about this new development in Duncan Wishart's past – certainly not Irina his wife, who had ordered him to forget the whole frustrating business.

That was easier said than done. The mission had become a matter of wounded pride. He'd always believed himself to be a sound judge of character and Wishart's recent behaviour had destroyed Andrew's faith in his own judgement. For all anyone knew the man had fallen out of a whole barrelful of bad apples. If he had, Andrew wanted to know about it.

On a cold December morning brightened by pale sunshine, he walked along Bell Street towards the police station, swinging his stick. Somehow he felt hopeful, though he hadn't informed Irina of his intended visit.

The desk sergeant looked up when Andrew entered.

121

Captain McLaren was a well-known figure in the city, so the smile was welcoming.

'What can I do for you, sir? If it's Lost Property you're seeking, that'll be next door.'

'Aye well, it is, in a way.' He launched into an explanation of his quest, ending apologetically. 'So I wondered if police records could throw light on the matter?'

'I doubt it.' The policeman shook his head. 'If the mother couldn't be traced there'd be no charges made and nothing put on record.'

'Hmm.' Andrew frowned. 'Then what about the bobby who found the bairn – Sergeant Duncan?'

'Oh, aye! I was just a young recruit at the time, but I mind the sergeant did take an interest in a wee foundling,' the man recalled.

'The orphanage named the baby Duncan, after the sergeant, I believe. He was upset when the foster parents did a moonlight flit and took the bairn away. He never did find out what happened to it.'

'I could tell him!' Andrew said grimly. He glanced at the policeman thoughtfully. 'Sergeant Duncan must have retired long since. He'd be an old man now. Is he still on the go?'

'Last I heard of him, he was hale and hearty and living on the Dudhope estate in Mavis cottage, a wee but an' ben on the slopes o' the Law Hill. He'd be interested to hear if the bairn survived. Thon foster parents were a bad lot!'

After thanking the sergeant for the information, Andrew stood outside the police station, wondering whether to admit defeat. There was so little to go on! Still, maybe he owed it to the retired bobby to set the record straight.

He set off up Lochee Road towards Dudhope, the pavements dirling beneath his feet to the relentless thunder of the jute looms. War had sent Dundee men to the trenches, but had brought plenty of work and employment for their womenfolk, in the mills.

Mavis cottage was a fair step up the steep hill. The

122

greenery of Dudhope rose above grey tenements and bare trees, giving Andrew glimpses of the slopes of the Law beyond. The climb was a good measure of his recovery.

When he reached the cottage he stood for a moment getting his breath back and noted fresh paintwork, a small garden neatly kept and a shipshape little cottage.

He went boldly up the path and knocked. The door was opened by a fresh-faced old man. Keen eyes beneath jutting eyebrows studied him curiously.

'Sergeant Duncan?'

'That was me a good while back.' The old man nodded. 'It's plain mister now.'

'Of course.' Andrew smiled. 'I'll come straight to the point, Mr Duncan. It's about a newborn baby you found abandoned on your beat around thirty years ago. The orphanage named the boy after you, D'you remember the incident?'

'It's something a man's no' likely to forget!'

'I can imagine!' Andrew nodded. 'It must've been a shocking experience.'

'Aye, well . . .' He looked away. 'A lot o' water's flowed under the Tay brig since then.'

Andrew could see that getting information out of this canny lad would be like plotting a course without a compass, but he persevered. 'I wondered if you'd any suspicion at the time who the mother might be – or the father, for that matter?'

The fierce old eyes remained expressionless. 'None whatsoever.' He hesitated. 'The baby went to foster parents that were scum. I heard the wee baby died.'

'No, Mr Duncan,' Andrew shook his head. 'He didn't.'

'What?' He stared, obviously shaken.

At that moment a woman's thin little voice called from inside the cottage, rather querulously.

'Eddie, please shut the door! I'm cold!'

'My wife,' Eddie Duncan explained hurriedly. 'Amy's an invalid. She mustn't catch cold. Sorry . . .'

The door closed in Andrew's face. He stood frowning at the glossy surface and heard the woman call out again. 'Who's that at the door, Eddie?'

'One o' my mates frae the allotments, love, just passing the time o' day.' He heard the old man answer.

A blatant lie! Frowning, Andrew walked down the path. Why had Edward Duncan lied to his wife? That was odd. Maybe he should have another chat with the old man – but on neutral ground, next time.

Stuck in Tanilov acting nursemaid to two sick youngsters, Archie's thoughts turned longingly to his hometown, Dundee. Which was strange when he thought about it. When he'd actually lived in the city he couldn't wait to get out of it.

A job as ship's cook on the *Pole Star* had seemed a heaven-sent opportunity to escape and see the world. Then the war happened and he'd found himself living precariously, sailing on the dangerous route between Dundee and Archangel with submarines lying in wait and a threat of conscription to the trenches if he didn't.

So Dundee figured nostalgically in Archie's dreams these days. He remembered the bonny silver river Tay with affection, and Saturdays in the narrow Overgate tainted with smells of fish and frying onions from buster stalls, as well as dancing at the Palais, all spruced up!

'Archie, I am hungry!' Marga whimpered.

He bent over her. Tonsillitis had made the poor lass very ill. She was thin and pale and Archie recognized she needed nourishing food. He frowned. Supplies were running low in their hidey-hole above the doctor's surgery. He could see he'd be forced to embark upon a risky shopping expedition.

'What d'you fancy, hen?' he asked kindly.

'*Kazoolies*, Archie!' She brightened.

'Whit kind o' beast's that?' He looked blank.

Michael looked up from the book he was immersed in and

laughed. Even Marga raised a smile. 'They are cakes with sugar and spice, of course!' the young lad said scornfully. He didn't like Archie, and made no attempt to hide it.

'Right!' Archie donned coat, hat, gloves and boots. He shrugged on the haversack which went everywhere with him. It was a worry leaving the twins on their own, but it had to be done. Hopefully, they wouldn't be disturbed. The downstairs rooms weren't occupied until the doctor arrived in the evening to commence his consultations.

'Lock the door behind me and don't open up to anyone!' he ordered, giving Michael a stern glance. 'Mind what I'm saying now, son!'

'I am not deaf! And I would not want to be your son!' the lad retorted rudely.

'Aye, well . . .' Archie shrugged.

The boy didn't like him. So what? He pulled a muffler across nose and mouth and went out into the freezing cold.

The shops were not far, only two hundred yards down the street. Archie found one that seemed better stocked than most and selected several nutritious items including bread, cheese, salted herring and a pot of caviar. He topped that up with pickled cabbage, beetroot and cucumber and a flagon of goat's milk. He grinned delightedly when he discovered Marga's *kazoolies* – liberally scattered with sugar.

He piled all the purchases on the counter and laid down a British ten-shilling note with a flourish. He estimated that should be more than enough to cover the cost.

The shopkeeper stared at the money. Barter was the usual method of payment these days and he'd been doing rather well out of it. He picked up the note between finger and thumb and regarded it suspiciously.

'*Nyet!*' he growled.

'What d'you mean, *no*?' Archie frowned. 'Can you no' recognize good British siller when it's put right under your nose?'

The man began an angry tirade in Russian. Archie didn't

understand a word. He lost patience with the daft gowk. 'Och, stop your blethers! You can keep the change.'

Ten shillings was more than generous! A week's wages in the Dundee jute mills. But the man turned scarlet with rage, yelling and shaking a fist.

'Away an' boil your head!' Archie growled in disgust. He swept the goods into the haversack and walked out of the shop.

The shopkeeper raced after him, shouting. In no time a noisy crowd had gathered around Archie, impeding his progress. Then someone grabbed hold of him. He swung round. 'Here, take your hands off me!'

His jaw dropped. His assailant wore police uniform. There were two of them. He was being arrested. 'Nah, nah!' he cried hurriedly. 'I paid the man fair an' square. You can't arrest me – I've two bairns to see to!'

The policemen paid no attention to his foreign tirade. Archie struggled, but they were hefty men and once they had him in their grip they marched him off down the street.

Archie spent a worried, uncomfortable night at the local police station, locked up in a cell reserved for disruptive prisoners. Archie could not imagine what Michael and Marga would do when he failed to return. The two youngsters must be distraught, wondering what had happened to him.

A slant of sunlight came through a high, barred window by mid-morning and heralded the arrival of the two guards from yesterday. They were grinning, and had brought a visitor.

'Michael!' Archie groaned. So they'd found the bairns!

'You look very awful.' The lad smiled. He sat down beside Archie on the wooden plank. 'You are free to go, they say.'

'Are you sure?' He eyed the guards warily. They seemed to be enjoying a joke. 'What did you tell them?'

'Not quite the truth. I tell them Marga and I live in Scotland and we are visiting our grandmama when the troubles started. I say you are Scottish man sent to bring us home and that is why you act mad.'

126

'And they swallowed it?' Archie said incredulously. 'What else did you tell them?'

'That you are very generous and have plenty British money,' he admitted. 'I found the shop you went to yesterday and the shopkeeper say British money is very good value at the bank. He apologizes to you and will make no charges.'

'Decent of 'im!' Archie growled.

'So the police say you can go, but—' he examined his fingernails intently – 'there will be a charge for overnight lodgings and a fine for wasting police time.'

'Oh, aye?' Archie sighed and reached resignedly into his moneybelt.

A free man once more, he paused outside the police station. 'I'm surprised the police didn't ask you more searching questions about me,' he remarked thoughtfully.

'They did.' Michael turned beetroot-red. 'I told them you are my Scottish father.'

They stared at one another, then slow grins spread across their faces. Archie clapped the young lad on the back. 'Good for you, son!' he chuckled.

Seraphima was having problems as the *vozok* travelled steadily onwards towards Murmansk. The journey itself was no bother. Vassily made sure she was as comfortable as possible. The problem was keeping secrets. Seraphima was a fine needlewoman and could make corsets of exquisite fit and comfort, trimmed with handmade lace and finished with embroidered silk or satin – but knitting was not her forte. The pattern she'd planned for Vassily's muffler was ambitious, involving symbols of Russian pine forests and Scottish heather moors. It was almost beyond her capability as a knitter and was driving her daft. Moussia's presence in the cab did not help. The playful cat found balls of coloured wool an endless source of fun. Seraphima was at her wit's end retrieving hard-won knitting from Moussia's claws.

And then there was Vassily's book. To please him, she'd

made an effort to be engrossed in his gift whenever they halted to let Osopa rest and Vassily come into the cab to thaw out. That meant bundling the knitting hastily out of sight and resulted in dropped stitches and tears of frustration afterwards.

Besides, reading *Tsar Ivan the Terrible's Reign of Terror* made Seraphima's hair stand on end. It was a very strange choice for a gentle lady!

The *vozok* had stopped that morning and Vassily would soon appear. She grabbed the book and read a few sentences. Seraphima's eyes widened, her cheeks paled and she gave an audible gasp at the horrific details of torture outlined on the page. Unfortunately, Vassily appeared in the doorway and noted her expression.

'My book distresses you!' he said. 'What is wrong?'

'Well . . . you know . . .' she began hesitantly, 'One does need strong nerves to read about Ivan the Terrible . . .'

Vassily sat down heavily. He felt quite sick. That greasy scoundrel in the shop had deceived him! A romance, he'd assured him, a pleasant love story in a beautiful binding to while away the hours! Never judge a book by its cover!

'I did not know what the title said!' Vassily groaned.

Seraphima gave him a puzzled look. 'But you went to school. You can read.'

'No, ma'am. I cannot.' He hung his head. His shame was pitiful to see.

She leaned across and took his hand. 'Vassily dear, why not?'

'Remember I told you once that my poor uneducated parents thought I was clever?' His eyes were wet with tears. 'Well, I was not so clever, after all. Words were a jumble beyond my understanding. When I tried to write, letters were back to front and made no sense. My teacher told me I could not be taught.'

'Your parents . . .?'

'They never knew.' He shook his head sadly. 'The teacher was kind. She let me stay on at school and do odd jobs about

128

the place. I saved the few kopeks I earned and bought my parents a Bible. They cried when they saw the Good Book. They were devout people, and they rejoiced because I could read the scriptures to them whenever they wished.'

'But Vassily, you couldn't read!'

'No, but I could remember almost word for word what the priest read out to us on Sundays and feast days.' He lifted his chin. 'I could pretend to read, and they never guessed the truth, God bless them.' Miserably, he met Seraphima's eyes. 'Now you will despise me even more, and that is what I deserve.'

'No! That's not so!' She looked at him earnestly. 'Listen, Vassily. My husband had a friend once, a very clever, intelligent man. But just like you, words made no sense and he could neither read nor write. Yet he designed and made surgical instruments with the greatest skill and precision. My husband said the brain is complex and all its functions are not understood. Maybe to you the written word is meaningless, but your memory fills me with awe. You could remember every stitch of your mother's knitting pattern. How clever!' She smiled, thinking about her own frustrating muddles.

They sat quietly hand in hand, then Vassily squared his shoulders. There was a subtle change in him, Seraphima thought. A change one would hardly notice, but Seraphima knew it had happened all the same. She recognized it as the banishing of shame and guilt and the realization of his true worth.

'Thank you, Seraphima.' He looked at her and smiled, then leaned forward and kissed her.

Aleksandr Rostovich did not sleep well that night. The commissar spent the small hours pacing the floor. He didn't know if Anna would go or stay.

Like a fool he had told her she was free to leave. Being a passionate and independent young woman, he realized that Anna would very likely take him at his word. Fool that he was! He should have bound her to him with

129

much stronger emotional chains, now that he had found her again.

But she had not gone – yet. He had checked that evening, and she was still with Katerina Orlov and the child in the apartment. Aleksandr's thoughts wrestled with possibilities.

The grandmother, Seraphima? If she could be found and brought to Petrograd, Seraphima would be a powerful bargaining counter to keep Anna in the city. He had agents at most northern railway stations on the lookout for the old woman, but she had vanished into thin air. It seemed inconceivable she was attempting to reach Murmansk by road, but it was a possibility that maybe should not be discounted.

Aleksandr flung himself upon the bed and lay staring at shadowy frescoes on the decorated ceiling. He was a man tormented by doubts since Anna McLaren had returned to Russia. He was dedicated to the revolutionary cause, and love and compassion had no part in the stern freedom fight. His friend Josef had told him so; the man with an impossible Georgian name they had nicknamed the Iron Man, Stalin.

Aleksandr was in high favour with leaders of the revolution. His future was assured, a position of authority in the Council of Soviets when the inevitable turmoil was over. And yet . . .

He turned his face to the wall. Would power bring him the pleasure he had known when he and Anna were young and in love?

Anna had not slept well either. She sat up with Katerina until very late discussing what to do. Anna faced a dilemma but Katerina's mind was clear. 'You must go to Murmansk,' she advised. 'You owe it to your grandmother Seraphima and your father and mother to arrive home safely. The Orlovs are incidental. We are not in the original scheme of things at all.'

'You're my friends. I promised to save you, and I will!'

130

But even Anna recognized desperation in the tone. She'd had no idea how it could be done.

She was no nearer a decision that morning, but her thoughts kept turning to Seraphima. What if her grandmother had reached Murmansk and found nobody there and the ship gone? The thought of dear *Babushka* wandering cold and lonely in that dismal port was more than Anna could bear.

If only Wishart had stayed! She could hardly believe he had abandoned her, yet what else could he do as time dragged by? She blinked away tears. Oh, if only Wishart had waited!

'Anna . . .' Katerina touched her hand. 'You mustn't cry. Nothing will persuade me to leave Petrograd while my husband is here, but it makes sense for you to go, my dear.'

'I . . . I suppose so . . .'

It was the ultimate defeat, she thought. She couldn't face Katerina, nor look at beloved little Basil. Still asleep, rosy-cheeked and innocent.

'Good!' Katerina nodded her satisfaction. 'Now you will eat a large breakfast while we plan your journey. I trust the commissar will provide transport to Finland Station, but he is such an awkward, difficult man!'

The awkward, difficult man arrived just as they finished breakfast. He barged in without knocking. An unusual occurrence.

'Anna, we must talk—'

Katerina rose and stood between them. Basil, newly wakened, clung wide-eyed to his mother's skirts. 'It's too late for talking, Commissar. Anna's mind is made up. She's leaving.'

'Stand aside, madame.' He eyed her coldly. 'I have a proposition to put to her first.'

'Relax, Katerina.' Anna smiled at her friend. 'I may as well hear what he has to say.'

'It is simple, my darling. Marry me!'

'But Aleksandr, I told you I could not—'

'Anna, listen to me!' he interrupted passionately. 'If you will promise to marry me I'll ensure that Ivan, Seraphima and the entire Orlov family reach Scotland safely. I swear I will do this for your sake!'

She stared at him and decided that he was perfectly sincere. She had no doubt he would keep his word – but on one condition only.

'No, Anna! Don't!' Katerina cried in distress. 'Marriage should be without any conditions, love should be the only bond!'

'Be quiet, woman!' Aleksandr rounded on her angrily. 'This is your last chance!'

'No!' Katerina said. 'There is still the collar of pearls. Set the menfolk free and we'll strike a bargain.'

He looked at her with a grim gleam of triumph. 'There's no need, madame. I've already guessed where one part is hidden!'

In a sudden quick move, Aleksandr snatched the wooden rattle from the little boy. Basil gave a piercing howl and Katerina cried out, 'Oh, please – no!'

The commissar shook the child's toy vigorously, listening triumphantly to the entrancing rattling sound. 'I have one vital piece of the collar right here in my hand, Madame Orlov – and very soon I'll have the rest!'

# Nine

Aleksandr paid no attention to Katerina's protests and Basil's howls as he examined the child's rattle. Unlike silver and coral trinkets with which wealthy families indulged teething babies, it was made from Indian rosewood, an extra hard timber. This toy had a sturdy handle and smooth egg-shaped top. The little boy's emerging incisors had made no impression upon the extremely hard surface.

'Of course, everyone knows the fable of the collar of pearls.' Aleksandr looked at Katerina and smiled. 'It's composed of many parts, and if one part is lost the family chain is broken forever. Let's see which part this little one has hidden here . . .'

'Please don't break it!' Katerina begged tearfully. 'His father had it made specially for him because he is an Easter baby and therefore doubly blessed. It is his only toy and very precious.'

'Oh yes, madame, I agree. Unique and precious!' He laughed. He struggled with the hollow top but could find no way of unscrewing it. Losing patience, he strode across to a marble-topped table and smashed the rattle down on its surface with all his strength. Basil's heartbroken wail drowned the sharp crack as the wood split neatly in two halves like a chocolate easter egg. A shower of beads scattered in all directions.

'Beads! Cheap worthless rubbish!' Aleksandr cried in angry disgust.

'I told you! It is only a toy!' Katerina screamed at him.

'What have you done with the Empress's collar? Tell me!' he demanded furiously.

'You will free the doctors and Ivan first,' she said more calmly. 'Give us safe passage to Murmansk and let us board a ship leaving for Scotland. Then I may tell you.'

'Sorry, madame.' He shook his head. 'Your price is too high.'

Anna had heard enough. 'Aleksandr, please listen to me . . .'

'Well?'

'What if I promise to marry you?'

'Anna, no! Please don't!' Katerina clutched her arm.

Anna smiled at her friend and turned back to Aleksandr. 'I promise you that when my good friends are safely aboard ship, I'll marry you, Aleksandr – if that's what it takes for a change of heart.'

'Yes,' he laughed jubilantly, embraced and kissed her, then let her go. 'That's exactly what's needed, my darling!' Then he paused for a moment and frowned. 'But negotiations will be tricky from now on, Anna. This is a police matter. It could be several days before the *Cheka* agree to release our prisoners.'

'What's a few more days?' Anna said blithely. 'We can wait!'

Katerina faced her angrily when Aleksandr had gone off to start negotiations. 'Are you crazy? If you marry this bolshevik you've thrown away any chance of happiness!'

'I loved him once, Katerina, I can love him again!'

'My dear, you may think you will change him, but you can't!'

'Yes, I can. Love conquers all!'

'Romantic rubbish!' she snorted. 'Look what he did to my beloved baby! Who could love a man who smashes a child's toy in cold blood?'

'I shall pick up the pieces and mend any damage done to the toy – and the man!'

'Ohh, you are so stubborn, like your grandmama!' Katerina

shook her head tearfully. 'If you marry this commissar and ruin your life because of the Orlovs, how can I forgive myself!'

Anna put an arm gently round her friend. 'Aleksandr's not a bad man at heart, you know. Please Katerina, I know what I'm doing. Won't you trust me?'

'I would trust you with my life and the lives of all my dear ones, Anna Androvna,' Katerina declared passionately, 'but do not ask me to trust your commissar!'

Aleksandr returned to the stateroom which served as the commissar's office.

His aide-de-camp looked up from the desk. 'You look pleased with yourself, Commissar!'

'Moderately pleased, Boris. But we have problems.' He seated himself on the corner of the desk.

'We?'

'Yes. How do we prise three prisoners from the *Cheka*'s grasp?'

The officer whistled through his teeth. 'The secret police? We *do* have problems! Is this strictly necessary?'

'Yes, unfortunately.' Aleksandr went on to detail the situation briefly for his trusted aide.

'All this trouble for a woman!' The aide shook his head in disgust.

'Don't forget the collar of pearls, my friend! I'll have one of Russia's treasures *and* a beautiful bride – if the Orlovs get safe passage from Murmansk.'

'What fuss and bother! Surely you've searched for the necklace?'

'High and low!' He shrugged. 'There's nowhere left to look. I thought I'd found one small piece, but was out of luck. The Orlovs have been too damn clever.'

'What about the missing grandmother?'

'Seraphima?' He glanced up quickly. 'What about her?'

'Her disappearance always struck me as odd, y'know. The Orlovs must know the risks of a train journey. Perhaps

135

it made sense to entrust the necklace to the old woman. Who would look twice at a poverty-stricken old crone travelling by road?'

Aleksandr nodded thoughtfully. 'It's a possibility! Red Guards and brigands don't bother with refugees tramping the roads.' He stood up purposefully. 'Maybe I should send out my scouts, with orders to find my dear old landlady and search her most thoroughly.'

Vassily was uneasy, though he could not explain why. Barring accidents they should reach their destination in under two weeks and he should have felt quite relaxed, but he sensed someone was taking unusual interest in the cab. Recently, he had parried searching questions about his passenger with vacant stares, but it worried him.

Vassily's inclination was to press on fast and ignore nightly stops at resthouses, but Seraphima's comfort was the main consideration. Besides, he didn't care to alarm her with fears which might exist only in his head.

Seraphima was knitting frantically and the muffler grew longer day by day. The pattern was erratic thanks to Moussia's claws, but the muffler felt warm and soft where it rested on Seraphima's lap. Though it was knitted without much skill, it was fashioned with love. Yes, love! her heart insisted, though she would never tell him so. It would only embarrass the shy man.

Today she bundled the knitting out of sight and rapped on the connecting window. 'Tea's ready!'

Presently he came in, unwound sacking from nose and mouth, removed snow goggles and rubbed his reddened eyes.

'Cosy in here.' He smiled and sat down.

'It should be, I've kept the stove going full blast for miles. I thought we were never going to stop! I believe you're keen to be rid of me!' she teased, handing him a steaming beaker.

'No, Seraphima, it certainly wasn't that,' he said gravely.

She didn't notice the grave look, rummaging in her bag for a book. They had agreed to exchange Vassily's gift for something more soothing and had come across the very thing while passing through a small village.

'Poetry!' Seraphima had pounced on the book of poems with delight, but Vassily had made a face.

'The cover's dreary. You should have gold!'

'Never judge a book by its cover.' She laughed. 'I thought you'd learned that lesson!'

'Yes,' he agreed sheepishly, 'but I never learned poems.'

'Then it's high time you did!' She had haggled with the shopkeeper and left him admiring a red and gold history of blood-curdling horror.

'Now, where were we?' Seraphima found the marked page and settled down to read aloud. Vassily cradled the beaker in his cold hands and listened intently.

But not to Seraphima. There were horses coming up behind, galloping fast. He could hear the muffled beat of hooves resounding on hard frozen snow. His heart began to beat faster in unison. The horses reined in close by. The cab rocked and shook as Osopa lunged and whinnied in fear. Vassily stood up.

'What's happening?' Seraphima looked terrified. She gathered Moussia in her arms.

'Shh! Maybe nothing.' He opened the door and looked out. Vassily's heart nearly failed. Two Red Army soldiers had just dismounted. He put on an indignant expression. 'You've frightened my poor old horse, comrades. What do you want with me?'

'Not you, old man!' One of them laughed. 'You have an old woman in there with you?'

'I do not!'

'Oh, come off it!' The other scoffed. 'We know you do.'

Vassily glared. 'My passenger is a *lady*.'

'There are no ladies now.' The first one grinned. 'The revolution did away with ladies.'

137

'Oh, did it indeed?' Seraphima had appeared at Vassily's elbow. She was a small but impressive figure. Old habits die hard. The soldiers muttered and shuffled their boots awkwardly in the snow.

'What do you want?' she demanded.

'Ma'am . . .' the senior man answered in a more respectful tone, 'we believe you carry a valuable object which is state property. We've orders to confiscate the package.'

'I see.'

This required careful thought. Seraphima was on the wanted list, but the few trinkets she had hidden did not merit much attention. Her thoughts turned to the collar of pearls, the Empress Catherine's gift to a favourite Orlov in bygone days. Now, *that* was priceless, its fame well known. Did the Bolsheviks believe she had it? If so, that must mean the necklace had not been found yet. She prayed that the Orlovs were safe, but had someone in authority remembered Seraphima, an innocent old friend of the family who might well be entrusted with the priceless heirloom? It was possible!

'A package, did you say?' She smiled.

'Officer said it wouldn't be easy to hide, ma'am.' The soldier nodded. 'We've orders to take the cab apart.'

Seraphima looked resigned. 'Oh, there's no need for that! If you'll just step inside I'll hand over the precious item.'

'Seraphima . . . don't . . .!' Vassily muttered, doubling his fists. She shook her head at him warningly.

The soldiers appreciated the warmth. They relaxed, seating themselves comfortably and looking around. 'It would certainly be a sin to destroy this cosy nest!' they laughed.

'Now, let us reveal the treasure!' Seraphima said.

The large cat basket lay on the seat beside her. She undid the straps. An angry Moussia scrambled out, spitting. Seraphima took no chances now with her beloved pet. Moussia was consigned to the basket every time the cab door opened. The soldiers recoiled in alarm. Seraphima reached inside. Reverently, she brought out the ikon of the

138

blessed Saint Stephen and unwrapped it. It glowed like a golden jewel in the cab's dim interior. The saint surveyed the two men with kindly, tolerant eyes.

'This . . . this is it?' one whispered in awe.

'Yes. It is a very great treasure and I am sad to see it go.' Seraphima wiped away a tear. 'But if the state has need of it, the state shall have it.'

She wrapped the ikon carefully in its canvas covers and handed it over. 'Take great care of it!' she said sternly.

'We will, don't worry, ma'am!' They snapped to attention and bowed themselves out.

Vassily watched the soldiers trot off into the distance, the ikon stowed safely in a saddlebag. He returned to the cab and sat staring at Seraphima. 'You will miss your plaster saint.'

'Yes, Vassily, I will.' She sighed, then grinned. 'I'm sure those poor ignorant souls were sent to capture the Orlovs' collar of pearls. But I think Russia has far more need of good St Stephen's guidance, don't you?'

'That's for sure!' he laughed. But inwardly Vassily was afraid for her. When the authorities discovered they'd been tricked they would come after Seraphima again And next time they would not be gentle.

He looked at her. 'We'll follow a different route now. It's safer, but there are no resthouses – no habitation.' He waited for that information to sink in.

She met his eyes. 'Good idea!' Seraphima nodded.

They both knew they must spend nights alone together. That was tempting fate and highly improper, but Seraphima did not care.

'Now where were we?' Calmly, she reached for the poetry book and continued to read aloud. And it was a love poem, as it happened . . .

Archie had decided to move out of the hiding-place above the doctor's surgery. It had become too conspicuous since the ill-fated shopping expedition. Word had got around

139

about the presence of sick children and motherly Russian women came sneaking up the outer stairs from the alleyway bearing soup, meat pies and spiced biscuits.

The twins snapped up every gift and were thriving. The Russians' generosity was heart-warming. Archie was touched, but apprehensive. They were sitting ducks if word happened to reach the wrong ears.

'Gather your gear, we're movin' out tomorrow,' he decided.

The youngsters didn't argue. They felt better and the stay in the small apartment was wearisome. They woke early next morning and Archie cooked a substantial breakfast to keep them all going. Michael checked a railway timetable. A train was due at midday, which gave ample time to reach the station.

They were just finishing the last slices of smoked bacon when Archie's sharp ears detected a furtive sound. He listened. Floorboards creaked, just outside the door. The others heard it too and looked at him, startled.

He put a finger to his lips, picked up the poker and tiptoed to the door. He wrenched it open, the poker raised.

'For heaven's sake! A dog!' Archie cried.

The poor thing crouched down cowering, expecting a beating. Its brown eyes looked up at him pathetically, without much hope. The twins rushed across the room.

Marga was down on her knees, in tears. 'Oh Archie, he is thin, poor, dear dog. He has smelled the bacon!'

The dog uncurled itself a fraction. Its tail gave one or two uncertain flops. Its drooping ears edged a little upwards, and its nose twitched at the smell of the cooked bacon. A drool of hungry saliva made a pool on the floor.

'We must feed him, Archie!' Marga declared.

'Now wait a minute!'

'Yes!' Michael said. 'There are bacon scraps left, and we can't take soup and half-eaten meat pies with us, can we?'

'No, but—'

'Pl-l-*ea-se*!'

140

Archie capitulated. The last thing they needed was a starving dog. But it was already too late to protest further. The mongrel sensed welcome and was on its feet with tail wagging. It was ushered in. Archie watched as it wolfed every scrap of perishable food and washed that down with gulps of water. Then the three of them sat around the dog and looked at it.

It was more presentable with its ears cocked and tail wagging. It wore an oddly engaging grin, but no collar.

'Where has he come from, Archie?'

'Dinnae ask me! His owner'll be looking for him.' Archie suspected the poor beast was in for a sound beating when found.

'He is a lovely dog!' Marga sighed. 'What do you think he is called?'

Archie considered the mongrel thoughtfully. It had a hopeful, affectionate look which reminded Archie strongly of his uncle Hamish, who had a habit of turning up at mealtimes at home in Dundee.

'If it was up to me, I'd say Hamish,' he said.

'Hamish is a good name!' She hugged the dog. It looked gratified. Maybe it was not used to tender loving care.

'Aye, well . . .' Archie cleared his throat of an unwelcome emotion. Time was running out.

The twins and the dog huddled together and stared pathetically. Archie hardened his heart. He opened the door and pointed. 'Home, boy!'

The dog became a picture of misery, ears lowered, tail between legs, skinny body hunched low to the floor. The pathetic mongrel cringed on trembling legs. Archie sighed and turned to Michael. 'Tell it to him in Russian!'

'He understands very well,' the boy said indignantly. 'It is cruel to put him out. He does not want to go.'

'Well, he cannae stay. For heaven's sake, son, a dog's the last thing we need!'

'I-I suppose so.' He patted the shivering dog reassuringly.

'He will go with me, Archie. I'll take him down to the street, then maybe he will go home.'

'Aye. Do that.'

Archie folded his arms and watched a tear-jerking display of fond hugging and kissing, then endured Marga's heart-broken sobs as her brother departed, leading the mongrel.

Archie closed the door and comforted the lass with a drink of tea and a spiced biscuit. Then they sat down and waited.

An uncomfortable space of time dragged by. Archie became more and more agitated as he watched from the window and saw no sign of the lad or the dog. He hauled out a pocket watch and stared at it in shock. The boy had been gone for more than an hour. What on earth had happened to him?

Marga began crying. She'd had nightmares since her mother and Elena vanished, and now Michael was missing. Another nightmare was beginning.

'Hush.' Archie hugged her. 'It's all right, hen. He'll be back soon.' He'd better be! he added silently.

'You won't leave me, will you, Archie?' She clung to him tearfully.

'Nae chance!' he declared fervently. He'd lost too many folk already.

'I love you, Archie.' She nestled closer. 'I think I will marry you one day.'

'Whit?' His voice rose to a nervous squeak and he released her smartly. Another complication. And a serious one, this time. He took another glance at the watch. They'd lost all hope of catching the Murmansk train now, and worst of all, they'd lost Michael . . .

Andrew McLaren was not a gardener although he liked everything in the garden shipshape. He'd engaged an old lad called Sandy Semple to come in once a fortnight, to keep the Peep o' Day garden tidy. A few days after his encounter with the retired policeman, Andrew wandered out to have a quiet word in Sandy's ear.

'What goes on in the Law Hill allotments on winter days?'

'No' much, Cap'n. A lot o' blethers in the huts.'

'That's a popular pastime?'

'Oh aye. Takes them out from under the women's feet.'

Andrew stored the information. One damp morning close to Christmas he slipped quietly out of the house. This was a busy season for Irina and Mina with corsetry orders and he was confident he would not be missed. He boarded a tram heading for Lochee Road. From there it was a trek uphill to the area recently set aside for raising vegetables, which were much needed because of wartime shortages.

It was a gamble finding Eddie Duncan there, but fortunately it paid off. Andrew was directed to a small hut where Eddie was potting cuttings. They stared at one another.

'It's yoursel', Cap'n.' The retired policeman frowned. His tone was not welcoming.

'Aye, Mr Duncan. We've unfinished business concerning an abandoned baby which is now a grown man.'

'And I wish I'd been left in ignorance!'

'I'm sorry. I thought you'd want to know.'

'Oh, I can see it was kindly meant,' he admitted grudgingly. He sighed and brushed spilled compost absently on to the floor. Then went on in a different tone: 'I've lost sleep over this. It opens old wounds, y'know. Is he a good man? Has he done well for himsel'?'

'Aye.' Andrew nodded. 'Duncan Wishart's a very clever lad. A ship's captain at thirty.'

'A captain? Fancy that!'

'Maybe you've always suspected who the parents were?' Andrew watched him shrewdly. 'Maybe you even knew the mother?'

'Maybe.' Eddie turned and looked at him levelly. 'But if I did, I'd tell the young lad, Cap'n. Not you!'

In Murmansk, Duncan Wishart had decided to give the loyal crew a Christmas dinner to remember. That seemed only

143

fair, after hours of boredom endured in this makeshift new port where the sun never rose above the dark horizon.

Once Elena had recovered from the terrifying events prior to her arrival aboard the *Pole Star*, she discovered she could indulge a passion for cooking. In happier times the kitchens of the Orlov mansion had fascinated Elena as a youngster. She had watched cooks at work and learned a great deal.

Archie's replacement was only too glad to have Elena's help in the ship's galley. The crew had already seen a noticeable improvement. They all enjoyed having a pretty young woman aboard. Elena's presence kept them on their toes, washing and shaving. She was obviously pregnant by now, and the whole crew was fiercely protective of the little 'Russian mother'.

Their captain was not so comfortable with the situation. Elena made Duncan wonder anew about his own start in life and the same painful question kept bothering him. Why had his mother abandoned him at birth?

Elena sensed a problem with him. It worried her. 'Maybe you do not wish me to work in the galley, Captain?' she ventured when she caught him on his own one day.

'Elena, if you enjoy cooking, please do continue,' he said warmly. 'The men are looking forward to a sumptuous Christmas dinner.'

'For me, it will be strange.' She sighed. 'Christmas in Russia is celebrated thirteen days later than your feast day.'

'Then we'll have another celebration when your family turns up.' He smiled at her.

He was a changed man when he smiled. She had not seen him smile much lately and it disturbed her. 'My presence distresses you, Captain. Why is that?' she asked.

He looked contrite. 'I'm sorry if I gave you that impression, Elena. It's nothing to do with you, it's just . . .' He hesitated, then went on lamely: 'I can't imagine what would make a mother abandon a newborn baby.'

Elena studied him thoughtfully. Could a cruel past explain

144

what ailed the man? A child needs to know it is loved and wanted, otherwise there will be lasting scars.

'I can only tell you how it would be for me,' she said gently. 'My Dmitri married me willingly because he loved me, and my loving parents stood by us, even though we had anticipated marriage and committed sin. Now I am alone, but I would not abandon my baby while there are still those who love and care about me and my baby.'

She looked at Wishart and her eyes grew dark. 'But if I were unmarried with nobody to love me, or care if my baby lived or died, then I might consider letting the precious child go. It would break my heart, but I might do it if I believed the little one would have a better start in life.'

Duncan nodded thoughtfully. He suddenly could see his unknown mother in a more sympathetic light. 'That's a helpful point of view, Elena. Thank you.' He smiled.

It was a warm and friendly smile. A pity it was so seldom seen! Elena thought.

The doctors had been well treated in prison, compared with others. Even so, Leon and Dmitri shared a cold dark room that was little more than a cell. Their diet was a monotonous one of weak tea, cabbage soup and stale black bread.

Their guards assured them they were given preferential treatment because doctors were in short supply, and for that they should thank the leader, Lenin. When they had served their sentence for neglect of duty they would be returned to the wards, where they were sorely needed.

So it was an unpleasant surprise when the door was flung open early one morning and the guards came tramping in.

'On your feet. Get dressed.' One of them flung down a heap of articles of outdoor clothing.

This was unusual behaviour. Leon Orlov did not know whether to be hopeful or afraid. He knew Katerina and the little one were in the city. Leon lived in hope they would be allowed to visit him. He frowned at the heap of clothing.

'What's this in aid of?'

145

'You're going on a journey, comrades. Your luck and our leader's patience has run out.' The guards laughed heartily. Good spirits in prison guards was not a good omen.

Leon and Dmitri shrugged on old greatcoats. They pulled on wool hats and mitts and draped moth-eaten mufflers around their heads and throats and were shepherded into a corridor echoing to the shuffling tramp of many feet. Their section of the prison was on the move.

Icy cold hit the group as they left the prison and straggled through massive gates on to the streets. There had been very little fresh snow since the blizzard, but roads remained treacherous and the march to Finland Station was an ordeal the prisoners would not forget.

The doctors arrival at the railway siding was unexpectedly happy, however, for they found Ivan in the crowd. Dmitri gave a delighted shout, and the two brothers embraced joyfully. The three made sure they were herded into the same cattle-truck. They had much to talk about in the dark corner they made their own.

'Where are they taking us, d'you know?' Dmitri asked his brother.

'North.'

'Siberia?'

'Where else?'

They fell silent. Siberia was a destination to silence the bravest.

'All I wanted was to see Katerina and the child, one last time.' Leon said sadly. 'And nobody listened to my prayers.'

Dmitri didn't even know where to find Elena his bride. Maybe their child would be born and never know its father. He was glad of the semi-darkness to hide the tears.

'You know, in prison I had time to think,' Ivan said, unsmiling. 'We were fools to trust Anna Androvna.'

'She was our only hope!' Leon Orlov stared at him.

'I know.' He nodded. 'She is pretty and charming and I fell in love. But I didn't know she had a Bolshevik boyfriend!'

146

'Ah, yes. I remember he was Seraphima's lodger.' Leon frowned. 'But I can't believe Anna would deceive us.'

'I don't want to believe it either, but look at the evidence!' he said grimly. 'Your house was destroyed soon after she arrived in Archangel. She promised safe passage, but there was no ship, only a stranger who talks weird English and has plenty of money for train fares. First Seraphima was snatched, then Katerina and the baby. Anna went with them on a Red Army train.' He sighed and shook his head. 'I didn't suspect her till we met secretly at the Smolny Institute. An hour or two later I was captured and the hunt was on for you two. Conclusive evidence of Anna's guilt, I think.'

Huddled in their dark corner, they looked at one another.

'If we can't trust Anna, who can we trust?' Dmitri said.

'Nobody!' his brother replied.

Anna had struggled for hours to mend Basil's toy, but found the repair beyond her. She lost patience with the task and put the pieces in the wastepaper basket while he slept. The maid who cleaned their apartment removed it with the rest of their rubbish.

Fortunately Basil didn't miss the rattle too much. Katerina was teaching him Russian nursery rhymes, and the besotted pair giggled and laughed together and played pat-a-cake as if they hadn't a care in the world.

Anna envied them. The constant waiting was driving her mad. Aleksandr hadn't put in an appearance for several days and she didn't dare venture through a confusing maze of corridors without him for a breath of fresh air.

When the familiar tap came at the door at last, she wrenched it open angrily. 'Have you freed them? Can we leave?'

'Calm down!' He looked at her with a teasing grin. 'Have patience, my sweet. I'm eager to be married too.'

'I-I wasn't . . .' She coloured and fell silent.

'I've brought something for you,' he announced cheerfully, stepping into the room. He put a cardboard box on the table. Katerina and Basil gathered round curiously.

'Behold!' Aleksandr produced the rattle, fully restored. He shook it playfully, bending down to the little boy. 'There you are! Good as new.'

'See Dada!' Basil yelled, grabbing it joyfully.

'Persistent little lad, aren't you?' Aleksandr smiled.

He turned to Anna. She couldn't read his expression, but the look in his eyes made her heart miss a beat 'Now, something for you, my love.' Carefully, he took out a flat package wrapped in canvas and handed it to her. 'Open it!' he commanded.

Wondering, she obeyed. Then her heart stood still. She held Seraphima's blessed St Stephen in her hands. She would have recognized the ikon anywhere. From childhood she had gazed at the kind old face illuminated in the lampada's glow. She knew every flaw and scratch on the gilded surface. She stared at Aleksandr with dread.

She could barely whisper, 'What have you done with Seraphima? Where is she?'

'Don't worry, my darling.' He looked amused. 'I promise she will be guest of honour at our wedding, whether she approves of your choice of husband or not.'

# Ten

'A plaster saint!' Laughing, Aleksandr kissed Anna lightly.

'Seraphima's wedding gift to us, my darling!' His tone was hurtful. The ikon had played an important part in her grandmother's life.

'It may not be worth much to you, but Seraphima valued it more highly than gold!' Anna said.

He shrugged and became businesslike. 'Be packed and ready to leave for Murmansk within the hour. An orderly will come for you.'

'Are our menfolk free, Commissar?' Katerina asked eagerly.

'Not yet. There's a problem. Perhaps it can be overcome.'

'Perhaps is not good enough!'

'Be patient!' he snapped. 'It's all I can say at the moment.'

Katerina turned to Anna after he had gone. 'How can you contemplate spending the rest of your life with such a heartless scoundrel?'

'He warned us it'd be difficult, Katerina! I'm sure he's doing his best.'

'And I'm sure he can't wait to get to Murmansk.' She shook her head tearfully. 'My dear, you don't understand! It's a God-forsaken region. Anything could happen to us there. Nobody would care!'

Anna sighed. 'Aleksandr mended Basil's rattle. You must admit that shows good faith.'

'Ahh, Annoushka!' Katerina shook her head sadly. 'He shouldn't have broken it in the first place.'

'See Dada!' The toddler waved the rattle happily. He sensed more travel in the air. His mother scooped him up and hugged him with tearful kisses. 'Perhaps, my darling, perhaps!'

Seraphima was plagued with doubt, but not about the times she spent in Vassily's arms. Nothing could mar the wonder of a companionship and love she'd found in frozen wasteland, in the winter of life. It had not occurred to her to question the wisdom of that love till the blissful journey was nearing its end and she was forced to contemplate the future.

While Vassily drove Osopa along silent tracks frequented only by fur traders, Seraphima sat and knitted the secret muffler and pondered options. She knitted clumsily in gloves, shivering because paraffin was running low and she saved what there was to make tea and warm Vassily when he came in from the biting cold.

'Your hands are freezing, my dear!' she exclaimed that morning. She held them in hers to warm them a little.

'Cold hands, warm heart, my lady!' He laughed, kissing her cheek with icy lips.

'Vassily –' she poured tea and handed him a steaming cup – 'I've been thinking. We're not too far from the Finnish border, are we?'

'No.' He sipped tea and watched her, waiting to hear what she had to say.

'I've a cousin in Finland who'd help us set up house together. We could find work there and make a good living. What do you say?'

'There is a granddaughter waiting for you in Murmansk.'

'We've been kidding ourselves!' Seraphima shook her head. 'Anna will be back home in Scotland by now. We've been weeks on the road. My son-in-law's ship couldn't possibly wait that long.'

'There are other ships. I believe Anna will wait,' he said.

'You can't be sure!'

'Yes, I can.' He smiled. 'She's stubborn. Like her dear grandmama who would wait forever, if the boot was on the other foot.'

Seraphima's eyes brimmed with tears. 'But I don't want to leave you, Vassily!'

'You would give up everything for an old peasant who cannot read and write?' he marvelled. He studied her thoughtfully for a long moment. 'Is that what you really want, my Seraphima?'

'Yes, of course!' She didn't mention marriage, though it was uppermost in her mind. They must marry or she would not be happy. But it was up to Vassily to propose. She looked at him fondly and waited.

'We'll see, dear lady.'

He kissed her and his lips were warm. Seraphima was content. She was quite certain he would propose, in his own good time.

Waiting anxiously in Tanilov, Archie was becoming increasingly desperate as time wore on and Michael had not returned. It was dark by 3 o'clock that afternoon. Marga sat huddled weeping miserably on the bed, convinced she'd seen the last of her twin.

'You've two options,' Archie told her. 'Either you stop here and blubber, or you come with me to look for the lad. So what's it to be?'

She stared and stopped crying. Her hero had never used that harsh tone of voice to her before. 'I will come with you, Archie.'

'Good-oh.' He nodded.

Swaddled up to the eyes, they ventured out. The street was well lit, in a town accustomed to winter darkness. The question was, where to start looking?

'See here, Archie!' Marga cried excitedly, examining a fairly fresh powdering of snow. 'Paw-prints. It is Hamish!'

'Aye. Could be.'

151

He wondered how many dogs were out and about in this neck o' the woods. Still, what was there to lose? Archie followed Marga, who had darted off down the street. They lost the prints at a road junction, but picked them up again in a narrow lane opposite. The prints were clearer here, accompanied by footprints which could be Michael's. These led through a gateway and up to a doorstep, where they disappeared inside a darkened house.

Archie frowned. They'd look a right pair of clowns if this turned out to be a wild goose chase. He eyed the door nervously and recalled the poor dog's beaten look. He was not keen to confront its owner.

On the other hand, Michael could be in there at the mercy of a cruel monster. Archie beat on the door panel with a fist.

A dog barked, and presently the door opened and a woman peered out. Marga broke into long explanations in excited Russian. The door was flung open and Archie found himself in the midst of a bewildering confusion of children aged from toddler to teen. Michael appeared with the dog at his heels and the twins embraced one another with shouts and tears, as if they hadn't seen one another for months. The woman, whom Archie assumed was mother of the tribe, grabbed his arm and hauled him inside, chatting away in Russian. He was propelled into an amazingly hot living room and seated in a chair. The dog set to work, rounding up children and setting them in place.

Then a speculative silence fell while the family sat and contemplated Archie. The mongrel flopped down on the rug with a lop-eared grin of recognition.

'You play-acting fraud!' He glared at it grimly.

'Er . . . Archie . . .?' Michael was fidgeting.

'Aye?'

'I have bought the dog.'

'Heaven help us!'

'I have to do it, Archie!' The lad protested. 'The poor dog bring me to his home. This kind lady weeps and tell me she has too many children and food is scarce. She love the dog dearly, but she must send him out to beg and forage for himself. She say he is clever dog and hard to resist. He make himself look . . . how you say . . .?'

'Pathetic!' Archie supplied dourly. 'So you bought it?'

'The lady tell me I make very good bargain.' The lad nodded proudly. 'He only cost a diamond ring Mama sewed in the lining of my hat.'

'Cheap at the price!' Archie groaned.

Marga had her arms fastened round the dog's neck and there was nothing for it but to take Michael's unwelcome purchase, and go.

The sobbing family produced a leather dog collar and lead and Archie was forced to witness another sorrowful farewell. The dog reverted to a shivering wreck of huddled canine misery and had to be dragged to the doorway on short trembling legs. Heart-rending sobbing followed it outside till the door closed.

Archie looked sourly at the cowering animal. 'OK, you big jessie, you can buck up now! You cannae fool me, Hamish.'

He flicked the choice titbits the family had provided towards the mongrel. It rolled its brown eyes, gave itself a vigorous shaking and showed a neat row of lower teeth in an apologetic grin. Then it wolfed down the treat and set off jauntily in the direction of their apartment, tail wagging.

Archie fixed the ecstatic twins with a stern glare. 'Tomorrow, no matter what, we catch the Murmansk train. Understood?'

'Hamish as well?' Marga demanded.

'Oh aye. It too!' Archie sighed.

Although the *Pole Star* was the flagship of Andrew McLaren's trading fleet he had other irons in the fire. A McLaren fleet of small coasters was doing very well around the British coastline, picking up coal and other essential commodities from the Fife coalfields and Dundee mills and transporting them to various destinations. Income from coastal trade and his wife Irina's corsetry enterprise had kept the McLarens solvent during this worrying time.

Christmas Day 1917 was an ordinary working Tuesday in Dundee. Bairns might find a gift in a Christmas stocking, a few sweeties, an apple and a sixpence in the toe, but otherwise there was not much to celebrate that wartime winter.

Andrew went down to the docks as usual. Neither he nor Irina felt much like celebrating. There had been no word of their missing daughter for weeks. However, Andrew found a brief message from Wishart waiting for him at the telegraph office: **All's well STOP Still waiting STOP Anna and Seraphima fine STOP Merry Christmas STOP Pole Star**

'Damn cheek!' he growled. When he felt a tap on the shoulder he turned round scowling. 'Och, it's you!'

'Aye.' Eddie Duncan was not put out by the curt greeting. The retired policeman eyed Andrew. 'I've been waiting a while but they said you'd probably be in sometime. I didn't want to come to the hoose.'

'What are you after?'

'The wife wants to meet you.'

That came as a surprise. 'Now why would she want to meet me?' Andrew asked.

'I tried to put her off but she wouldna budge.' He sighed. 'I wish you'd left us in ignorance about that bairn! I felt duty bound to tell Amy.'

Andrew considered the request. He was reluctant to face the invalid, yet it was an interesting development. Perhaps Mrs Duncan would be more forthcoming than her husband.

'When's a good time to come?' he asked.

'No time like the present.' The old man shrugged.

The two elderly gentlemen set off by tram and on foot till they reached the little cottage nestled in the shelter of the Law. Eddie opened the door, wiped his feet on the doormat and called out, 'Amy, I've brought Captain McLaren wi' me.'

Andrew removed his hat. The living room was cosy with a fine view through the yellow smoke of Dundee's factory chimneys towards the river and the Fife hills. Amy Duncan was small and delicate-looking. Two sticks resting at her side hinted at an invalid state but her eyes were bright and clear as she shook Andrew's hand.

Once he was seated comfortably she came to the point. 'So the wee foundling survived!'

'Indeed he did! Duncan Wishart's a true survivor, ma'am.'

She eyed him shrewdly. 'Maybe you were the saving of him?'

'Och no! The wee lad saved himself. I just had the opportunity to set him on his chosen path.'

Andrew launched into an account of Duncan Wishart's attempt to stow away, and the fine training in seamanship he'd arranged for the waif aboard the *Mars*. When he'd finished the elderly couple were silent for a long moment.

'The sea in his blood, Eddie!' the old woman murmured.

'That's not unusual in the port o' Dundee, love!' the old man said, with a warning glance at his wife.

Andrew noted the reaction. 'That might give a clue to his parentage I suppose, Mrs Duncan. But so far I've met a blank wall.'

'Because it's none o' your business!' Eddie retorted.

His wife rounded on him. 'If Captain McLaren hadn't shown an interest we'd never have known the baby lived.'

'What's the use of knowing, after thirty years? Much better not to know.'

'How can you say that!' Her pale cheeks reddened.

'Don't upset yoursel', Amy dear!' her husband said anxiously. 'This is just what I feared would happen. I was reluctant to tell you, but I thought it might set your mind at rest.'

'Rest?' She shook her head wildly. 'How can I rest, now we know?'

'Because there's no future in it! That bairn belongs only to the past, Amy, and that's where it should stay!'

They'd momentarily forgotten all about Andrew. He cleared his throat awkwardly. 'I didn't mean to upset you, Mrs Duncan. I'm sorry. I'd better go.' He stood up and reached for his hat.

'Aye, maybe you'd better,' Eddie said.

He saw Andrew to the door and the two men faced one another. The soft sound of Amy Duncan's sobs whimpered in the background.

'You realize I'll not give up till I know what's behind all this, Mr Duncan?' Andrew warned.

'Aye. You're a stubborn auld devil. Like mysel'.'

Andrew thought there was a hint of grudging admiration in the old policeman's eyes, as Andrew headed off down the path.

'By the by, Captain . . .' Eddie called after him.

'Yes?'

'Merry Christmas!' he shouted ironically.


On Christmas morning, Duncan Wishart had been amused and touched to find a bulging stocking hanging outside the cabin door. He took it inside to examine the contents, a pleasure he had not enjoyed as a deprived little boy at the cruel mercy of a foster father.

To his delight he found a penknife with an array of useful gadgets. In a small box tied with ribbon there were sweets and spiced biscuits. He smiled. Elena, of course! A well-wrapped parcel revealed a cake of Lifebuoy soap from Jock, the medical orderly, and in the toe nestled an apple and a silver sixpence for luck.

He spread the gifts upon the bunk and looked at them with a full heart. For the first time in years he struggled with tears. He'd nothing to offer in return except a weary vigil that kept loyal men from the arms of their loved ones. He pulled himself together and left the cabin.

Elena was in the saloon, the crew grouped around her. She greeted him with eyes like stars. 'Look at the present these dear men have given!'

156

She held up bootees, vests, matinee jacket and bonnet, a complete layette for a tiny baby.

Duncan examined the tiny garments. His thoughts flew back thirty years. How was he dressed when they found him? 'What a thoughtful gift!' He smiled warmly.

'Aye,' Somebody laughed. 'The whole crew's been behaving like auld grannies since the wee mother came aboard.'

'You'll recognize my white cardigan in a new guise, skipper,' Jock said proudly. 'I volunteered the wool. A local lass did the knitting.'

In gratitude, Elena excelled herself with the Christmas feast. Two roast chickens with all the trimmings appeared on the festive table. These had arrived aboard ship mysteriously. None of the crew divulged the source. There was Russian fare too, in the form of *pirozhkis* – delicious pies filled with chopped meat.

When the plum pudding arrived the captain poured a measure of vodka over it and set it alight. The raw spirit flickered a bright blue flame across the surface and the crew cheered. It was a good omen.

Elena had made party hats out of brown paper. She settled a paper crown upon the captain's dark head and kissed him on both cheeks.

'Thank you for saving me. And thank you for waiting to save all the others.'

He nodded and paid attention to the feast. It would not do for the crew to see their captain in tears.

When the mood was most relaxed and the pudding reduced to crumbs, a naval officer appeared unexpectedly in their midst. He had found his own way down the companionway to the saloon, guided by sounds of merriment. He wished everyone Merry Christmas, but he brought an icy air with him. The laughter faded.

'Pull in a chair, sir, join the party!' Duncan Wishart said cordially.

'Thanks.' The officer glanced around the table. 'I've

good news for you all. You can be on your way home within the week.'

Duncan frowned. 'I have permission to stay at this berth and wait for refugees to arrive.'

'Yes, I know.' The man nodded. 'But I'm afraid that's been cancelled. Merchant vessels are ordered to leave port right away. The Russians signed an armistice with Germany ten days ago and we lost an ally at the stroke of a pen. Murmansk is the only port we can use to land forces to intervene and fight the Bolsheviks.' He met Duncan Wishart's gaze squarely. 'I can give you one week to prepare your ship and get out of here, Captain!'

'Seven days? Impossible!'

'It's not negotiable. Those are my orders.'

A heavy silence fell. Nobody moved a muscle. Duncan's crew watched him, hardly daring to breathe. To a man they were longing to leave this dismal place. He couldn't blame them.

Seven days! And then he would have no option but to leave. Without Anna. And that would break his heart.

Coaling began on the second day, dockers moved in, bent double under the weight of coal sacks, the snow blackened, and there was a steady thunderous roar as the bunkers filled.

Duncan supervised the operation.

'Odd dockers they have in this place!' the first mate remarked. He'd been studying the quayside through glasses. He handed the binoculars to Duncan.

An odd little group was just emerging from a cloud of coal dust and heading for the ship. He focused on the tallest.

'Archie!' He felt a heart-stopping jolt of joy. Was she there – had Archie brought her with him? He trained the glasses on the two smaller figures, so wrapped in furs it was hard to make out features. He lowered the glasses slowly. One thing was certain: neither of them was Anna.

Archie's arrival was greeted with loud cheers from the crew and an ecstatic display of hugging and kissing from

Elena, who kissed Archie on both cheeks and hugged his two companions with wild cries of joy and floods of tears in a heart-warming display of emotion.

'It's her brother and sister,' Archie told Duncan. 'Awfy sorry about the McLaren lassie and her auld granny, skipper, but I lost 'em.'

'Lost them? Where?'

'Somewhere along the way.' He looked sheepish. 'They'll maybe turn up yet.'

Duncan's attention was attracted to the cowering animal Archie had dragged reluctantly aboard. 'What's that?' He pointed. The mongrel cringed.

'Och, it's just Hamish needing his tea.' Archie sighed. 'Dinna pay attention to the beast.'

'The poor dog's half-starved!' Duncan frowned.

'Don't you believe it! Its mother was a whippet.' Archie eyed the trembling wreck. 'Buck up, Hamish! I ken fine you've had a whiff o' the galley.'

When the excitement of the arrival had subsided, and the two Orlovs had adjourned to Elena's cabin where they were talking ten to the dozen, Jock the medical orderly waylaid Duncan. 'A word with ye, skipper,' he said kindly.

As senior member of the crew, Jock was entitled to air his views. He had a high regard for their young captain and had formed certain opinions which he'd kept to himself concerning the young man and the boss's bonny daughter. Jock believed the romance was ill-fated.

'Now that Archie's aboard, the men want to leave. That was the bargain,' he said.

'I still have five days, Jock!'

'Son . . .' Jock put a hand on his arm. 'She won't come now. She's chosen to stay in Russia wi' the Russian boyfriend. You may as well up anchor and forget her. You owe it to your crew.'

'Five more days, Jock!' Duncan Wishart's expression set hard. 'Is that too much to ask?'

'I don't know. It could be.' The older man sighed.

Anna, Katerina and the child were on a train speeding north. It was a fast train equipped with royal compartments and it travelled at imperious speed, a large red flag whipping in the wind at the head. Slower trains made way.

Katerina was in high spirits now they were on their way, confident that she and her husband would be reunited. With Anna's help she spent time increasing her vocabulary with words and phrases she imagined they would need in Scotland.

Anna wondered what her own future would be like in Russia. She had assured Katerina the planned marriage to Aleksandr would be a success, but she couldn't ignore certain doubts and fears. She told herself it was natural for brides-to-be to suffer pre-wedding nerves.

She already knew she could never share his enthusiasm for this cruel revolution, and yet not long ago he had begged her to marry him and save him from the man he might become. There was still hope!

However, Katerina believed it was too late and he would never change. Not even Anna's love could save him. Who was right?

Restlessly, Anna left the compartment where Katerina was patiently teaching Basil to count in English. She had drawn faces on her fingernails and the two were giggling together. They didn't even notice she'd gone.

Anna stood in the empty corridor watching the featureless landscape rush by. It was good to be alone after weeks of close confinement, but her solitude did not last. Aleksandr's aide approached her.

'Ah! The blushing bride!'

'Not a bride yet!' she said coldly.

Anna did not like the man. He was Aleksandr's close friend and confidant, but he treated her with thinly veiled insolence.

'Ah yes! I forgot this marriage hangs upon certain

conditions.' He grinned. 'I hope the commissar finds you worth the trouble.'

'I promised to save the Orlovs. Then you people interfered. It wasn't my fault my father's ship left Murmansk.'

'But it didn't!' He chuckled at her astonishment. 'Your lover, the captain, is more persistent than I thought. Captain Wishart still waits patiently in port. But for how much longer?'

She stared at him. His expression was full of malice. She would never trust this man. 'I don't believe a word you say. You are trying to give me false hope, and that is cruel. I know Wishart has gone, but there are other British ships,' she told him angrily. 'All I want is to see my grandmother and the Orlov family safe in Scotland!'

'I wouldn't count on that.'

'What do you mean?'

'Aleksandr hasn't told you yet?' He raised his brows. 'The doctors and your friend Ivan are on their way to a labour camp and we all know the Orlov woman won't budge from Russia without her husband. You see the problems you have given the commissar?'

'Can-can he save them?' Anna cried in deep distress.

'Why do you think the train flies like the wind?' He shrugged. 'He'll try.'

'He must love me to do this!'

'Don't flatter yourself!' The aide laughed. 'There is more at stake than a pretty bride. There is the collar of pearls!'

With a mocking salute he went off smiling along the corridor.


The doctors and Ivan had been travelling for days, but not so comfortably. The train stopped now and then at the back of beyond where escape was pointless, and the prisoners were ordered to cut wood to refuel the engine. They took the chance to collect branches and twigs to stoke the old rusty stoves which stood in the centre of the trucks, relics of peasants travelling the hard way.

The extra wood proved a blessing. Now the prisoners could melt snow for drinking water and washing. Leon Orlov took command in the truck; the doctor was a stern taskmaster where hygiene was concerned.

Even so, Ivan fell ill. It was a fever that left him tossing and turning, hot and shivering. On the long journey, fevers were common under crowded conditions, but Ivan's seemed more virulent and the doctors feared it could be the influenza already rampaging across European battlefields.

'Anna!' The sick man muttered her name constantly and the doctors exchanged a worried glance. Her betrayal preyed upon his mind. Sometimes he shouted, sometimes pleaded softly, more often he sobbed. It would break the hardest heart, just listening to him.

The prisoners had no idea where they were headed but at least it was not to Siberia. Leon and Dmitri had noticed that after travelling due north for several days the train suddenly changed direction and was now steaming north-west, faster. That could mean their final destination was the coast. Were they to be shipped to Germany as labourers? That was not a pleasant prospect.

They had lost count of time when the train stopped, days later. The truck doors were flung open and they were ordered out.

'Where are we?' someone asked.

'Murmansk,' one of the guards answered. 'You should be thankful for friends in high places. You'll be deported to Sweden and after that it's up to you. Russia doesn't want scum like you.'

Leon and Dmitri prepared to join the others, Dmitri supporting his sick brother. Ivan was recovering, but still weak.

'Not you three!' The guard intervened, shoving them aside.

They stood by, watching a straggling column of prisoners wend its way out of sight. Leon took a deep breath. He could smell the sea. More importantly, he could hear surf break on a distant shore. This sea was not frozen.

'Follow me!' the guard ordered.

They were taken to an old wooden house with heavily carved gables and put into a sparsely furnished room. Dmitri lowered his exhausted brother on to a chair, and turned to the guard. 'Why are we here?'

'To witness a marriage.' The man laughed. 'You are the commissar's special guests, comrades. I doubt if he will let you kiss the bride.'

The guard left them and presently the door opened and Anna walked in. She paused in the doorway and stared in disbelief. Nobody had prepared her for this meeting. She and Katerina had arrived in Murmansk yesterday and their train had rested in a siding overnight. Anna had found the delay infuriating. She wanted to go to the harbour to make sure the *Pole Star* was there, but Aleksandr forbade it. He'd given no hint that Ivan and the doctors were due to arrive. He had merely asked her to accompany him to the office of foreign affairs that morning, to make sure her papers were in order.

Anna's heart sang. Aleksandr had prepared this wonderful surprise to delight her! He was standing beside her watching the reunion with a smile. She swung round and kissed him. 'You did it! Oh, thank you, thank you!'

Laughing, she ran to embrace her friends. She took three or four steps towards them before hesitating. They were not welcoming, staring at her, cold and unfriendly.

'What's wrong?' she faltered.

'I trusted you,' Ivan told her bitterly, 'and landed in prison.'

'That wasn't my fault!' She glanced at Aleksandr.

'And now you mean to humiliate me, Anna!' Ivan cried.

'Of course not!' She looked bewildered.

Leon Orlov intervened. 'You can't deny we've been brought here to witness your marriage to our worst enemy. Do you want us also to witness his power?'

'Of course not! I only agreed to marry him to save you . . .!' She suddenly realized what she'd said and broke off in dismay.

Aleksandr gripped her wrist and pulled her round to face him. 'Was that the only reason?' he demanded.

She looked at him helplessly. This was a dangerous slip of the tongue spoken in the heat of a moment. Anna was indignant. Why should she justify her reasons for marrying Aleksandr? She glared at him.

'You spring this surprise upon me, then pounce on a slip of the tongue! I admit I'm marrying you because you have the power to reunite this family. You kept your promise, Aleksandr, and I love you for it. Now I will keep my promise to marry you. What's wrong with that?'

'Nothing.' He smiled.

'Everything!' Ivan scowled. 'There should be no bargains if you love one another. This man does not propose marriage, only a monstrous form of blackmail!' He looked at Anna and his tone softened. 'I apologize, my dear, I blamed you for everything, but now I can see this Bolshevik traitor took advantage of your loving nature. He guessed you would sacrifice your own happiness to save your friends.'

'A rejected lover *would* say that!' Aleksandr scoffed.

'She did not reject me!' Ivan struggled to his feet. 'You stole her away. Ask her which of us she would choose, if she could. Go on, ask if you dare!'

'Ivan, don't!' Dmitri warned.

The commissar's expression had darkened and their freedom hung in the balance.

Leon Orlov intervened swiftly. 'Commissar, I'm impatient to see my wife and family. Could that be arranged?'

'Certainly, doctor.' Aleksandr turned to him. 'The *Pole Star* is still in port and her captain has permission to take refugees on board.'

'He didn't abandon us!' Anna exclaimed. Oh, she should have known Wishart would wait. For once, she should have believed Boris, Aleksandr's perfidious aide.

'I have another surprise for you, my darling.' Aleksandr smiled. 'I've decided to hold our wedding ceremony aboard your father's ship.'

She stared at him. 'Will Wishart agree?'

'I'll see he does!' Aleksandr sounded amused. 'I've arranged for a priest to be on board tomorrow. The church's blessing doesn't matter to me, my love, but I know it will please you.'

'Tomorrow?' she said blankly.

'Yes. I too am sorry it couldn't be today!' He laughed. 'I long to leave this gloomy place. I'm eager to be back in Petrograd to show off my beautiful bride.'

Anna smiled uncertainly. She was imagining marrying Aleksandr with Duncan Wishart looking on. He would not approve of this situation, and the thought was somehow devastating. Another disturbing flutter of pre-wedding nerves, but the feeling of panic was real.

Duncan Wishart had retired to the bridge to think. It was cold and dimly lit but he felt in control here – of the ship, that is, if not his emotions.

Two days to go, and Anna had not returned.

Archie's mongrel sneaked in at Duncan's heels. It had taken a shine to the *Pole Star*'s skipper and followed him around with a deferential air. A lesser man would have been flattered.

'What are you doing in here?' He frowned at the dog.

It put its head to one side and looked blank. Duncan smiled.

'Sorry. I forgot you don't understand English.'

The dog accepted the smile as permission to stay. It settled down at his feet.

Duncan had been seeking solitude but somehow the dog's presence did not intrude. It offered undemanding companionship. He wondered if the animal sensed that he was a man who'd been alone too long. Alone as a small child working long hours in his foster-father's dark

165

workshop, repairing old jute sacks for potato merchants; alone as a young man struggling to overcome the stigma of being an unwanted baby abandoned in a gutter.

He studied the mongrel thoughtfully. He'd never owned a pet, because he'd never had a home. A room in Rosie Heron's boarding house didn't count. His landlady would probably have chucked his few belongings in the bin by now and let his room to someone else. He didn't bear Rosie a grudge. It was time to move on anyway.

He'd decided if he arrived back in Dundee safe and sound he would find a nice house with a garden and view of the Tay. If he couldn't marry the only girl he'd ever loved and raise a secure and happy family, he'd settle to becoming a crusty old bachelor with a faithful hound . . .

The dog suddenly growled, deep in its throat, interrupting his reverie.

''Scuse me, skipper,' Jock put his head round the door. 'There's a foreign gent to see you.'

'Show him in.'

The dog snarled when the visitor was shown in. Its hackles rose.

'Oh, it's you!' Duncan recognized his old enemy, the Red Army officer. As before, the man was dressed like a local and would pass for a fisherman.

The officer scowled at the dog. 'Tell this brute to stop its snarling.'

'You tell it. It only understands Russian.'

'*Stoy!*'

The dog crouched silently at Duncan's side. It watched the visitor's every move.

'I am Commissar Aleksandr Rostovich's personal aide, Captain. He has sent me to tell you to expect company tomorrow.'

'Pleasant, I hope?'

The man's lip curled. 'Bourgeois refugees.'

'I hope for your sake Anna McLaren is with them.'

'Don't worry. Anna will arrive for the ceremony.'

166

'What ceremony?'

'The commissar and the lovely Miss McLaren will be married tomorrow aboard her father's ship.'

'Over my dead body!' Duncan said.

'Funny you should say that!' The officer smiled. 'Russia made peace with Germany. We are in close touch with German U-boats now. Your ship's safety cannot be guaranteed when you leave port. You'd be wise to co-operate, Captain.'

The threat was not lost upon Duncan. The lives of everyone aboard lay in his hands, not to mention the fate of Andrew McLaren's prized flagship. He had little choice.

'Get out!' he said bitterly. 'Go on, leave my ship!'

'Till tomorrow, then.' He sketched a mocking salute. He knew he had won.

The dog stalked him to the door with bared teeth. He pointed a finger at it. '*Umer!*'

The dog checked suddenly, rolled over and lay rigid.

'What did you do to him?' Duncan cried angrily.

'I told the dog to die.' The officer laughed.

'Nobody dies on my ship!'

'There is always a first time, Captain!' He chuckled and quietly closed the door.

The dog came to life again. It put a paw on Duncan's knee and looked at him apologetically. He sighed and fondled its ears.

'She's broken my heart, Hamish,' he confessed. 'Why must I love that girl so much?'

The dog gently licked his hand. Strangely enough, he was comforted.

Andrew McLaren's meeting with Amy Duncan had left him with a possible clue to Duncan Wishart's parentage.

The sea was in his blood! The old lady had let the information slip before Eddie stopped her. It confirmed what Andrew had already suspected. The Duncans knew more about the foundling than they were telling him.

167

Was the father a sailor? Andrew wondered as he relaxed one evening in the week bridging Christmas and Hogmanay. His slippered feet were stretched out to a blazing fire.

'I am sick and tired with you, Andrew!' Irina eyed her husband with exasperation 'You sit like a big dummy. We have no interesting conversation any more.'

'Sorry, love. I was thinking.'

'I know what you think!' she scolded. 'You think about our darling Anna, your precious ship and Duncan Wishart!'

'Quite right, Irina. I'm no nearer finding out where the man came from and it worries me.' He frowned. 'He's made me look a fool. I trusted him and he ran off with our daughter. If that man came out of a barrelful of bad apples, I want to know!'

'I know all I need to know about Wishart.' She glanced at the baby's bonnet taking pride of place in the display cabinet. 'Somebody loved him.'

'Aye,' Andrew sighed. 'But who?'

Next day, without saying where he was off to, Andrew headed for the office where old Dundee shipping records were kept. He was given ready access, being a well-known fleet owner. He settled down at a desk, faced with a formidable bundle of documents relating to 1887, the year the infant was born. He'd no idea what he was looking for.

Amy Duncan had been quite definite. The sea was in Duncan Wishart's blood. Andrew himself came from a long line of mariners and knew the truth of that. Somewhere in this mound of tedious information might be something that rang a bell. Grimly, he set to work.

Dundee harbour was busy in 1887. The docks must have been a veritable forest of masts. Andrew waded through lists of tonnages, cargoes, bills of lading, supplies, complaints, claims for damages, settlements, wage bills, jute inventories and, of course, lists of whalers, their crews and catches.

A note stated that since gas lighting was introduced in 1817 demand for whale oil had dwindled. However, makers of umbrellas and ladies' corsets still needed whalebone for

168

stays and ribs, and jute mills used whale oil to soften brittle jute fibres. There was still a small but active whaling fleet in 1887. All Dundee whaling ships were listed, together with crews' wages and bonuses.

Andrew ran an eye perfunctorily down the lists. He had given up hope of finding anything useful and his head ached. Then a name caught his eye. It was in a list of crewmen who had signed on in March to sail with the whaler *Greenland* bound for Arctic waters: John Albert Duncan of Lawside, Dundee. Andrew stared, the headache forgotten. Could this be a relative of Eddie Duncan's? Now here was an interesting possibility!

When Katerina Orlov awoke that morning she found it hard to believe she had spent her last night in captivity. Today she would be reunited with husband and family, the commissar promised – if he could be trusted!

They had travelled from the railway station by sleigh yesterday and were installed overnight in a house close to the harbour owned by bolshevik sympathizers. She and Anna and the little one had been treated kindly by their enemies, which was just as well, since the port of Murmansk was under British and French control.

Basil was fast asleep, exhausted by yesterday's journey, but Anna was awake and dressed, sitting in front of a mirror staring at her reflection. Katerina's eyes misted. The poor girl looked so beautiful! Last night, the commissar had brought his bride-to-be the gift of a red gown and thick black velvet cloak lined with ermine and white satin.

'For our wedding, my darling,' he'd said.

Katerina had to restrain herself at that moment from blurting out the old wives' warning:

Marry in black, wish yourself back,
Marry in red, you will wish yourself dead—

169

This morning, despite these misgivings, Katerina admitted the red dress looked wonderful. It was simply cut with a low neckline and fitted slender Anna to perfection.

'You should have a necklace to set it off,' she remarked.
'I have one.' Anna smiled.

She produced the gift her mother and father had given her on her 21st birthday. Her eyes filled with tears as she fastened the clasp and studied the effect in the glass. The precious necklace had been sewn into a seam of her coat for safe keeping and she'd forgotten how significant its message was.

A brilliant star fashioned in dazzling diamonds: the Pole Star! Beneath, on the starboard side an emerald twinkled green and to port a bright red ruby gleamed. Its message was as plain as a compass reading. She could almost hear her father say, '*It will show you the way, my dear!*'

She wondered sadly if she would ever see her parents and Scotland again, once she had married Aleksandr.

'You're crying!' Katerina hugged her. 'How can I be happy if you are crying?'

'Brides are allowed a few tears, Katerina. It's traditional!'

She laughed and dried her eyes. Today was her wedding day and this afternoon she would marry the man she would soon love again. Of course she was happy! Aleksandr turned up later. The two women and the little boy were dressed and waiting when he walked in.

'You have a cheek, Aleksandr Rostovich!' Anna scolded, smiling. 'You're not supposed to see the bride till the ceremony begins. It's unlucky!'

'Superstitious nonsense, my darling!' He laughed, then caught sight of the necklace. 'What's this?'

She explained its significance. 'Isn't that a lovely thought, Aleksandr?'

'I'm sorry, it won't do.' He shook his head. 'I have a better plan. My bride will wear the collar of pearls.'

'Afraid not, Commissar.' Katerina said. 'You can't have that till Seraphima comes.'

170

'Seraphima!' He frowned in exasperation. 'So that sly old vixen has it after all, just as I suspected!'

'Don't you dare insult her!' Anna cried.

'Calm down, darling. I assure you I have the greatest respect for foxes! I'm disappointed you can't wear the collar on our wedding day, but there will be other occasions. Seraphima will turn up eventually.' He turned to Katerina with a gleam in his eye. 'You did not keep your part of the bargain, madame. That is unfortunate.'

'You have Anna. She is a far greater treasure,' Katerina retorted.

'Yes, I'm a very lucky man.' He smiled equably. 'And no doubt I will have the Orlov treasure later when we find Seraphima. It was a clever trick to entrust Imperial Russia's precious gem to a poor old widow. I admire your impudence, madame!'

Seraphima had finished Vassily's muffler. There was just enough wool to make fringes at the ends. She examined the finished work critically. The pattern was certainly original! You could see where Moussia's playful paws had sent Seraphima's stitches haywire. Vassily's gifted mother would have laughed her efforts to scorn. Still, she'd done her best. She smoothed the scarf lovingly with cold hands and hid it away.

It was only then she realized there was something unusual going on. There was little daylight these days and precious little fuel, so the interior of the *vozok* was lit sparingly by the carriage lamp. It was difficult to see through the frosted windows but she was sure she glimpsed houses and dimly lit windows. She heard voices, the thud of hooves and the swish of a sleigh gliding by. What was happening? They'd seen no human habitation for days!

'Vassily!' She opened the connecting window. 'Is this Finland?'

'No, ma'am.'

'Where are we?'

'Murmansk.'

'Vassily! Come in here at once!' she cried angrily. The cab came to a halt. He spent time attending to Osopa's comfort, while Seraphima fumed.

'I thought we were going to Finland to start a new life?' she said furiously when he appeared at last.

'That's what you thought, Seraphima.' He nodded. 'But it was not a wise thought.'

'Why ever not?'

'My dear, Finland is too far,' he said gently. 'The mare has the heart of a lioness, but she is growing old too. She would trot till she dropped if I asked her, but I could not demand that of her. Could you?'

She was silent. She stroked sleepy Moussia, who was purring on her lap. Seraphima remembered her distress when she'd lost the beloved pet. She remembered the incredible joy when she discovered Vassily had saved her cat.

'Very well.' She sighed deeply. 'I agree Finland is too far. We will find a ship to take us to Scotland. My daughter is happily married to a Scottish man. They say Scotland is very beautiful. You will be happy there with me, Vassily!'

'No, my dear.' He shook his head sadly. 'I will not.'

'Now you tell me the truth!' she sobbed tearfully. 'You bear a grudge because I called you peasant once! You want rid of me!'

'Seraphima, stop yelling, you'll frighten the cat!' Moussia was bristling on her knee, all teeth and claws. 'Of course I bear you no grudge! I am a good, hard-working peasant and proud of it.'

'Then why won't you come with me?'

'Because my mind would never be at rest, dear lady.' He held her hands. 'Listen to me, Seraphima. I can't abandon Osopa after all she has done for us. She has given me precious time with the lady I love. How could I be happy if I thought the mare was starved and ill-treated by bad masters? Don't you understand?'

172

'Of course I do! But Murmansk can't be the end of the road for us, Vassily!' Seraphima wailed.

'Of course it's not the end, my lady!' He laughed and kissed her hand. 'Love goes on. Love is neverending.'

He would have left her with a kiss, but she stopped him tearfully and produced the muffler from its hiding place.

'I made you a present. It's not well made. Not like your mother's beautiful work,' she warned.

He took the scarf and felt its warmth. He pictured the effort that had gone into the wavering pattern. He saw its endearing flaws, stitches dropped, pulled and twisted by Moussia's playful claws. Vassily held in his hands the essence of the delightful woman that was Seraphima. Beauty, warmth, strength . . . aye, and endearing faults too! He smiled tenderly though his eyes were wet. When he wore the scarf on the coldest winter days, Seraphima's warmth would always embrace him.

'It's perfect, my dear. My mother would approve of you,' he said simply.

'You think so?' Her cheeks were rosy with pleasure. 'I would like to give you the poetry book, but . . .' She stopped.

'I can't read!' He laughed, something he could not do at the start of the journey. He tapped his brow. 'No matter, dear lady. I have all the poems stored forever, in here.'

Vassily kissed Seraphima's cheeks, wound the precious gift around his throat and went out into the bitter cold.

Duncan Wishart stood on deck watching the first refugees arrive. These consisted of three men escorted by his old adversary, the commissar's aide.

Some members of the crew had gathered curiously to watch the arrival, Archie among them. Aromas of the cookhouse lingered around the young cook and Hamish attached himself hungrily to Archie. The dog spared a snarl and a few cautious growls for the Russian officer bringing up the rear.

173

'Do you know these men, Archie?' Duncan frowned.

'Just the tallest young chap, skipper. He's called Ivan somebody or other and was one o' the Tsar's officers. I'm surprised the Reds let him go. Anna must've spoken up for him. He was head over heels in love with her.'

'How many Russian boyfriends has Miss McLaren collected on her travels?' Duncan demanded darkly.

'It's not her fault men fall for her. She has a winning way with her,' Archie said, speaking from experience.

'I've noticed.' The captain turned up the sheepskin collar of his coat against a flurry of stinging snow.

Elena had been looking out for the refugees. She came rushing on deck, the twins hard on her heels. 'Papa! Papa and Dmitri, my own darling!'

The ecstatic cries of Elena and the two youngsters echoed across the dark water as the whole family fell into one another's arms and hugged, kissed and wept. In a frantic babble of Russian they yelled their joy and happiness to a sunless sky. It was a magical display of exuberant emotion which left the more restrained Dundonians clustered on deck, open-mouthed.

None more so than Duncan Wishart himself. He watched the family's outpouring of uninhibited joy, and though he struggled to remain detached, a curious ache centred in the region of his heart. So this is how families behave. This is how life would be for a loved and wanted child! The sight was absolutely heartbreaking to a man who had no roots.

'Is everything ready?' He came to with a start to find the commissar's aide confronting him.

'Ready?' He frowned.

'For the wedding!' the officer said impatiently. 'The commissar and his bride will be here any minute.'

'The saloon is warm and the cook has prepared a feast. What more can I do?'

'You can put on a braver front, Captain. You look like the cat that lost the mouse,' he laughed.

Duncan liked Leon Orlov on sight, although the doctor

had a limited command of English and the two men could do little more than exchange a few words, when everyone gathered inside.

Marga and Michael clung either side of their father as if they intended never losing sight of him again. Elena and Dmitri whispered lovingly together in a quiet corner and had eyes for no one else. Archie hovered nearby, looking rejected. He and Elena had been getting along famously. He had been teaching her the finer points of Scottish cooking.

The dog gave the cook up as a bad job and attached itself once more to Duncan, who was supervising proceedings and seemed a better bet, foodwise. Duncan had met Dmitri's brother, Ivan, who had embraced the captain gratefully in an effusive Russian manner. Duncan had some sympathy for this man. The tall Russian looked sick at heart, as well he might, since he was another of Anna McLaren's discarded conquests, forced, like Duncan himself, to watch the object of their adoration married to another man.

'Here they come!'

One of the crew had been keeping lookout on deck. Duncan braced himself to meet the woman he had loved and lost.

He wasn't sure what effect it would have on him. Would loving Anna McLaren turn out to be a lonely man's daydream, a sea mist vanishing to leave no lasting impression? He prayed it would be so.

An older lady had appeared, leading a small child swaddled in furs. She paused in the doorway, blinking in the light.

'Katerina, my darling!' Leon Orlov cried, bounding towards them.

Husband and wife hugged and kissed in an ecstasy of tears and laughter. There was a time in the depths of despair when neither had expected to see the other again.

Of course, their children joined in, clustering around crying and exclaiming, hugging and kissing parents and one another, all talking ten to the dozen.

175

But not Basil, the baby! The toddler took one terrified look at the strange man advancing upon him with open arms and dived underneath his mother's ankle-length coat. The shaggy-haired stranger dressed in shabby clothes looked nothing like the photograph of the handsome Dada which Basil's mama kept tucked away to kiss every night Basil said his prayers.

Nothing would tempt the little boy out to meet his father. Still, everyone was too happy to mind one small cloud. Katerina shrugged off the coat, removed the little boy's furs and left him in a quiet corner sleepily clutching the rattle and wrapped in the security of his mother's coat.

Duncan Wishart slipped quietly away, unable to face another family reunion. The dog had abandoned him to obey an inherent herding instinct and had rounded up and penned all the Orlovs into a loving little group in a corner of the saloon.

Stepping into the corridor, the captain found himself face to face with Anna. 'You!' he said blankly.

'Nice to see you, too, Captain Wishart!' she said, looking hurt.

'I didn't mean . . .' He stopped.

What was the use? Words could not express what he felt, meeting her with such breathtaking suddenness. He studied her in silence. She looked beautiful in a black cloak trimmed with white fur which she'd flung back over her shoulders to reveal a red dress.

'Married in red . . .?' He lifted his brows.

'Oh, don't *you* start!' She sighed. 'Katerina has been bombarding me with dire predictions. Fortunately, Aleksandr's not superstitious.'

'I don't care tuppence about Aleksandr! Only about you . . .'

It was a revealing remark said with revealing passion, and she stared at him. He was past caring.

She looked pale, her eyes dark and shadowed as if she'd been crying recently. He wondered if she found

176

family reunions as difficult as he did. She must know that when she married her commissar she might never see her parents again.

'They tell me you sing love songs,' she said softly. 'I wish I'd heard you.'

'So do I.'

He wondered what difference it might have made. The familiar theme returned to torment him: *'and I will love thee still, my dear, till a' the seas gang dry . . .'*

'Why on earth are you marrying this Bolshevik?' he demanded, a harsh tone disguising a fair depth of emotion.

'Aleksandr was my first love,' she said.

'I thought you'd recovered from that infatuation!'

'Are you trying to annoy me, Captain Wishart?'

'No, of course not. Just trying to understand why you're doing this. When I go back to Dundee without you, what shall I tell your parents?'

Anna sighed, a weary and resigned little sound, he thought.

'Tell them I'm happy to stay in Russia,' she said. 'Tell them I'll look after Seraphima. Tell them, tell them I love them . . .' Her voice broke. She couldn't go on.

Anna had known the moment she set foot on deck that holding the wedding aboard her father's ship was a bad idea. An impersonal office in Petrograd would have been much more fitting. She loved this ship. It had been her refuge on stormy voyages with her father in command on the bridge, Wishart at his right hand. The *Pole Star* had always brought her safely home. Anna's hand went involuntarily to the necklace designed to guide a cherished daughter home. But not this time! She couldn't hold back tears.

'Oh, Wishart . . .'

'Don't cry! Please!' He pulled her into his arms though he knew it was a mistake. She laid her head on his shoulder. That was the precise moment his heart broke.

He drew back and looked at her. 'You haven't said you're

177

marrying this man because you love him. Do you really love him, Anna?' he asked urgently.

An icy draught hit them both suddenly. A door closed and Aleksandr came down the corridor. 'A fond farewell, my darling?' His eyes narrowed as he studied Duncan intently.

Anna stepped back hastily, her cheeks flushed. 'This is Captain Wishart, Aleksandr.'

'Nice to meet you, Captain.' He dismissed Duncan with a nod and turned to Anna. 'I brought the priest with me, my love. Everything's ready. Shall we go in?'

He led her into the saloon. The Orlovs fell silent but the assembled crew raised a cheer. The priest stood robed and waiting beside a table serving as an altar. The scent of incense hung heavy in the hot air.

Aleksandr's aide came forward, his gaze faintly mocking as usual. 'We have plenty candles, but you'll have to do without orange-blossom and golden crowns,' he whispered.

'Never mind the trappings!' Aleksandr frowned. 'Get on with it!'

Bride and groom joined hands before the priest and the room became hushed. All that could be heard was the soft sound of Katerina's sobs. Duncan Wishart forced himself to watch impassively.

There was a sudden commotion in the doorway. The door swung open, the dog barked, everyone turned to look.

'What is this? What is going on?' Seraphima demanded. She stood in the doorway, taking in the scene and her expression was one of utter dismay. Vassily towered behind her. He carried a large lidded basket from which came loud, angry mewing. The dog pricked up its ears.

'*Babushka!*' Anna's incredulous cry of joy resounded across the room.

Seraphima hurried forward and she and her granddaughter hugged and wept and kissed one another. Presently Seraphima dried her eyes and looked Aleksandr up and down.

'Anna, what are you doing? Why are you marrying him?'

'I can tell you, Seraphima!' Katerina cried. 'He wants Anna and the collar of pearls as well. She made a bargain. She promised to marry him so that we can all go free.'

'What? I can hardly believe my ears!' Seraphima cried angrily. She rounded on Aleksandr. 'Even as a student you were devious and greedy for the good life, Aleksandr Rostovich!'

'A poor man can dream!' he said. 'Of course I want Anna for her beauty and intelligence . . . and of course I want the collar of pearls, who wouldn't?' He glared at Seraphima. 'And as for you, old woman, you dare not preach to me! You want a pretty granddaughter to look after you, and a precious jewel as security. You've hidden the collar, haven't you?'

'Oh yes, Aleksandr, I've hidden it where you can never find it!' Her eyes gleamed. She thrust her face close to his. 'But you cannot have both my granddaughter and the collar of pearls. It must be one or the other. Choose carefully, my boy!'

Aleksandr looked around the crowded room. Nobody moved or spoke. He could see now the error of marrying in a foreign ship on alien soil. There were no Red Army guards here to support him.

Aleksandr turned slowly to face the stern old lady. 'No, Seraphima,' he told her calmly, 'I refuse. I will not choose!'

# Eleven

'Your granddaughter also has a choice, Seraphima,' Aleksandr said quietly. He turned to Anna, who stood mesmerized beside the astonished priest. 'Your *babushka* thinks I don't love you enough.' He smiled. 'She thinks all I care about is the Orlovs' collar of pearls and you are only part of the bargain.'

'She could be right,' Anna said.

'Of course not, my darling!' He laughed. 'Let's have no more talk of bargains. In the presence of all these witnesses I want you to choose freely whether you will marry me or not.'

Ivan broke away from his brother, who had been keeping a watchful eye on him, and shouldered his way to the front. 'This is your chance to get rid of this Bolshevik, Anna. Tell him to go!'

Aleksandr looked amused. He was very confident as he pulled Anna into his arms and kissed her. But as he did so, the gold necklace dug into Anna's neck, the pressure of her father's guiding star marking her skin so uncomfortably she couldn't ignore it.

'Make your choice, my love!' he whispered in her ear. 'Tell them what you want to do.'

'I want to go home!' she cried tearfully.

'What?' He released her, shocked.

'I'm sorry, Aleksandr. But it's the truth, and I can't marry you now.' Gingerly, she rubbed her neck, though miraculously, the pain had gone. 'I want to go home, to Scotland.'

180

'It's this damned ship!' he stormed. 'It was a foolish decision, bringing you here!' He rounded on Wishart and yelled in English. 'Why did you wait, Scotchman? A wise man would have gone long ago!'

'Ah, but we Scots are stubborn!' The captain smiled.

Ivan couldn't hide his delight. 'Hard luck, Commissar. Anna has chosen me!'

'No, *boyar*, she has not!' Aleksandr retorted bitterly. 'She has chosen her native land. I'm broken-hearted, but I can still find it in my heart to applaud her choice, for I'm a patriot too. I would not steal away from Russia to save my own skin, if my country needed me.'

Ivan flushed. That was too near the mark for his comfort.

Aleksandr glanced swiftly around the assembled company, weighing up the chances of removing Anna from the ship's potent influence to more neutral ground. He saw right away that could only be achieved by battling a path through the *Pole Star*'s crew. It was not an option he relished. He turned his attention to the Orlovs. They were crying for joy on one another's shoulders. There was little chance of grabbing members of that family and holding them hostage once more.

He sighed. Murmansk was not a friendly haven and he had no intention of starting fights he could not hope to win. Resignedly, he turned to Anna. 'Very well, my darling. I accept your decision although it breaks my heart.'

He kissed her on both cheeks and looked at her intently for a long moment, willing her with all the power of his forceful personality to change her mind.

But she stood firm. She wiped away tears and whispered the hallowed Russian blessing, 'Go with God, Aleksandr!'

He shook his head sadly and slowly. 'Without you, my love, there is no God!'

Then he and his aide headed for the doorway without a backward glance. Aleksandr paused when they reached Seraphima. 'Satisfied?' he demanded with a wealth of bitterness in the tone.

'A wise decision.' To his surprise she reached up and kissed him.

He eyed her tentatively. 'You know where the collar of pearls is, don't you?'

'Indeed I do!'

'I wish I could see even one small piece!' he said.

She hesitated, glancing at Katerina Orlov. Katerina stood very still, quite impassive, then gave a small, quick nod.

'Very well then, so you shall!' Seraphima turned. 'Vassily, bring the cat basket!'

He obeyed, placing it on the floor. Inside, Moussia began mewing and scratching at the long-suffering lid. The dog bounded over and sniffed curiously at the heaving basketwork. Seraphima swiftly undid the buckles and out leaped Moussia, ears flat, back arched and tail bristling.

The dog jumped back and the two animals confronted one another, employing every canine and feline danger signal in their repertoire. Then nerves broke and courage failed. The dog scurried beneath the table where the wedding feast was, while Moussia clawed her way upwards to crouch on top of a locker.

Meanwhile, Seraphima was busy easing aside the felt lining of Moussia's carrying basket. A few minutes later, she produced a jewel case triumphantly.

Anna gasped. The last time she had seen this beautiful leather case was on Elena Orlov's wedding day. On that occasion it had contained a glittering collar of matching pearls, interlaced with sparkling diamonds. She would never forget the sight.

'Here, Aleksandr. Take it!' Seraphima handed the case to him.

He fumbled excitedly with the golden key and flung back the lid. 'Empty!' he cried wrathfully.

'Of course,' Seraphima said. 'You wouldn't expect Madame Orlov to ask a poor old widow to risk her life carrying such a treasure, would you? I was honoured to be asked to look after the empty case. But maybe if you ask Madame very nicely you may be permitted to keep it, since you're so very keen to own a small piece of Russian history.'

Aleksandr snapped the lid shut angrily, with a noise like a gunshot. He strode across the room and stood in front of Katerina Orlov. 'You are very clever, madame!' he said. 'I salute your cunning, but I still say the Empress's collar of pearls should stay in Russia.'

'That's for me to decide, Commissar.'

'Then decide wisely, madame!'

He gave a mocking bow and flung the empty case down at her feet. He waited a moment to see if she would stoop before him, but she did not. Aleksandr spun on his heel and marched out, his aide following. For a moment nothing could be heard but the creak of the swinging door and the usual sounds of the ship at anchor.

Archie was first to break the silence. 'After a' this carry-on I don't suppose anyone has remembered this is Hogmanay.'

'What is Hogmanay?' Elena asked curiously.

'The last day o' the old year and the bringing in of the new. Dundee folk always put on a great show.' His eyes sparkled.

'You mean a party, with singing and dancing?' Marga said eagerly.

'Not half!' Archie recalled overheated rooms packed with people, sentimental songs sung off-key, hot pies and shortbread, port for the women, and drams for the lads. 'There's a wedding feast going to waste here,' he said. 'How about having a wee bit of a do to see in the New Year?'

There was a roar of agreement from the crew. All eyes turned to Wishart. Duncan longed to celebrate. He had a good grasp of Russian and recent events had left him feeling light-hearted and not a little light-headed with overwhelming relief. He had not lost his beloved Anna after all. Incredibly, she had chosen to go home.

On the other hand, he knew they should leave port as quickly as possible. He could not overlook the threat to the ship now that the commissar's wedding plans had foundered. It was possible the Russians would seek revenge.

However, then Duncan looked at Anna and could think of nothing else but how much he longed to dance with her and hold her in his arms. For a short few hours he longed to shed his weighty responsibilities and be a young man in love.

'Very well, lads!' He smiled. 'Let's show the Russians a real Dundee Hogmanay!'

His crew let out a skirling yell. Somebody produced a fiddle and someone else a mouth organ and they struck up the lively chords of a popular reel.

'C'mon, skipper! Start the ball rollin'!' Jock roared, stomping his feet.

Laughing, Duncan headed for Anna. 'Shall we dance?' He held out his arms.

'Dance?' She stared at him, outraged. Her eyes filled with tears. 'How could you even suggest such a thing?'

'I thought . . .?'

'No, you didn't think, Captain Wishart!' she cried passionately. 'You didn't consider my feelings at all!'

'I . . .' He stopped.

She was right. He'd merely considered his own joyful relief at the outcome. He'd completely overlooked the fact that Anna had just made a heartbreaking decision. Of course she couldn't dance!

She wrapped the black cloak around herself, hiding the red gown. Seraphima made a move to comfort her granddaughter, but Anna had already rushed to the doorway and was gone.

The music played on. Wild music that pulsed cheerfully throughout the ship, but ached painfully with every beat of Duncan Wishart's heart.

In Dundee the last few sombre hours of 1917 had been subdued, only memorable for longer butter queues, but Captain Andrew McLaren had plans for New Year's Day. War news at the start of 1918 was not heartening and the

184

McLarens had not planned a New Year dinner, which left Andrew at a loose end that afternoon. Irina preferred the Russian celebration which took place later on, when Dundee festivities were all over.

So Andrew sneaked a cake of his wife's freshly made butter shortbread into a paper bag, wrapped a small piece of coal in a twist of newspaper, and slipped a hip flask into a back pocket. He kissed Irina, who was finishing an urgent order for corsets and scarcely noticed, then he went out into the cold sunshine swinging a walking stick. He would need its help on the steep incline he planned to tackle.

Eddie Duncan answered his knock once Andrew had reached the cottage door. 'Och, it's you again!'

'A good New Year to you too, Mr Duncan!'

'What's good about it?'

But he stood aside and ushered in the visitor. At least Amy Duncan was pleased to see their first foot. She was delighted with the shortbread.

'Real butter shortie! My, what a treat!'

'Long may your lum reek, Mrs Duncan!' Andrew put the wee bit of coal on the fire for luck. It blazed with a nice yellow flame. Eddie watched the pantomime dourly. He only relaxed once Andrew produced the flask and the two men sat down by the fire to enjoy the whisky.

'By the by, Mr Duncan,' Andrew ventured after more general chat, 'does the name John Albert Duncan strike a chord?'

There was a sudden stillness in the room. The elderly couple made no move for a moment or two.

'Maybe.' Eddie savoured the whisky, rolling it round the tongue.

'Your son, perhaps?'

Amy gave a small sound like a whimper. Eddie put the glass down with a clatter. 'Our only bairn lies sleeping in Balgay cemetery, Captain McLaren! Our bonny laddie remains forever twelve years old and we grudged him sore to the angels.'

185

'I'm so sorry! Forgive me, but I had to ask.' He was deeply saddened. He hated to intrude upon such tragic grief.

'Och, man, you'll never change! You're of the bulldog breed.' Eddie shook his head wearily.

There was a tear in his wife's eye. 'Infantile paralysis, the doctors said it was. I caught the infection too, but I survived. I've been in and out of hospital ever since, and now I'm housebound. If only it was me that died, and not my bairn!'

'But you wouldn't wish your fate upon that lively little lad, now would you, my love?' Eddie said gently.

'No, Eddie. You're right, I wouldn't.' She dried her eyes.

Andrew waited a minute or two. He topped up Eddie's glass. 'So who's John Albert Duncan?'

'My older brother,' the retired policeman said, reluctantly.

'Well now!' Andrew was pleased; this was a real advance. 'Records show that your brother John sailed from Dundee with the whaler *Greenland* in March 1887, bound for Arctic waters. Duncan Wishart was born eight months later in November. Could there be a link?'

'Maybe.'

Andrew sighed. Getting information was worse than pulling teeth, but he continued patiently. 'Where's your brother now, Mr Duncan?'

'If you'd checked the records more thoroughly, you wouldn't be asking.' Eddie retorted scathingly. 'The *Greenland* foundered in a storm in the Davis Strait, and went down with all hands in September 1887.'

'Och, man, I'm sorry!' Andrew exclaimed wretchedly.

'So you should be!' Eddie glowered over the rim of the glass. 'And you had the nerve to come here and wish us happy New Year!'

'Just tell me, and it'll go no further . . .' He took a deep breath. 'Was your brother the foundling's father?'

186

'John?' The old man leaned forward angrily. 'Now you listen here, Captain! My brother was a decent man and pillar o' the kirk. He was a widower who never looked at another woman once his dear wife died. John devoted all his energy to bringing up their lass.'

'He had a daughter?' Andrew said sharply.

'Aye, he did.' Eddie scowled ferociously. 'A happily married daughter and hard-working son-in-law, devoted to her. So don't you dare think ill o' my kin!'

'But were they Duncan Wishart's parents?'

'That's for the young man to ask, not a nosey auld sea dog!' Eddie snarled.

Andrew was more confused than ever, but he couldn't let go. 'Let's say for the sake of argument that this devoted, happily married couple *were* Wishart's parents. Why the devil would they abandon their wee baby in the gutter?'

Frostily, Eddie raised an empty glass to him. 'If you dinna mind my saying so, Captain, you've long outstayed your welcome here. And a happy New Year to ye!'

It was well after midnight before New Year festivities aboard the *Pole Star* ended and Duncan Wishart was free to go looking for Anna. She wasn't in the cabins allocated to his Russian passengers. He searched the fo'c'sle discreetly while arranging a berth for Ivan with the crew, and even glanced hopefully in cupboards and storerooms. He cast an eye round the engine room where engineers and stokers were building up a head of steam ready for departure.

Usually the engine room's oily heat, gleaming brass and the smooth power of the ship's engines evoked strong emotions of pride and anticipation, but there was no sign of Anna down here in the warmth, and all he felt was emptiness.

From the heat of the engine room he wearily climbed companionways and went out on to the freezing deck. Signs were confusing here. There had been no fresh snowfalls recently and the deck and gangway were covered in hard,

187

trampled snow. Seraphima's driver had been the last to leave, his footprints easy to follow in a track across the quay towards lodgings with a friendly fisherman, where horse and cab were stabled.

The imprints of Anna's light footfall were impossible to decipher. Duncan stared into darkness illuminated by the glitter of frosted snow. It seemed likely she'd had a change of heart and gone chasing after Aleksandr.

Duncan cursed his thoughtlessness. He had been alone too long. Selfishly, he had forgotten that she must love the Russian commissar and was heartbroken, too.

The only place Duncan hadn't searched was the bridge and wheelhouse, and he went there without much hope. As he'd expected, the heart of his ship was dark, cold and empty. She really had gone.

He was suddenly dead tired. All he wanted was deep dreamless sleep. He had to be alert and on his toes in a few hours; ready to leave port – an icy wind whispered in the rigging – *without her*!

Usually, Duncan relished the sound of the ship coming to life before a voyage but as he trailed wearily to his cabin he scarcely noticed the engines pulsing like a heartbeat.

He was mildly surprised to discover he'd left the cabin light on, something he was careful about. It took fully a minute for his tired gaze to focus on a huddled figure in black cloak and red silk gown lying on his bunk.

Duncan shut his eyes and opened them again. He was not dreaming. Anna was lying there, sound asleep. The closing door wakened her with a start. She sat up, yawning sleepily.

'I must've dozed. Where on earth have you been, Wishart? The party ended ages ago.'

'Looking for you.' His legs felt suddenly weak. He collapsed into an armchair.

'I've been here for hours!' She sounded aggrieved. 'I wanted to talk to you in private and this was the only place I could think of.'

'You can say that again!' he said. 'All the passenger cabins are packed and your boyfriend Ivan is bedded down in the fo'c'sle. I was sure you'd changed your mind and gone off with Aleksandr.'

'I did consider it.'

'I'm glad you didn't.'

'Why?' She stared at him attentively.

'Because the marriage wouldn't have worked.'

'You sound like my grandmother.' She frowned. 'I do love Aleksandr, you know.'

'Then for heaven's sake don't marry him!'

'Don't be horrid, Wishart! You make me so mad!'

'Exactly!' He nodded grimly. 'Married to your commissar you're bound to witness cruelty and injustice sooner or later. You'd make an angry outspoken fuss, and the masters Aleksandr serves won't tolerate criticism. The pair of you would very likely end up digging salt in Siberia.'

She lay quite still. 'You're saying I'm the wrong wife for him,' she said slowly. 'You're telling me I would probably ruin him.'

'Yes, I think you might.'

She turned her face away into the shadows. He couldn't see if she was crying or not. He thought perhaps she was.

'Just as well I chose to go home, wasn't it?' she said in a choked little voice.

'Yes, it believe it was.' He yawned. He was content to have her near, even though she loved another. He could hardly keep his eyes open. He stretched out in the arm-chair.

'Wishart!' Anna sat up. 'I can't stay here! What will the crew think?'

'The very worst. They're sailors.'

'Where shall I go?'

'There's the store cupboard. You know the way.'

'That's not funny!'

'Lie down and go to sleep, will you?'

'But the crew—!' she wailed.

189

He was already fast asleep, head resting on the buttoned leather. It was strange to watch him sleeping, she thought. He seemed vulnerable with the hard angles of mouth and jaw relaxed in utter exhaustion. She decided a blameless reputation was of lesser importance than letting him sleep. Let the crew think the worst! Anna snuggled down in the bunk and pulled the blankets round her. But it was a long time before she slept.

Seraphima was up smartly next morning. She shared a tiny two-berth cabin with Marga and the cat. Moussia approved the arrangement, scorning the hated basket and spreading herself heavily across the bunk, nearly shoving Seraphima off.

At Archie's suggestion, Marga's twin brother was housed in a hammock slung from coat hooks in a cupboard intended as a cloaks store. Michael was pleased to have his own small space, and delighted with a swaying hammock which made him a true seafarer.

The ship throbbed with life. With less than two hours to departure, crew members had scraped the decks clear but Seraphima's felt boots still skidded on ice when she went outside. She hung on to the ship's rail with clumsy mittens and scanned the quayside looking for Vassily.

The *Pole Star* had become a well-known feature in the port over the past weeks and news of her departure drew a small crowd of Navy men and local fishermen. There was muted excitement in the air, rumours flying that a large fleet would soon arrive bringing British and American troops to help Russian resistance fight the Bolsheviks.

Vassily was standing back, beside the cab. He was holding Osopa's head and staring quietly at the ship.

The *Pole Star* was a brave sight. Her flags were flying and every light was lit, brightening the perpetual darkness.

Seraphima made her way down the gangway and found Vassily waiting at the foot.

'There's no need to risk breaking an ankle!' He scolded her.

'Now there's a thought!' She smiled. 'I would have to stay with you then.'

The joke could only raise a weak smile. She looked at him with tears in her eyes. 'My dear, I wish you would come with me. I worry about you so much. How will you survive?'

'Don't worry, my dear lady!' His eyes danced. 'I will be a professional cab driver. The *vozok* will carry plenty customers till the thaw comes, then I will sell it and buy a small coach. Osopa and I will have a stance beside Tanilov railway station. No matter what happens to Russia, people will still want transport. There will be wealthy Bolsheviks and Red Guards on leave trying to impress girlfriends. I could make a fortune. One day, perhaps, I will own a fleet of cabs and drivers, and Osopa and I can go out to grass.'

'Oh, Vassily! I pray it will be so!' Seraphima sighed.

It was just a dream of a rosy future, but it was a good dream, and sometimes dreams can come true for good people, she thought.

Seraphima slipped her hand out of the mitten and searched in a pocket. She produced a brown paper bag tied with a scrap of pink ribbon.

'A present,' she said.

'For me?'

'No, you have yours!' She laughed, lovingly arranging the warm scarf cosily round his neck. 'This is for Osopa.'

The moment of parting had arrived. They stared at one another with much love and great sadness, but they would not spoil this special moment with tears.

'Go with God, my beloved,' Seraphima said.

She kissed him Russian fashion, very gently on both furrowed cheeks.

He only nodded, for Vassily was a shy man at emotional moments. He made sure she climbed the gangway safely then turned and trudged his lonely way back through the crowd to where the cab and the patient sledge-horse waited.

He rested his forehead against the mare's neck and untied Seraphima's ribbon.

The little bag contained a feast of sugar lumps. Then Vassily did cry. Warm tears coursed down his cheeks and turned to sparkling ice, shining like stars on Osopa's snow-white blaze.

Anna eventually slept soundly and wakened with a start. She found herself alone in Wishart's cabin, with the throbbing beat of engines intensified. The captain had gone, and the grinding rattle of anchor chains had wakened her. The *Pole Star* was close to departure.

Anna clambered out of the bunk and cautiously opened the cabin door. She had tiptoed, shoeless, into the empty corridor and was in the act of closing the door when Ivan came clattering down the companionway and stopped dead.

Anna put a hand to her tousled hair and tugged the cloak closer around the crumpled gown. She looked the picture of guilt, yet was completely innocent.

'So!' Ivan said grimly. 'I searched everywhere but didn't think to look in the captain's quarters!'

'I can explain!'

'Don't bother. The crew make jokes about you and him. I may not speak English very well, but I understand more than they think. They say he sings love songs and the only woman he loves is you.'

'What rubbish.' She laughed awkwardly. 'Wishart and I fight all the time.'

'Because you Scots are passionate people beneath the ice!' he said.

He looked so woebegone she was sorry for him.

'Cheer up, Ivan! The passenger cabins were full and Captain Wishart's bunk was free. He slept very gallantly in an armchair. Satisfied?'

'Forgive me, dear one. I'm a jealous man where you are concerned,' he said.

'I know.' Anna sighed.

Ivan's jealousy was a complication she could do without. Her emotions were still raw and painful after Aleksandr.

The remaining passengers had congregated in the brightly lit saloon to view the ship's departure. It was a subdued group this morning. They knew that they were leaving their Russian homeland for years, perhaps forever.

Seraphima's eyes were dim with tears, but she could just make out Vassily beside the solid outline of the cab. It was not a day for standing idly around and onlookers were dispersing now the hawsers were cast off. Seraphima saw a small family group approach Vassily's cab. She watched bargaining take place, then they all piled inside. She saw Vassily pause for a moment to stare towards the ship, then he pulled the muffler warmly over mouth and nose and took the driver's seat. Seraphima watched the *vozok* move off, sure-footed Osopa trotting briskly along the snowy track. She watched with a hopeful heart. Who knows? Dreams *can* come true.

There were others on the shore, watching the *Pole Star*'s departure with keen interest. Aleksandr and his aide, muffled to the eyes, mingled with the locals.

'Do you mean to let that woman get away with humiliating you, Commissar?' The aide gave his master a searching glance.

'What do you suggest, Boris?' Aleksandr's tone was mild.

'We know the course the ship is heading. We could tell our German friends. They'd be interested.'

'No! Let her go. Let them take their chances with the sea.'

'Huh! You grow soft in your old age!' the aide said sulkily.

'That's enough!' The commissar rounded on him wildly. 'You have no love in your cold heart for anyone, my friend!'

'Why, you-you're crying!' the man whispered.

'Yes. Take a good look.' Aleksandr's tear-stained gaze

was fixed upon him, dark and cold. 'You are privileged, comrade! These are the last tears anyone will see from me.'

He turned his back upon the ship and walked away. His aide paused, then followed hesitantly, keeping a few cautious paces behind his leader.

Captain Wishart would not have chosen to round the North Cape in the depths of an Arctic winter, but the circumstances were unusual. The full howling force of an Arctic storm hit the *Pole Star* in the Barents Sea as she crept round the Norwegian coast bound for Narvik. Norway was neutral – which was all that could be said in favour of this route.

Duncan blessed the stout construction and top of the range equipment installed in Andrew McLaren's flagship as the *Pole Star* ploughed through rising seas.

Officers and helmsman glanced at their young captain with growing respect. He was cool in command, calm and decisive. They recognized great skill, and an intuitive understanding of the elements. His passengers did not fare well. The first casualty was Michael, tipped out of the hammock with a badly sprained wrist. Fortunately, there were doctors aboard, and the youngster was soon comfortable on a makeshift mattress on the floor.

All the women were seasick except Anna, who had as usual quickly gained her sealegs. Elena's husband, Dmitri, succumbed and so did his brother, Ivan, but Leon Orlov was a good sailor. Surprisingly, so was Basil, his tiny son.

However, Basil's beloved mama was badly afflicted. She was too ill to change a nappy or pick him up when the ship rolled and he fell in a wailing heap. Too ill to sing and play with him or even feed him, she lay dead to the world and he was miserable.

Help came from an unexpected quarter. The strange man who shared their cabin picked him up and hugged him. 'There, there, my little man! Uncomfortable, are you?' Leon pressed a whiskery kiss on to Basil's cheek, then set about

194

attending to his needs in a skilled, professional manner. Afterwards, he sat the toddler on his knee and showed him a bird fashioned from brown paper with flapping papery wings. Basil looked at the stranger, starry-eyed. Suddenly recognition dawned.

'Dada!' The toddler smiled contentedly.

The storm formed strange alliances. Archie had procured a nanny goat to cope with the toddler's needs. He had stabled the animal in a small section of the hold packed with straw bales and sawdust to protect the precious beast. First of all, the frightened dog crept down to the makeshift stable, followed by Moussia, temporarily abandoned by her seasick mistress.

The animals huddled together, drawing warmth and comfort from one another, and settled down to sleep and endure the storm.

Anna had borrowed trousers and jersey from Archie, who was of slender build. Clad in oilskins, she succeeded, with a struggle, to make her way to the bridge.

Wishart raised his eyebrows when he saw her. He looked exhausted, eyes deeply shadowed with lack of sleep.

'What on earth are you doing here?' He frowned.

'I'm a sailor's daughter, remember? Hot cocoa's impossible, Archie says, but he's sent a tot of rum.'

She dug into the pocket and produced a bottle. The warming rum was handed gratefully round the cold, tired men.

'How's Ivan, by the way?' Duncan asked. 'Is he seasick or lovesick?'

'Recovering from both ailments.' Anna gave him a look. Ivan's infatuation was a sore point with both of them.

While the captain's attention wandered momentarily, the sea had withdrawn into a trough of strangely calm water and the *Pole Star* wallowed awkwardly for a moment or two before the full force of the gathering swell descended upon her in a monstrous wave. She could not escape, her bows ploughed into a wall of water and were totally submerged.

The occupants of the bridge, all but the helmsman clinging

195

to the wheel, went tumbling helplessly. The captain anticipated calamity and seized Anna, clasping her protectively
against his chest and falling with her.

The struggling ship yawed and rolled and flung them to
the floor. Terrified, Anna clung to him and looked into his
eyes. They shone with a light that made her heart lurch.
He smiled. 'Don't be afraid. She's a stout ship, she'll
survive!'

Then Anna glimpsed a truth she'd hidden even from
herself. The memory of it came racing from years ago,
reaching back to a time when she was only a young girl and
her hero was an ambitious deck officer who'd had no time
for distractions. How she'd adored him, and how cruelly
his indifference had hurt her vulnerable young heart! Badly
wounded, she'd given him a wide berth ever since.

But now, held safe in his arms, the past faded into
insignificance.

'I love you,' she murmured, surprising herself.

'What?'

The ship rolled, the helmsman fought the wheel, heading
the bow into the turmoil. The sound and fury of the storm
pounded in Duncan's ears. He couldn't trust his senses
any more.

'What did you say?' he shouted. He knew it was important, but he couldn't hear her.

Another monstrous wave thundered and frothed across
the decks. Anna screamed, 'Nothing! It doesn't matter!'

Nothing mattered any more, she thought confusedly,
because she would die in his arms. She was a sailor's
daughter and had weathered many storms, but this time
she was sure the *Pole Star* was sinking.

196

# Twelve

'Heave ho, lass!'

Cautiously, Anna opened her eyes. One of the crew was grinning at the captain and herself, sprawled together in a corner of the wheelhouse. The man put his arms under Anna's armpits and set her on her feet. The ship was still rolling wildly and the wheelhouse was a shambles. Despite the chaos the sailor looked remarkably cheerful.

'I – I was scared,' she admitted.

'I don't blame ye. That was a massive lump o' water. I was a wee bit concerned mysel'.' He gave the captain a hand to rise off the floor.

'Thanks.' Frowning, Duncan Wishart surveyed the storm. 'Is it my imagination or is it not quite so wild?'

'We've rounded the cape under the lee o' the land.' He nodded and eyed his exhausted captain. 'You've been on the go a while, skipper. Why not tak' a rest till it's time for the next trick?'

Duncan was sorely tempted. Rest made sense and he had complete faith in these fine seamen. At the moment they would be more alert than he was if an emergency arose. He agreed, and turned to Anna. 'I'll see you safely below, then make sure the hatch covers are sound.'

'Never mind me. The ship comes first.'

'Passengers and crew are high on my list!' He smiled.

'But I'm just . . .' She stopped, on the verge of tears.

'I know. You're a stowaway, but you're still the boss's daughter!' He slid open the wheelhouse door and helped her out.

197

The storm had been fearsome viewed from inside, but it was ten times worse outside. A howling gale wrenched at Anna's oilskins and seared any unprotected skin with a vicious chill. She grabbed Duncan's arm in terror. She had weathered many storms at sea, but none of this ferocity. Lifelines had been rigged around the decks in anticipation of severe conditions and shadowy figures were working on deck now the weather had improved slightly.

He yelled above the clamour. 'Anna, don't worry. We'll be sheltered if we go aft.'

Clinging to a lifeline, they reached the head of a companionway leading below to passengers' quarters, just as the door swung open and Ivan stepped over the coaming. He was in a foul mood, one eye closed and a livid bruise visible beneath the brim of a sou'wester.

'This wretched man will drown us all, Anna!' he yelled, glaring at the captain with one baleful eye.

'Of course he won't! He's a wonderful seaman.'

'You think he's wonderful?'

'Yes, I do!'

'That's not the crew's version!' He scowled. 'They say you've chased him since you were a little girl, and the man only tolerates you because you're the shipowner's daughter. You think he's so wonderful now?'

'Oh, shut up and take her below!' Wishart spoke in fluent Russian. He shoved Anna impatiently into Ivan's arms then grabbed the lifeline once more and ventured out into the full force of the gale.

During the day, the worst of the weather passed away to the far north as the ship hugged the more sheltered Norwegian coastline. Wishart set course for Narvik to refuel and pick up the remainder of the *Pole Star*'s cargo, which had been left in store.

It was a relief to all aboard when the ship berthed in the neutral port of Narvik. They found the atmosphere ashore quite different. Even the air felt milder despite a covering of snow. Anna's spirits lifted and she readily agreed to Ivan's

198

suggestion of a walk into town to explore the shops while the crew attended to coaling and cargo.

Strolling arm in arm around well-stocked shops was a delightful experience for both of them, after all the trials they'd been through. Anna bought hand lotion for Katerina and Elena, a pink lipstick for Marga and a compass for Michael to follow the course. She ended the shopping spree with a wooden boat for Basil, the baby of the family.

With some trepidation she tendered a British one-pound note and some coins she'd kept hidden, but the beaming shopkeeper accepted the currency willingly while Ivan watched with amusement.

'You've bought nothing for yourself,' he remarked.

'I'm going home!' She smiled joyfully. 'Everything I need is there.'

'You are a very sweet girl!' he said, and kissed her tenderly in front of all the shop assistants and customers.

Anna left the shop covered in blushes, but Ivan fell strangely silent.

When they were approaching the ship again, he stopped her with a hand on her arm. 'Wait. I have something for you, dear girl. I hope you'll accept it, before we join the others.'

'Is it bananas? I haven't eaten one for ages!' Her eyes danced.

'No. Not bananas.' He laughed and tugged the mitten off her left hand in order to slip a circle of glittering diamonds on to the third finger.

'This was my mother's, an anniversary gift from my father, God rest them both! I sewed it into the collar of my shirt. Fortunately the Bolsheviks never offered to wash it!' He smiled.

'Ivan . . . that's the engagement finger! I can't accept this!' Anna looked at him in dismay. How could she tell him she loved Wishart? Surely not another broken heart laid at her doorway?

'It's not intended as an engagement ring, my darling. It's

199

an eternity ring! My future's too uncertain to make lasting commitments, but my love for you will last forever.'

'No!' she cried tearfully. 'Please don't say that!'

'Listen, my *Anglichanka*.' He took her hands and gazed at her earnestly. 'Soon I'll be fit again. Then I'll go back to Russia to fight against our enemies. If you will only keep my mother's ring safe and think about me sometimes, then I'll bc content.'

Anna was deeply touched. She hugged and kissed him emotionally. 'Of course I will! I'll take the greatest care of it, Ivan dcar. I'll pray that one day you'll come and claim your mother's ring back again, to give to the woman you'll marry.'

'God willing,' he said quietly, and kissed her on the lips.

Duncan Wishart had been on the lookout for Anna for some time. Earlier, he'd noted she had gone walking with the Russian and had been pleased to see she'd had the sense to take an escort with her into town. Duncan had also stretched his legs in the outskirts of Narvik, the dog Hamish at his heels, and he'd had a stroke of luck.

In a tiny shop filled with vases and flowerpots and garden implements he'd spotted a bunch of fresh red roses, produced by the florist's green-fingered wizardry. The roses had cost most of the British currency in his possession, but he reckoned they were worth every penny.

'You see, I'm a dour devil, Hamish old chap,' he'd informed the dog, while heading back to the ship clutching the fragrant bouquet. 'I'm tongue-tied, trying to think of sweet nothings to whisper to my lady-love, But red roses say it all, don't they?'

Sensitive to happy moods as always, Hamish had yapped a response and rolled himself over with legs in the air, in a heap of muddy snow. And now, in a state of high tension and with the roses hidden behind his back, Duncan stood watching coal-heavers making tracks from storage bunkers to hoists.

They were trampling pristine snow into a sooty mush while Duncan stood at the quay and kept a weather-eye open for his beloved. He was confident she would understand the significance of red roses as a profession of his true love. Even more so in January, amidst snow and ice.

But when he saw her appear with the Russian, an unusual intimacy about the pair sent a chilly foreboding down Duncan's spine. His happy anticipation faded. From a distance, his hopes began to founder and sink as he saw his rival slip a ring on to her finger. He watched her surprised reactions, then, with a dreadful sense of loss, he witnessed the inevitable, emotional acceptance.

The rose stems were crushed to pulp in his grasp as he watched them kiss. A sharp thorn pierced his palm and he didn't even notice. Drops of blood reddened the snow as Duncan watched the young couple mount the gangplank, laughing. They did not even notice him, standing at the edge of a cloud of black coal dust. He let the roses drop into the blackened slush.

One of the coal-heavers deliberately trampled the slender stems in passing, stamping on the fragrant petals with filthy boots. He gave the desolate captain a sly grin as he plodded by, bent under the load. 'Forget about love, Scotchman! Someone does not like you. U-boats keep an eye open for your ship.'

This was the last straw. Duncan drove thoughts of love from his mind. He strode back on deck, his features cold and expressionless. The dog followed, ears drooped pathetically.

The ship left port in a frantic hurry. Duncan was keen to put to sea and pile on as much speed as they could muster in an attempt to outrun any submarines which may be lying in wait.

The coal-heaver might be a German sympathizer and the threat merely a spiteful one with no real foundation. Then again, given past events, it could be genuine. Duncan could not afford to ignore it.

Aleksandr might not be a vindictive man, but his henchman certainly was. The captain shuddered, recalling the Red Army officer's pitiless, ice-cold gaze. He picked up the speaking tube and whistled down to the engine room, 'Give me more speed, boys!'

The passengers had recovered from seasickness and the effects of the storm as days passed and the sea stayed calm, but they remained subdued. Archie had taken on the self-appointed task of educating the Orlovs in Dundee dialect and held daily sessions in the saloon. They now understood that a 'peh' meant a meat pie, and 'awfy no' weel' merited either a dose of medicine or a trip to the doctor. Possibly both.

Ivan was Anna's constant companion, but when they walked on deck warmly clad against the cold, her gaze would stray to the bridge. Wishart would be there, but he would never reveal by so much as a smile or lift of the hand that he noticed her. She laughed and smiled and pretended that his indifference didn't hurt, but it broke her heart.

Then at last, she and Duncan Wishart met unexpectedly, all alone on deck in the gloaming. Anna had wrapped herself in a warm cloak and slipped away quietly to be by herself. The others were seated cosily chatting in a warm fug which all Russians, the dog and Moussia appreciated. Out on deck, she could hear the lilting murmur of Russian voices blending with the steady beat of engines and the eternal sound of the sea. It was peaceful. Yet oh, so lonely.

'What on earth are you doing? You'll freeze out here!' The captain loomed out of the semi-darkness like a shadow and stood frowning at her. She almost retorted that she was warm and only his coldness froze her. Instead, she said nothing.

She pulled the cloak closer to her chin and he noticed her left hand was bare.

He frowned. 'Where's your ring?'

'Too precious to wear.'

'Yes. Much too flashy.'

'Don't be nasty! It's Ivan's mother's eternity ring, a gift to her from his father!' she said indignantly. She looked down at her empty hand and suddenly wanted to cry.

Duncan eyed her averted profile despairingly. What chance had he, a foundling, of winning Anna McLaren? The Russian had wealth and family links stretching way back into a dim and distant past. More importantly in Duncan's eyes, he'd had parents who loved one another and were honourably wed. Why should she bother with a nobody?

'Go inside!' he ordered sternly. 'Don't wander alone on deck. You might fall overboard and nobody would know.'

'Or care!' She gave him a glance smouldering with resentment, and obeyed without a backward glance.

A message had arrived for Andrew McLaren at the Dundee telegraph office: the *Pole Star* was heading home. But far from reassuring the captain it threw him into a state of alarm. Fishermen reported a typhoon in the north and some ships had foundered. There was no word of the *Pole Star*'s condition or the safety of passengers and crew.

Andrew's main consolation at this worrying time was the Morris motor he'd bought, with the idea of taking housebound Amy Duncan out for a spin.

He'd paid five bob for a driving licence, taught himself to drive in a couple of sessions, then joined the growing number of motorists cursing jute carts and tramcars on Dundee's congested roads.

Irina had grumbled about the expense at first, but had soon realized the motor car was excellent therapy for a worried man. Her husband spent hours washing, polishing and tending to the vehicle. She decided that anything that kept him occupied and out from under her feet was an asset.

One day in late February, Andrew had driven down to the docks once more, a daily ritual. He was sitting in the car staring moodily at his flagship's empty berth when a shout arose.

'Ship's coming in!'

Andrew climbed out and watched the pilot tender head out towards the bar. His stomach was tied in knots. There was a smirr of mist out there on the river estuary. He could only make out a shadow of a ship. It seemed like hours before the vessel came gliding towards the dock. Andrew's sight of her blurred with tears and he closed his eyes and almost dropped to his knees there and then, to thank God.

It was the *Pole Star* at last! His ship was home. He was aboard her before the gangway was properly in place. The crewmen stepped hastily aside, the greeting dying on their lips, for Andrew's expression was now thunderous.

His keen eye noted rust, storm damage and breakages. There was no sign of his beloved daughter. Andrew headed grimly for the bridge.

The ship's officers had completed docking procedures and there was an air of relief and jubilation when Andrew burst in. The men looked thin and worn out with the strain of long, dangerous days at sea, but he was too furious to take note of such details. He glared at the captain and waved the others out, peremptorily.

'Where's my daughter?'

'Down below, sir. Helping the others to pack.'

'Others?' He frowned. 'But Anna and Seraphima are safe?'

'Oh yes, they're fine . . . and so's the cat.'

'Just as well, Wishart, otherwise I'd have the law on you.' Andrew scowled. 'How dare you let Anna sail on my ship when I'd expressly asked her not to? You made her face appalling danger!'

Duncan Wishart stiffened resentfully at the accusation. 'Your daughter is a determined young lady!'

'That's beside the point! You were duty bound to alert me to her plans, not encourage her to rebel against my wishes!'

'So in your opinion I'm guilty, without hearing a word spoken in my defence!' the young man said angrily. 'It's obvious you've no faith in me, Captain McLaren. In that case I can't possibly work for you. I'll save you the bother of dismissing me, sir. I resign!'

He flung open the door and stepped outside, yelling for the mate to complete the formalities before striding resentfully off towards his quarters.

Andrew remained leaning against the chart table, all anger spent. He found he was trembling with emotion and close to tears. He'd had a real fondness for the ill-treated little boy and great respect for the man he'd become against all the odds. Andrew was desperately sad to see it end in bitterness and recrimination.

The news had reached Anna that her father was aboard, and she came racing to the bridge. She burst into the wheel-house and Andrew opened his arms and his daughter flew to him, laughing and crying at one and the same time.

'Darling *Papachka*! It's so good to be back home!' she sobbed.

'Not before time, my dearest lass.' He wiped his eyes. 'You've given us months of frantic worry, Anna dear! Still, we know how much you love your grandma, so your mother and I forgive you. It's more difficult to forgive that man Duncan Wishart, though!'

'Why? What has he done?' Anna stared at her father in astonishment. Before Anna had appeared, Andrew had watched the young man descend the gangway and head for the dock gates, his seabag slung over his shoulder. It had been a sad sight, but Andrew had hardened his heart.

'It was Wishart's duty to tell me you intended to sail with him. If I'd known, we could've worked something out and spared you a long dangerous trip, but he never said a word!'

'That's because he didn't know!' she cried. 'He'd no idea I was aboard till five days after we sailed, Dad. I stowed away!'

205

'What?' The colour left his cheeks.

'I stowed away in a store cupboard and Archie helped me. Duncan was furious when he found me. It was too late to turn back by then, though he did threaten!' She smiled. 'But he was wonderful to me afterwards. He waited faithfully in Murmansk for weeks on end and then battled through atrocious weather to bring us all safely home. Oh, *Papachka*! He is such a special, wonderful man!'

She glowed with the depth of her emotion. Then it struck her that he should be here, on the bridge. 'Where is he?' She frowned.

Her father couldn't meet her eyes. 'We had a blazing row. I accused Wishart of taking you away without telling me what was going on. He was deeply offended by my lack of trust and so he refused to work for me and resigned. He's gone ashore.'

'But it's all my fault, not Duncan's! He's innocent. Everything that happened was my own fault!' Tears spilled down her cheeks.

Her father took her in his arms and she sobbed brokenly against his shoulder. He'd never seen her in such a state. There was more to this than met the eye? he wondered. Had she grown more than a little fond of Duncan Wishart?

'My dear, why not chase after Wishart and tell him I'm sorry? Tell him I had the wrong end o' the stick all along.'

'Should I?' She looked up.

'He'll listen to you.' He nodded. 'Tell him your father did him an injustice, and if he'll overlook it I'd be proud to have him in command of my flagship again.'

Andrew smiled and pushed her gently towards the door. 'Go on, dear. He can't have gone far!'

Anna left the ship and ran across the uneven dockside cobbles, her head still swimming with the rhythm of the sea. It made her unsteady and the chase across dry land seemed nightmarish after weeks spent at sea.

She searched for Duncan when she reached the busy

dockland road, and didn't know which way to turn. Then she caught sight of him in the distance and she stumbled on. But she caught him at last. Out of breath, she caught hold of his jacket and held him fast.

'I thought I'd lost you!'

He looked down at her darkly. 'Would it have mattered?'

'Of course it would. I'm in love with you. Don't ask me why after the way you've treated me!'

'Wait a minute! You wore Ivan's ring.' He looked quite dazed. 'Aren't you engaged?'

'Of course not!' She shook her head. 'Ivan plans to go back to Russia to fight when he's well enough. I only agreed to keep his mother's ring safe for him.'

'So that's all it was!' He sighed. 'I got the signs wrong!'

'Yes, you did – and you told me once not to jump to conclusions!' She stared at him. 'Is that why you've been acting so cold?'

'Yes, but that wasn't the only reason,' he admitted, looking down at her. Dock workers crowding the pavement at the end of a shift were forced to dodge around the couple. Duncan and Anna scarcely noticed. He took her by the hand.

'Come with me, Anna. There's something you should see.'

Wondering, Anna followed him.

He led her along a narrow lane redolent of Dundee's whaling past and stopped when they came to an ancient stone arch straddling a squalid street.

She stared at the weathered stone and shivered. This was a cold, comfortless place. She recalled the old legend that long ago plague victims had been thrown out of town through this ancient gate, to live or die outside.

'The Wishart arch, Anna.' Duncan lowered the seabag to the ground and laid a hand against the crumbling stone. 'This is where my mother abandoned me when I was a tiny baby. I don't know who she was or why she did it, but I've hated her ever since. The knowledge I was unwanted was hard to bear. I was determined to succeed.'

He turned and looked at her. 'Then you came along, a bonny little girl who teased and tormented me and followed me around when I was trying to get on. I sent you packing, didn't I?' He smiled ruefully. 'But when you'd grown into a beautiful woman once more aboard my ship, I discovered that if you were in danger I lost my appetite and couldn't sleep. When I thought I'd lost you to Aleksandr, my future was bleak. How happy I was when you decided to come home! I planned to tell you then that I loved you, but Ivan slipped that ring upon your finger, and again it seemed life had dealt me a bitter blow.'

He reached for her hand and looked into her eyes. 'That's how much I love you, my darling. I long to spend the rest of my life with you, but could you marry a man who came from nowhere – a nobody?'

Anna flung her arms round his neck. 'Wishart, I know who you are. I've known since I was a little girl!'

'Who am I?' He kissed her quickly, enchanted.

'You're my own true love!' She laughed, her brown eyes dancing.

He sighed quizzically, shaking his head. 'Why on earth did it take so many years, mistakes and misunderstandings before we found one another?'

'Who cares?' Anna said. 'We reached safe harbour in the end!'

They looked at one another and smiled with complete understanding, then they hallowed the ruins of the grim old Wishart arch with their first long ecstatic kiss.

It was a rare, balmy day at the end of March, when the month that had come storming in like a lion trotted out like a lamb. Andrew McLaren had driven his three passengers out into the Angus countryside. The scene before them was bathed in mild sunlight. Eddie Duncan sat fidgeting in the passenger seat, Anna and Duncan Wishart sat close together

208

in the back, holding hands. Duncan's grip was even firmer than usual on his fiancee's hand.

Today, he was going to meet for the very first time the woman who was his mother and his emotions were in a turmoil, not to mention panic. Andrew's precious car had laboured up the hilly winding pass through the Sidlaws at Lumley Den. At the top, the radiator was steaming. He pulled into the side. From this vantage point there was a wonderful view of the valley of Strathmore and the snow-clad tops of the Grampians beyond.

'We'll stop and let her rest awhile,' he said.

The two older members of the party settled down for a smoke to steady their nerve. Anna and Duncan clambered out of the car and walked hand in hand to the grassy verge. Listening to birdsong, the bleat of a lamb, the vast silence, and the peace.

He was very nervous, wondering if he could trust himself to restrain the resentment of thirty bitter years. 'I still don't know why she did it, Anna. The old man wouldn't say. He wanted her to tell me herself. He said she needed time to adjust to the fact her baby lived, after all.'

He took a long, deep breath of the pure, cool air. 'I've hated her for so many years, my darling! What if I say something I regret? All I have to show for my birth is this.' He reached into a pocket and brought out the tiny bonnet Irina, his future mother-in-law, had given him.

'Look how beautifully it's knitted, love,' Anna said. 'If your mother knitted it for the baby she was expecting, it was knitted with loving care.'

'Perhaps.' He shrugged, not convinced.

He tucked the bonnet away and turned to Anna for her kiss. He needed her strength and love to carry him through today. It seemed to him the most crucial day of his life.

Eddie watched the young lovers as they stood locked in one another's arms, quite oblivious to gorse bushes sprouting tender yellow blossom all around them.

'When the wild gorse don't bloom kissing's out o' fashion, Andrew!' he remarked with a grin.

'Aye.' Andrew knocked out his pipe. 'Better get moving.'

They drove down into the little village of Glamis, past the school and round to the right, keeping in the shadow of the castle wall. Following Eddie's directions, Andrew pulled up beside a neat red sandstone cottage.

Duncan climbed out of the car. He found he was shaking as he helped Anna out. He stood for several long moments staring at the cottage, and hesitating.

'Go on, lad. In you go. You're expected,' Eddie urged.

He and Andrew brought up the rear.

There was a brass plate on the wall and Duncan's eyes widened in surprise as he read it: *Margaret Lorimer L.R.A.M. Pianoforte*.

He'd hardly had a chance to reach for the doorknocker before the door was whisked open.

There stood the woman who was his mother. They stared at one another. She was tall, like himself. She had grey-blue eyes, like himself. Steel-grey hair gathered in a knot at the nape of the neck. She was a pretty woman with a kind expression, but he thought he could detect in her expression deep, underlying currents of hidden emotion. Like himself?

She put one hand to her heart, the other to her face and whispered, 'Dear God! Marcus!'

'Yes, Margaret love, I saw the likeness too!' Eddie nodded. 'The lad's the dead spit o' his father.'

'Come on inside.' Margaret Lorimer recovered quickly, ushering them in. She made no attempt to kiss or hug her son.

To be honest, Duncan thought his mother looked as awkward and scared as he was. She took them into a pleasant sitting room, a fine upright piano taking up the corner by the window.

She followed the direction of his eyes and smiled. 'I teach

210

music at the school and take private pupils as well. It gives me quite a decent living.'

'My niece has worked hard at her career. She's done very well for herself,' Eddie said proudly.

When they were seated, an awkward silence fell. Margaret Lorimer turned to her son. 'You must have wondered about me, Duncan. You must have often wondered why you were abandoned.' She stopped.

'You bet I did! You left me in the gutter!' He couldn't restrain his anger.

'No, I didn't!'

'Someone did!'

Eddie laid a hand on the angry young man's arm. 'Be quiet and listen to the facts!' he ordered sternly. 'My brother John, Margaret's father, sailed with the whaling fleet and so did Marcus Lorimer, her husband. There was still good money to be made in that risky trade in the 1880s and my brother John and his son-in-law Marcus were well-off.'

He paused and glanced at his niece. He knew this must be hard for her to hear. Eddie sighed and continued, 'Aye, well, just before their last trip on the *Greenland* the two of them were persuaded to invest all their money in an income trust for Margaret and her unborn baby. It seemed a wise move on the face of it. They'd be at sea from March till October as usual, and she'd have a regular income to pay for food and rent. But it didn't work that way . . .' He paused and shook his head, suddenly overcome.

His niece patted his hand and took up the story. 'They never came back,' she said sadly. 'The *Greenland* foundered and her crew went down with her. The income trust was a fraudulent scheme. I was left penniless and when my baby's birth was imminent I was far behind with the rent. The landlord evicted me.'

She stared at Duncan, her eyes dark. 'I went to my neighbour and begged for help. She was a motherly soul with a daughter of her own. We'd been friends. I trusted her.' She wiped away a tear.

211

'Aye, but when poverty comes in the door, friendship flees out the window!' Eddie said grimly. 'It was a long hard labour and a difficult birth and Margaret lay half-dead at the end. The woman took fright when she found herself wi' an unconscious mother near to death and a squawling newborn boy. So she dressed him in the clothes his mother'd made and crept out at the dead o' night and left him in the shelter of the arch. When the mother rallied later on, that besom told her the bairn was stillborn and the infirmary disposed of it!'

'It's strange,' Margaret said softly, staring at her grown son. 'I thought I'd heard a baby crying. The sound haunted me for years. I thought I'd dreamed it.'

'It was no dream!' Eddie said. 'Thank heaven the woman had a decent daughter! The lassie came running to me in tears to let me know what her mother had done. I went out right away and found the wee mite fast asleep.' He paused and shook his head. 'I was in a right pickle! Amy and I had just lost our own dear boy to infantile paralysis and Amy was in the isolation hospital gravely ill with the same terrible infection. I daren't take the bairn home mysel'. So then I remembered Carolina House, the orphanage. I knew they'd take good care of him, and later on it might seem natural for the man that found him to take an interest in his welfare. I planned to return him to his mother, once she'd made a new life for herself. But the orphanage gave him to foster folk who were a bad lot. We were told the baby had died, so we never had the heart to tell Margaret the truth.'

He glanced at Andrew with a smile. 'Then you came along, Captain McLaren, sticking your nose in, and wouldn't be silenced!'

'Thank goodness!' Margaret Lorimer said warmly.

'Aye,' Andrew nodded towards his future son-in-law. 'You have a clever lad here, Mistress Lorimer. Musical too. You should hear him sing!'

'I'd love to!' She laughed and seated herself at the piano.

'Duncan, my dear, will you sing for me?'

Duncan looked at his mother, then smiled at the beloved girl he would marry in April when the old family house they had chosen together, beside the river, was made ready for them.

He went and stood by the piano, at his mother's side. For Duncan, the choice of a song was easy.

'"My love is like a red, red rose," please, Mother.'

Margaret Lorimer looked up at her son with pleasure. Mother! She would enjoy hearing that word. She would hear it echo in her head and in her heart. She would never tire of hearing him say it. Mother!

Then her son's glorious tenor filled the room and echoed across the peaceful village. Those out walking on that pleasant afternoon paused to listen in wonder, then went on their way heartened.

But for Anna, the words held more significance, as he sang softly for her alone—: *'And I will love thee still, my love, till a' the seas gang dry . . .'*

Duncan and his mother smiled at one another with complete understanding, as the last plaintive notes of the famous old love song faded away into silence.

Anna watched them together and wiped away a tear. God willing, she thought, there would be many happy years ahead for this mother and son. They had found one another, at last.

The house at Peep o' Day Lane positively buzzed with activity, on the sunny April morning Anna McLaren had chosen for her wedding day. The upstairs rooms resounded to the lilting sound of excited Russian voices. The female Orlovs were all crowded into Anna's bedroom, offering Irina and Seraphima advice on the wedding gown, the drift of gossamer veiling, the circlet of orange blossom on Anna's dark hair, on this, that and every detail of the approaching ceremony.

'Oh, Mama dear, do stop it!' Elena laughed at last. She

took no part in the activity, sitting nursing her tiny daughter and watching all this carry on. Baby Catriona was Dmitri and Elena's little Scottish baby, born only three weeks ago.

'Don't listen to her, Katerina!' Anna laughed and hugged her dearest friend. 'We need all the advice we can get. I doubt if Dundee has ever hosted a Russian Orthodox wedding before.'

'Do not hug! You will crush the beautiful gown!' Katerina gave a scream and pushed her playfully away.

'No, madame!' Seraphima looked up. She was down on her knees, fussing with the veil. 'Finest satin will not crush.'

'The sun's out!' Marga reported. She was on the window seat, stroking Moussia on her lap. Marga's nose was pressed eagerly against the window pane, on the lookout for her hero, Archie. She spotted him just at that moment and her lovelorn heart swelled with pride. Didn't he look fine in the kilt?

'Here comes Archie to collect Michael,' she cried. 'They'll make such handsome attendants for you and Duncan, Anna!'

'Nearly ready, ladies?' Andrew McLaren appeared in the doorway,

Andrew found himself facing a roomful of busy womenfolk gathered around a radiant bride, so beautiful she took his breath away.

'Oh, my dear lass, you're lovely!'

'So she is, this girl I love like a daughter!' Katerina nodded. She smiled at Andrew. 'I must tell you, Captain, I wanted your daughter to wear the Orlovs' collar of pearls, because we love her so, but she would only wear the pretty jewel her mother and father gave her, more precious to her than diamonds and pearls. That is a measure of the fine person she is!'

Katerina turned to her tiny grandchild, asleep in Elena's arms. 'Well, it does not matter!' She smiled. 'God willing, this little Scottish Orlov will wear the collar of pearls on her wedding day, true to our family tradition. When that happy day comes the collar will be a symbol of unity for us in a new homeland. It will remind us of our Russian roots for generations to come.'

Katerina crossed to the dressing table and opened the jewel case lying there. She stood back, so that they could view the collar of pearls, restored in all its glory. The room fell silent. Diamonds sparkled like fire, cooled by the pale lustre of five hundred perfectly matched pearls.

Andrew drew in a breath. He had never seen anything quite so wonderful. 'Just one thing puzzles me, Katerina,' he said at last. 'You told me Red Guards searched everywhere for the collar, and yet they never found it. I can't imagine where on earth you hid it!'

The womenfolk exchanged wide grins. Marga took a fit of giggles and Katerina gave Seraphima a most wicked and unladylike wink. Elena hugged her precious little daughter and laughed heartily at the captain's baffled look . . .

They were recalling the memorable scene which had taken place in this very room, shortly after their arrival in Scotland, two or three months ago. On that occasion the bedroom door had been locked against male intrusion. Seraphima, Irina and Anna were working busily upon three pairs of wellworn corsets. Katerina and her two daughters stood by, clad only in vest and knickers.

'Do hurry up, my dears!' Katerina begged impatiently, watching the skilled corset-makers' patient work.

'Less hurry, less worry, madame!' Seraphima went on calmly snipping. But at last the task was finished. They all gathered around the bed. Waiting, holding their breath.

'Behold!' Seraphima cried.

Holding up the corsets, one by one, she shook them vigorously over the counterpane.

A dazzling array of diamonds and pearl jewels spilled out upon the bedcover and lay glittering in the light of day. The women let their breath go in a sigh.

'The collar of pearls!' Katerina said. She felt vast relief, tinged with some sadness. This marked the end of an era for their dynasty. Still, they had much to be thankful for, she thought.

The cherished collar had been saved from theft and greed and the family remained united – thanks to the endurance of its womenfolk!

'I'll have diamond-shaped bumps and bruises for weeks to come!' Katerina smiled, rubbing her hips.

'And what about me, with my very large tummy, Mama?' Elena smiled. At that time she'd been quite close to giving birth. It was a wonder little Catriona wasn't born with goose bumps and pearly teeth! she'd laughed, afterwards

'Mama, do look!' Marga giggled, examining her bare posterior in the mirror. 'I have orange blossoms imprinted all over my bum!'

'Never mind, my brave darlings!' Katerina swept her two daughters into her arms. 'I'm proud of you. You bore discomfort without a murmur, and fooled all our enemies . . .!'

Recalling that delightful incident, Anna took pity upon her puzzled father, and explained, 'You see, Dad, we had dismantled the collar of pearls into three separate parts. Then Seraphima sewed all the various pieces into the linings of Katerina's, Elena's and Marga's corsets. We guessed that nobody would think of looking there!'

Andrew's brow cleared. He laughed delightedly, 'They hid the collar of pearls in their corsets!'

'Where else?' shrugged Seraphima, the corset-maker. Irina kissed her beloved daughter and hugged her wily little mother. 'My clever *Mamushka!*' She smiled, wiping away a tear.

Andrew looked at his watch. 'Time we were moving, ladies!'

He approached his darling daughter, the bonny bride. Anna gave her father a special, misty smile and took his arm. Bursting with emotional pride, Andrew headed the merry wedding procession outdoors.

Anna made him pause for a moment in the sunlit front

doorway. They glanced across towards the harbour, where the masts and funnel of the *Pole Star* could just be seen. The sight overwhelmed Anna with happiness. She had found love aboard that fine ship, and the guidance that had brought her, and the dear man she loved, safely back home.

Her father surveyed his flagship with quiet satisfaction. He visualized a bright future for its young captain, Duncan Wishart – not to mention an extraordinary past for his future son-in-law to put behind him, for good!

The wedding cars were waiting in Peep o' Day Lane, white ribbons fluttering in the breeze. Crowds of Dundonians would be gathered round the kirk door to catch a glimpse of this popular bride. Andrew glanced at his watch again.

'Full steam ahead, my lass!'

'Aye, aye, skipper!' Anna McLaren laughed and kissed her father's cheek. Always a sailor's daughter, she thought, and very soon to be a sailor's wife . . .